SCENE OF THE CRIME

"What now?" I demanded when Zack came strolling back into the bar.

"All of a sudden, that smell in my car stinks worse than a road-killed skunk, Charlie. Car's been sittin' out there in the heat of the day since I got here this mornin'. Seems like maybe somethin's gone rotten."

"Did you check the trunk?"

"I can't get the trunk open, the catch is jammed."

"It's a new car. Why would the catch be jammed?"

"I wish you'd come take a sniff, Charlie. I'm sorta worried."

Angel was our worrier. Not Zack. "Worried about what?"

"I just want you to come see what it smells like to you."

I followed Jack outside. His gleaming new luxury car was parked well away from the other cars. A little breeze had come up and it felt good wafting on my face. At least it felt good until we came close to the Lexus and I caught a whiff of the odor Zack had talked about. That wasn't new car smell. Nor was it mildew. Or BO.

My stomach did a double somersault. I stopped walking as suddenly as if I'd crashed into a brick wall. All the blood left my head.

Zack scanned my face. "That's what I thought," he said.

Once you've smelled death you don't ever forget it; you can't mistake it.

Something or somebody dead was in the trunk of Zack's car.

Books by Margaret Chittenden

DYING TO SING

DEAD MEN DON'T DANCE

DEAD BEAT AND DEADLY

Published by Kensington Books

MARGARET CHITTENDEN

Dead Men Don't Dance

KENSINGTON BOOKS

http://www.kensingtonbooks.com

This book is dedicated with great affection, to my far-flung—
sometimes far-out—friends on Dorothy L.

KENSINGTON BOOKS are published by

Kensington Publishing Corp.
850 Third Avenue
New York, NY 10022

Copyright © 1997 by Margaret Chittenden

All rights reserved. No part of this book may be reproduced in any form or by any means without the prior written consent of the Publisher, excepting brief quotes used in reviews.

If you purchased this book without a cover you should be aware that this book is stolen property. It was reported as "unsold and destroyed" to the Publisher and neither the Author nor the Publisher has received any payment for this "stripped book."

Kensington and the K logo Reg. U.S. Pat. & TM Off.

First Kensington Hardcover Printing: July, 1997
First Kensington Paperback Printing: August, 1998

Printed in the United States of America
10 9 8 7 6 5 4 3 2 1

CHAPTER 1

You'd expect that finding a dead body on your premises would be a once-in-a-lifetime experience. That's certainly what *I* thought when an earthquake split open CHAPS' flower bed last August and part of a skeleton popped up. You probably read about the subsequent investigation. As usual, I did the work; Zack hogged the credit.

But after it was over, I thought, well, that was a sad, terrible, traumatic experience, but certainly not one that would ever be repeated. One newspaper reporter asked Zack and me if our lives might seem a tad boring in the future. "I sure hope so," I told her.

Ha!

I'm getting ahead of myself. Here's some background. I'm Charlie Plato, a thirty-one-year-old divorcée possessed of a Netherland dwarf rabbit named Benny, frizzy orange hair that Benny mistakes for carrot shavings, blue eyes, a tall skinny body, and an attitude.

The attitude includes a vow to stick to celibacy for the rest of my life, at least where Zack Hunter is concerned. You may have guessed by now that the Zack Hunter I'm talking about is *that* Zack Hunter. The TV actor. *People*'s sexiest man of the year—a few years back.

A year and a half ago, Zack created, and now owns half of, CHAPS, a very large country-western tavern/dance hall on Adobe Plaza, an historic paved, tree-shaded square, which is situated in upscale Bellamy Park just before it leaves off and shabby old Condor begins. Bellamy Park is on the San Francisco peninsula, between the San Andreas and Hayward faults, which explains the aforementioned earthquake.

The other half of CHAPS is equally divided between me, Angel Cervantes and Savanna Seabrook. The four of us constitute a typical American team: I'm female, part Greek/part Scot; Angel's an Hispanic male; Savanna's African-American and *all* woman; Zack, in his own words, is an "overprivileged white dude from Beverly Hills." None of us has what you'd call a real family. Well, I have Benny the bunny, and Savanna has a three-year-old daughter, Jacqueline, but her relatives wrote her off thirteen years ago when she married a white man. He's also history now. Orphans of the storm, Savanna calls us.

This past spring, Zack appeared in a TV infomercial for a local environmental group—Citizens for a Livable City (CFLC). It showed Zack riding horseback alongside a river, looking depressed when he passed a clear cut, dismounting to pick up an aluminum beer can someone had tossed.

After CFLC received more applications for membership in one week than they'd handled in a decade, eager representatives of the group talked Zack into running for a seat on Bellamy Park's city council. He persuaded me to manage his campaign. (I have a lot of weak moments where Zack Hunter is concerned. Fortunately for my self-esteem, though, I've so far bravely resisted the weakest of all.)

Angel and Savanna agreed to help out. CHAPS became the campaign headquarters. And that's where we all were when the first clue that my life was *not* going to become boring appeared on the scene. "There's a funny smell in my car," Zack said. I regret to say I failed to recognize this immediately as a clue, until it upped and hit me in the nose, so to speak.

I'm getting ahead of myself again.

CHAPS has a large open interior that is crowded every night but Monday, with cowboy and cowgirl wanna-bes. There are two dance floors, the larger of which we quaintly refer to as the main corral.

On the extremely hot Sunday afternoon when that first clue sneaked past me, CHAPS was occupied by a slightly different crowd. We were hosting Zack's campaign kickoff, and the interior of the building was draped with bunting. In addition to the four partners, there were twenty women of various ages present who belonged to Zack's fan club; a dozen Adobe Plaza neighbors; the entire membership of CFLC; a couple of Zack's Hollywood friends who were in San Francisco for some summer theater; and Sundancer Brown, CHAPS' eccentric but brilliant deejay who is also a member of the Bellamy Park Irregulars—Zack's poker buddies. On poker nights we have to use a replacement deejay. No one could replace Zack, of course.

Macintosh, another of Zack's poker gang, was helping me distribute bundles of the campaign poster that I'd designed and Zack had autographed.

"This poster is smashing," Macintosh said as we arrived together in front of the stage, where the bundles were laid out. A sixtyish roly-poly man with spaniel-brown eyes, a fuzzy brown beard and matching hair, he was peering up through his metal-rimmed spectacles at the enormous screen where Sundancer had projected a Big Brother blowup of the poster. Macintosh hadn't yet mastered his new bifocals.

Patting my arm gently, he gave me his tentative smile. "You're really getting the hang of desktop publishing, Charlie. And the idea is brilliant. You're a clever lass."

Who was I to disagree? The idea for that flyer had come to me a week or so earlier in the middle of the night. It looked exactly like an old Western poster, featuring Zack, of course, complete with western shirt and cowboy hat, squinting at the camera in the way that always makes my stomach go *whomp!* Above the picture huge black capital letters spelled out "WANTED." At the bottom were the words, "Zack Hunter, for Position 2, Bellamy Park City Council."

"It's a remarkably fine photograph," Macintosh went on, his soft Scottish burr giving emphasis to all three r's. His hint of an accent always made me think of the mist over the water, and the heather on the hills, that my mother used to talk about. She was a Scot, too. That's where I came by my orange hair and blue eyes.

"Not that it would be possible to get a *bad* photo of Zack Hunter," Macintosh continued. "The camera loves our friend, don't you agree?" Glancing from side to side, he added under his breath, as if passing on a secret, "If you've no objection, lass, I'll nip outside for a puff."

"I'm sorry you can't do it in here, Macintosh," I said. We'd decided CHAPS would go smokeless from the beginning, but I always felt sorry for the people huddled around doorways or leaning against walls outside almost every public building or office. Such gatherings seemed to have become social in a way, though, a meeting place for like-minded souls, something like the way people used to exchange news in the post office or country store.

Smiling mournfully, Macintosh moved on, apologizing to everyone who got in his way. As far as anyone knew, Macintosh didn't have a first name. A few months ago, he'd moved his highly rated, extraordinarily gentle children's television show—*Spreading Circles*—from L.A. to San Francisco. He produced and starred in the show, which featured a lot of educational stuff and animals. The program was warm and soft like a koala, like Macintosh himself.

Besides being a friend, he was also my computer guru. Anyone who owns a computer needs a guru—someone to call when the little hourglass thingamajig freezes up, or disappears, or when the screen pops up a message that says "Error # 1024," or "Can't find winsock.dll."

"Macintosh is so cute," Savanna said as I handed her a few bundles to pass out. "You ought to go out with him, Charlie."

Savanna says that about every guy who stops to exchange the time of day with me, including the tattooed hunk who empties the Dumpster in the parking lot every week. "Macintosh hasn't asked me," I told her. "Also, he's a little old for me, don't you think? And I'm pretty sure he's gay."

That was a major faux pas. Savanna's ex-husband was gay, a facet of his character she discovered when she came upon him frolicking in their bed with a twenty-two-year-old truck driver.

Savanna craned around a few people to take another look at Macintosh as he wended his way through the crowd. She even looked beautiful doing that. Zack says Savanna is the African-American answer to Dolly Parton—big hair, big bosoms, big smile, big heart. We all wear western gear, but Savanna's shirts are red and drip fringe, and she wears her cowboy hat on the back of her head. She's thirty-seven but looks twenty-five. "Macintosh does hang around CHAPS a lot," she murmured. "You suppose he has a crush on Zack?"

I laughed. "If he has, I hope he never makes a pass at him. Zack would pound him into the ground like a fence post."

There was no response. Savanna's lovely face had gone all blank, her eyes glassy like those of a doe caught in headlights. She was gazing toward the entranceway. Sure enough, there was Taylor Bristow's bald but shapely brown head looming above the crowd.

Zack insists his good buddy Bristow looks like Michael Jordan, but then Zack compares everything and everyone to something or someone connected with TV or the movies. Bristow does have a wonderful off-duty smile and no hair, and he's well over six feet, so I guess that's a resemblance. He's one of Bellamy Park's finest—a detective sergeant. We met him when he was investigating our skeleton. One look at Savanna, and his bacon had been fried to a crisp.

He'd caught sight of Savanna now. His face softened to a vacant expression, which matched hers. You can be pretty sure when people with high IQs look vacuous, hormones are on the march. As I watched, the two of them moved toward each other in slow motion, as if their locked glances were cords reeling them in. I'm not exaggerating, that's how they behave whenever they see each other. I wouldn't have been surprised to see Savanna's long dark curls streaming out behind her cowboy hat, as though caught in a soft summer breeze.

Bristow looked lean and dangerous in blue jeans and a yellow polo shirt, which clung to his muscles.

I moved on, handing out my nifty posters, until I caught sight of the star of this whole proceeding, his tough, rangy body leaning in its own macho way against the main corral's bar, one foot on the rail. Zack was, of course, wearing the signature clothing he'd plagiarized from Johnny Cash—black jeans, black western shirt, black cowboy hat and boots—and was squinting sexily at Lauren Deakins, who worked in the local drugstore.

Lauren was a somewhat statuesque young woman with thick dark eyebrows and a prominent nose. She had no idea of how to dress. Today she was wearing a full black skirt with an uneven hem, and a sweater that was much too skimpy for her fairly full figure. The sleeves were too short and showed the large bones in her wrists.

Lauren was a fan with a capital F. She became emphysemic whenever she entered the great man's presence, which she did as frequently as was humanly possible. "Adorin' Lauren," Savanna and I called her. "Dip her backward and hear her plead, Let me lie down at your feet!"

We were pretty sure Lauren had not yet become a member of what Savanna and I called "Zack's doll brigade"; she wore her virginity on her back like one of the damsels from *Don Quixote of the Mancha.* I figured it was only a matter of time, though.

"How about handing out some of these stacks for Zack?" I asked her sweetly, thrusting my remaining bundles at her. It took her a moment to focus on me. The woods were full of does caught in headlights today.

"Maybe I'll paper my bedroom with them instead," she

said breathlessly, convulsively pressing the flyers to her not-inconsiderable bosom.

To show his gratitude for this indirect compliment, our man in black bestowed on her his famous thin-lipped, bad-boy smile. While she was still hyperventilating, I turned her around and gave her a little push toward the rest of the crowd. "Give a bundle to anyone who'll take one," I instructed her briskly. "Tell them to pick up a few signboards from the stacks in the lobby and staple posters on them, front and back, stick 'em in people's yards. After asking permission, of course."

"Hey, Charlie," Zack said as Lauren wandered away, with many a yearning backward glance.

"Hey, yourself," I said. I hate to admit it, but the man makes me breathless, too. I've studied survival technique, however, so I know that attack is the best method of protection. "If you don't watch out, that child's going to take your flirting seriously. She's surely not experienced enough to realize you turn on the charm for any woman of any age, race, or creed, whether she's married or single or militantly lesbian."

This is not just my observation—one of the tabloids once wrote of Zack that he'd never met a woman he couldn't bed. I was married for a time to a man who came close to matching that description. That is one reason why I am mentally armored to resist Zack's blandishments. (I would be much safer if I could seal myself in a stone tower surrounded by a moat stocked with piranhas, but moats are hard to come by nowadays.)

Zack smiled lazily. "I've never laid a hand on her, darlin'," he drawled. He does a great drawl, even though he was born and raised in Beverly Hills. "I can hardly prevent her from frequentin' CHAPS, accordin' to her ID she's over twenty-one."

"You checked her ID? Why? To make sure your buddy Bristow couldn't run you in for messing with a minor?"

Once again, his grin lifted a corner of his extremely sensual mouth. "*Angel* carded her, darlin'. He's the one serves beer and wine around these parts, remember? Anyhow, even if Lauren was to stop comin' in, I'm forever runnin' into her at Dandy Carr's."

Dandy Carr's gym is a Bellamy Park bodybuilder hangout that features vein-gorged muscles and power breathing. It's also where Zack works out regularly. Maybe Lauren was in danger of becoming obsessed. Fans do. "Does she just hang around, or actually pump iron?" I asked.

"She pumps. Very well, too," he added, with an appreciative gleam in his green eyes, which he then turned on me. There's something about green eyes. They evoke images of tropical lagoons, palm fronds swaying, warm water lapping at your thighs—well, you get the picture. "You sure are cranky today, darlin'," he said.

Zack always calls me cranky when I criticize him. It's occurred to me to wonder if he's studied survival techniques himself.

He waved a languid hand at the assembled throng, who were presently devouring the heavy hors d'oeuvres supplied by Dorscheimer's Restaurant, one of the concessions in CHAPS' lobby. "Great turnout," he commented. He's also good at changing the subject.

"I'm still not convinced you're running for the council out of any political conviction," I said, deliberately putting him on another hook as punishment for wriggling off the last one.

"That's not fair, girlfriend," Savanna said from behind me. "Zack's as interested in protecting the environment of Bellamy Park as the rest of us."

"He wasn't worried about our environment when he took off to do that pilot last October," I pointed out.

The pilot was for a musical country-western mystery series. That's the sort of hokey thing Zack gets involved in. Unless you're one of the handful of people in this country who doesn't watch TV, you'll remember that Zack portrayed Sheriff Lazarro in the wildly popular, totally improbable TV hit series, *Prescott's Landing*. It ran for seven years but collapsed soon after the writers killed Lazarro off—an occupational hazard in La-La land. The reruns will probably go on till the end of time.

The truly tasteless musical pilot had proven to be a great success, to the astonishment of thinking people everywhere. (I include myself.) I shouldn't have been surprised. Remember H.L. Mencken? "No one in this world, so far as I know, ever lost money by underestimating the intelligence of the great masses of the plain people."

It may have been successful, but the pilot had not yet spawned its hoped-for series, which was why Zack was back in Bellamy Park. And possibly, I thought abruptly, the reason why he was running for office—to prove to himself that he was still beloved? A thought worth pondering.

"Well, everybody else looks like they're getting revved up to support you, Zack," Savanna said. She seemed to have recovered from the erotic trauma of Taylor's arrival, but the tall detective hadn't yet managed to unglue his gaze from her fabulous face.

If a genie were to grant me a wish, I'd ask to spend twenty-four hours being Savanna, just so I could know what it's like to have the mere sight of my face and body make strong men ricochet off the walls. About all I ever rate is a cheery buddy grin.

Savanna was smiling her killer smile at Zack, and he was gazing fondly at her. Which doesn't really mean a whole lot. Zack looks fondly at all women.

"Leastways I've got you and Angel in my corner," he said to her, zinging me a sideways glance from under his eyelids.

"Me too," Taylor Bristow chimed in. He was finally emerging from his amorous trance. I watched him take charge of the world, glancing swiftly around to make sure no bad guys had sneaked up while he was hors de combat, his right hand hovering at his currently gunless hip. "A lot of us liked what you said about cooperative efforts between the community and local law enforcement," he went on.

I should mention that Bristow has a wonderfully deep and vibrant voice. Very attractive. "I'm working on getting the Police Officers Association to endorse you," he added.

Savanna beamed. So did Zack. As Zack's campaign manager, I had to admit that was really good news for all of us. At the same time I realized I hadn't seen our other partner for some time. "Where's Angel?" I asked.

"He's fraternizing with Gina from Buttons and Bows," Savanna answered, pointing toward the main bar.

"Aha!" I said. Buttons & Bows was the country-western store that was the other concession in CHAPS' lobby. Gina was the manager, an attractively petite, though somewhat brash, young woman with a punk haircut, which had gone through the entire rainbow spectrum since I'd first met her. Today it was short, spiky and burgundy colored on top; long, brown and striped with blond in back.

Catching Angel's eye, I waved him over. Gina came with him. She was really hanging in there. Where Angel was concerned, hanging in there took a lot of patience. Angel had dated Gina sporadically since the previous fall, but none of us knew how far their relationship had gone. Angel wasn't exactly the communicative sort.

Angel has a wonderfully strong face and body that could have been hacked out of a single piece of mahogany with a chain saw. He's Hispanic, always polite, not too forthcoming about his past history, and meticulously clean. He wears a fine straw cowboy hat that always looks new, and white western shirts that surely just came out of a really good laundry. Of average height and sinewy, he has high, sharply sculpted cheekbones, a Pancho Villa mustache and black hair drawn back in a neat ponytail. His eyes, as you might expect, are dark and deep. At first glance he looks vaguely sinister, which makes him a good bouncer. When you get to know him you find out he's loyal and kind, which makes him a good friend. He's also a loner. As a rule.

Patty Jenkins, known as P.J.—one of our regular patrons who lived in the Granada apartment complex across Adobe Square—had set her sights on Angel at the time of the skeleton. Angel had politely slow-danced with her whenever she asked him, but every time the music stopped, he had taken her back to her table and walked away. There was a whole indirect characterization of Angel there.

"Detective Sergeant Bristow thinks he can get the Police Officers Association to endorse Zack," I told him as he and Gina joined us. "Isn't that great?"

"I thought you just indicated you weren't all that enthusiastic about me runnin'," Zack said.

"I'm worried you don't know what you're getting into,"

I said. "You're an actor, not a politician. You've already got people attacking you. Gerald Senerac. Opal Quince. Once you actually make it onto the council, you'll have even more enemies. Doesn't matter what city you're in, if you're on the city council two thirds of the residents are going to hate you. You'll become one of the rascals people want to throw out. It'll be traumatic for you. You're used to being adored, not run out of town on a rail."

The bad-boy smile tugged at his mouth again, and he took his cowboy hat off, ran a hand through his deliberately shaggy black hair and set the hat at its jauntiest angle. One finger lightly rubbed the faint scar that zigzagged down his left cheek. He always said a rambunctious bull had given him that scar, which I didn't believe for a minute. It was more likely an outraged husband with a bread knife. I got the message, just the same. Anyone who tried to run Zack Hunter out of town would be dancing with danger.

Angel shook his head at me, his ponytail wiggling. "Sonny Bono was an actor before he got into politics," he pointed out.

"Clint Eastwood likewise," Gina put in. "I really like Clint Eastwood," she added, rolling her eyes. "I used to make up sex fantasies about him all night long. Until I met Angel."

Gina was not one to censor her thoughts. Whatever came into her mind came out of her pouty mouth. It was a refreshing, though sometimes disconcerting, attitude.

We all looked with interest at Angel, whose ears had suddenly acquired a tinge of red.

"How 'bout Ronald Reagan?" Zack said with an air of finality. "He was an actor, too."

Who could question Reagan's success as a politician?

Well, actually, *I* could. However, at times I manage to exercise restraint.

"Ronald Reagan was involved in politics from way back," I pointed out. "He was president of the Screen Actors Guild in the fifties."

"Yeah, well, Reagan wanted to be governor of California and president of the United States," Zack said. "I just want to get elected to Bellamy Park City Council."

Most of the time Zack's logic escapes me.

I became aware that we had been joined by a presence that exuded Old Spice. The only person I knew who used Old Spice was Winston Jermaine, who was running for the other open position on the city council, opposed by Opal Quince.

There wasn't a whole lot to choose between Opal and Winston as far as personality was concerned. It wasn't going to be a major contest like the one between Zack and his opponent Gerald Senerac.

"Hey, Winny," Zack said.

"A word, Hunter?" Winston asked, and Zack put a hand on his shoulder and took him some distance away from my inquiring mind.

Zack was one of the few people who actually liked Winston. True to his habit of relating everything to the wacky world of Hollywood, he'd determined that Winston reminded him of George C. Scott playing General Patton. Winston was a retired engineer, a tough-looking old guy, big as a bear. He wore bow ties, a flattop, and a pocket protector full of pens and mechanical drafting pencils.

Savanna and Taylor had gone back to looking at one another in their loopy way. Beside me, Angel tugged worriedly at his Pancho Villa mustache while Gina glowed up at him. I was beginning to feel surplus.

"Mr. Jermaine went fishing with Zack and me yesterday," Angel said, sotto voce. "I think maybe he's loco."

"There was some doubt in your mind earlier?"

"I didn't know he was *really* loco," Angel said, his dark eyes intense. "He's trying to get Zack to join him in chaining himself to those railings at the side of that marsh Mr. Senerac wants to build on. He kept yelling, 'We have to stop the bulldozers.' Got himself so worked up he got seasick."

I laughed. "Sounds like a relaxing time was had by all." I touched Angel's shoulder lightly. "I don't think you need to worry about Zack doing anything dumb. He doesn't go looking for trouble in real life."

Even as I said this I remembered Zack leaping forward to take a pistol away from a potential murderer last fall and getting shot for his pains. Fortunately, he'd healed fast. And anyway, I'd leaped forward myself and *I* wasn't about to do anything as dramatic or dumb as placing myself in front of a bulldozer.

The dramatic part of that image did worry me a little. If anyone were to persuade Zack that a scene had potential drama, he'd probably go for it, no matter how dangerous.

"Talk to him, Charlie," Angel urged, evidently interpreting my thoughts accurately. "Mr. Jermaine has a bad aura. Very dark."

I studied his face. In the shadow of his cowboy hat, his bronze skin stretched tight over his high cheekbones. "I didn't know you were into mystical stuff," I said with interest.

He shrugged and narrowed his eyes at me, which I took

to mean he regretted the revelation and wished I'd drop it, at least for now.

I wrinkled my nose to let him know I'd let it pass, but I was intrigued. None of us knew much of *anything* about Angel: He'd worked on a ranch in Texas at one time, he'd competed in rodeos. At the time of the skeleton, he'd revealed that he'd discovered a dead body when he was a kid. He had since consistently refused to talk about that incident. That was his entire history, he'd have us believe, all the rest—he claimed—was too dull to talk about.

"Have you given any thought to Senerac's aura?" I asked him. "He may be a handsome devil, but he's one hundred percent malice under the skin."

Angel shrugged. "Mr. Senerac hasn't had anything to say since Thursday's debate. I understand he hasn't even been seen around town. Probably too ashamed to show his face after the facts and figures Zack threw up at him over that proposed shopping mall he and his backers are so keen on."

He frowned, then suddenly gave me his rare smile. You have to really watch for Angel's smile. It's magic. Now you see it, now you don't. But while it's there, it lights up his face. "The facts and figures *you* gave him," he amended. "You really had Zack primed, Charlie."

"What worries me," I admitted, "is that if Zack wins I can't be sitting behind his left shoulder dictating answers to every question that comes up. Once he's on the council he'll have to go it alone."

"All politicians have speechwriters," Angel said. "And Zack's a quick study." He put his big warm hand on my shoulder. "Mr. Senerac's not going to get on that council, Charlie, you can count on it."

One thing that comforted me about this whole project was that however poor a politician Zack might turn out to be, Bellamy Park would be a lot better off with him than with Gerald Senerac, whose main motivations seemed to be lining his own pockets and destroying Zack Hunter's reputation.

In various media interviews ahead of last Thursday's banquet and debate, and during the debate itself, Senerac had threatened to reveal certain unspeakable secrets about Zack before the campaign was over.

Unfortunately, Zack did have a secret or two—including a sixteen-month gap in his recent history that was so far unaccounted for.

Secrets make campaign managers nervous, I had learned since I became one. Secrets have a way of coming out when people run for office.

CHAPTER 2

I glanced at my watch. It was time for Zack to make his speech so everyone could go home and we could get the place cleaned up for tonight's opening time. Sunday evenings weren't as popular as Wednesdays, Fridays, and Saturdays, but we still drew a good-size crowd.

Catching Zack's eye, I tilted my head toward the mike. He nodded and climbed up on stage to stand directly below the blowup of himself. Very dramatic. "Y'all listen up now," he said in his nice folksy down-home drawl.

Everybody started applauding as if he'd said something immensely clever. The fan-club members stood up straighter, a few with hands to their hearts as if they were saluting the flag.

"It sure is nice of y'all to help me out here," he added before starting in on his prepared speech, which he'd memorized like a movie script. Angel was right, Zack was a quick study. He talked earnestly and well, with appropriate gestures, slipping easily into his old Sheriff Lazarro persona.

It was a good speech; thoughtful, intelligent, laying out his position on the future of Bellamy Park, covering the hot issues he and Winston stood for. Yes, of course I wrote the speech. What did you think?

When the applause finally died and people headed for the exits, all pumped up to begin campaigning, I took myself off to the office to add some names to our telephone tree. I hadn't even got the computer booted up before Zack and Macintosh and Winston wandered in.

"I wanna show the guys the dartboard," Zack explained.

I sighed. We'd hung the dartboard on the back of the office door so we could let off steam once in a while—there's something very satisfying about the thunk of a heavy brass dart embedding itself in a boar-bristle board. Once in a while the four of us held a minitournament while discussing business decisions or problems.

Recently Zack had transformed the dartboard by pinning one of Gerald Senerac's campaign flyers over it. Winston did his imitation of a neighing horse when he saw the darts sticking out of Senerac's patrician nose. Macintosh looked embarrassed—maybe over the darts, maybe over Winston's laugh.

Pulling the three darts out, Winston stepped back and plunked them one at a time into Senerac's high forehead, then removed them and handed them with a flourish to Macintosh, who accepted them reluctantly.

It took a couple of minutes for Macintosh to get the board in focus, then he flung the darts in a floppy overhand. Two bounced off the board and onto the floor, one stuck to Senerac's right cheek. Macintosh walked over and yanked it out right away.

Zack took it from him, gathered up the other two and fired each one into Senerac's throat. "Straight to the jugular," he declared, setting Winston off on another whinny.

"I never thought I'd wanna get me a picture of Opal Quince," Winston exclaimed.

Opal Quince was Winston's opponent—a seriously weird real-estate lady, with formidable teeth, who had made something of a career out of writing letters to the editor of the *Bellamy Park Gazette*.

"Opal hasn't said anything really bad about you so far," I pointed out to Winston.

"There isn't anything bad to say," he said with a smug smile. "Besides which, you're not up to date, Miss Plato—Opal has a letter in this week's *Gazette* accusing me of being in cahoots with Zack to take over the town and use it as a set for television movies, like *Northern Exposure* did to Roslyn in Washington state."

Zack smiled wryly. "Opal says *I'm* an agent of the devil, like all other actors who portray violence on TV."

This campaign was shaping up into a battleground for crazies, I thought as Zack escorted his buddies out.

I was sliding open the window to clear out the odor of Old Spice when Zack returned. Heat poured in, causing the air-conditioning to cut off. The sun glinted on the windows of the Adobe Plaza bank next door. For all of ten seconds I thought longingly of cavorting in the waves at Half-Moon Bay, then I closed the window.

"I've been wantin' to ask you somethin' all day, Charlie," Zack said as I turned around. He was leaning back against the doorjamb. He sure did know how to lean.

I did some leaning of my own, settling my elbows behind me on the windowsill. "Ask away."

"You happen to know a good deodorant?"

"Your social life falling off, Zack?" I was doing restraint well today.

He squinted at me. At least I *thought* he was squinting. It's hard to tell with Zack, because he's perfected this way

of narrowing his eyes that makes him seem to be gazing off
into a dust cloud created by stampeding cattle. "I'm talkin'
about my new car," he said. "It has a funny smell. It must
be fierce for me to even notice it, considerin' I got my nose
busted on *Prescott's Landin'* and I don't have much sense
of smell."

A month earlier one of the guys in our cleaning crew,
leaving after a hard night's work, had absentmindedly put
the group's van in reverse instead of drive, then stomped
down on the accelerator. The resulting backward leap had
flattened Zack's old pickup against CHAPS' very sturdy
adobe wall. The new car was a Lexus Zack had purchased
a week ago right out of a swank automobile showroom in
Menlo Park.

"Why don't you get one of those little green paper trees
you can hang on the rearview mirror," I suggested. "Probably it's just new-car smell. It'll fade in a few days. Unless
there's something wet in there. Mildew makes for a pretty
foul odor."

Zack frowned. "I was thinkin' maybe it's BO. You remember that episode of *Seinfeld*—the valet at a restaurant
brought Jerry's car around front and there was this tremen-
dous stench of BO after. They built the whole episode on
tryin' to get rid of the smell, but it kept gettin' stronger
even after Jerry had the car ionized at the car wash. Everyone who sat in it carried the smell away with them."

Sometimes Zack has difficulty drawing a line between
real life and television. While I was trying to think up an
answer that would be suitably insulting, his eyebrows
slanted up in the puckish way they had, and a glint showed
in his green eyes. Evidently he'd been teasing me.

Ambling across the office, he put a hand on the windowsill

on each side of me, and leaned in so that his face, and body, were barely an inch from mine. "What do you think, Charlie? How *do* I smell?" he asked softly.

He smelled *clean. Masculine.*

I read recently that a human's blood-vessel system is sixty thousand miles long and has more than an acre of surfaces. All of my sixty thousand miles had their surfaces pulsing.

"I wanna thank you for all your help gettin' today's shin-dig off the ground, darlin'," he said, looking at my mouth. "That poster is a real winner, Charlie. You are a woman of a thousand talents." His eyes glinted. "Maybe a thousand and one?"

Images of Scheherazade danced in my head. Like her I was constantly thinking up ways to stay out of the sultan's bed. Well, at least half of me was. My physical self kept saying go for it; my mental processes had a lot more self-respect.

"I have to get back to the computer," I said lamely. "I have to update the telephone tree. Several people volunteered this afternoon."

"Is it truly urgent?" he murmured.

Luckily, at that moment, I caught a slight movement in the vicinity of the doorway and glanced sideways to see Zack's friend, Marsh Pollock, looking in.

"Come on in, Marsh," I said hoarsely.

Zack looked over his shoulder, but didn't move away.

Marsh was thirty-nine, three years older and a couple of inches shorter than Zack, which put him right at six feet. His thick, prematurely grey hair was cropped short and curly, a look that was devastating with his tanned youthful face. Zack had good muscle tone. Marsh was buff. As the new owner of Dandy Carr's gym, he had to be.

Marsh had bought the gym from Dandy in February, after the old man suffered a minor heart attack and decided to retire to North Hollywood to be near his daughters. He'd kept Dandy Carr's name for the place—out of respect for the old guy, he'd told me. When Zack had met Marsh at the gym, he'd invited him to take Dandy's place in the Bellamy Park Irregulars, who used to play poker on Wednesday evenings but now got together on Sundays.

Marsh was wearing a white polo shirt with Dandy's logo on it, tan walking shorts, and boat shoes, a nice change from the western outfits I was usually surrounded by. He always looked as if he'd just walked off a yacht, and he had the kind of vivid blue eyes some sailors have when they've spent years looking at the vastness of the ocean. Though when I told him that, he laughed and said he'd never been to sea in his life.

Right now his eyebrows were climbing. "Should I come back later?" he asked.

"Much later," Zack murmured, looking at my mouth. "Two, three weeks. A month maybe."

I gave him a push and he shifted to one side, smirking. "He's harassing me," I told Marsh, making my voice brisk, aware I'd probably colored up. "I'd report him to my boss, but I don't have one. Did you come to volunteer for the campaign committee?"

"Sorry, Charlie. I've made it a practice never to get involved in politics." He switched his focus to Zack. "I was in the vicinity, dropped in to tell you I can't host tonight's poker game in the gym office even though it's my turn. I'm having the office painted tomorrow and the workmen cleared all the furniture out today."

Zack shrugged. "My house then? I can probably catch Macintosh and Sundancer if I hustle." He glanced at me sideways. "If Charlie can bear to let me go," he added.

"I'll try to soldier on," I said.

I fully expected Marsh to leave with Zack, but he remained in the doorway. I purposely moved over to my desk, sat down and booted up the computer, hoping he'd take the hint. But he didn't.

A couple of times Marsh had come close to coming on to me, but I'd bristled in time and he'd backed off. I hoped he wasn't going to try again today. I had enough to do fighting off Zack.

Besides which, I wasn't quite sure what I thought of Marsh Pollock. I pride myself on my ability to read people but I couldn't seem to get a handle on him. He always had a sort of knowing smile hovering around his mouth, which was attractive, but irritated me no end. Which probably meant I was also attracted to him, I admitted to myself with a sigh.

He perched himself on the edge of my desk. "Are you and Zack ... ?" He let the question hang.

"No," I said, more explosively than was warranted.

He let the silence grow. "How come you don't work out in my gym, Charlie?" he asked. He had a gravelly sort of voice, which made everything he said sound as if it had hidden meanings.

I kept my gaze on the computer screen as I retrieved the telephone-tree file. "Your gym is always crowded with perky young things in spandex, and macho guys spattering sweat on the mirrors," I said. "I prefer the gym in Condor.

It has all this neat old equipment—separate bench presses with long handles, old-style leg-lift and leg-press machines. I especially like the rowing machine and the treadmill; they don't have any monitors that check your pulse rate or tell you how many calories you're burning. And the place is usually empty at the time I work out."

I always babble when I get nervous, and something about this man made me nervous. When I finally managed to stop, he leaned forward and said in a conspiratorial way, with that funny little smile in place, "You'd look great in spandex, Charlie."

A line of zzzzz's appeared on my screen. I hit Backspace several times to wipe them out. Once again I caught movement in the doorway. Busy as Union Square today. This time it was Lauren Deakins, Zack's fan. For once I was glad to see her. "Hi," I said. "Can I help you?"

She stammered something about Zack. Apparently she'd come looking for him. Darting glances from me to Marsh, who had twisted around to see who I was talking to, she gripped the doorjamb and looked as if she were about to burst into tears.

"I think Zack probably left," I lied. I was beginning to worry about this young woman.

"Oh well . . . okay, I guess . . . thank you." Flushing miserably, all the way up to her thick eyebrows, she finally managed to detach herself from the doorjamb and take herself off.

"One of Zack's fans," I explained to Marsh.

"An apparently proliferating breed," he said with a grin, then went on as if there'd been no interruption. "I could work with you on a program as your personal trainer, Charlie, no extra charge. You really need to bulk up a little."

"In other words I'm too skinny? Don't you worry yourself, Marsh, I'm very healthy. I eat right and I eat regular."

Stand by for a minihistory here. I'm actually almost obsessive about eating regularly. After my parents demolished themselves and their Cessna in a thunderstorm near Tahoe during my last year of high school, I'd gone into a tailspin and had apparently decided to starve myself by the time I graduated from the University of Washington. At that time, I fortunately took a job with a doctor in Seattle. Though he was a plastic surgeon, he recognized anorexia when he saw it and got me into therapy.

Unfortunately, he also married me, then periodically forgot that fact when his more glamorous patients came up from Hollywood (in disguise) to consult him. I decided that in this age of AIDS his little hobby was probably even more hazardous to my health than anorexia. So I divorced him and answered an ad Zack had spread around a few newspapers, which, of course, had led me to my current situation.

"What do you say, Charlie?" Marsh asked, leaning closer.

My patience, never my primary virtue, was wearing thin. There'd been enough testosterone floating around in this office for one day.

"Thanks, but no thanks," I said sharply, then added for good measure, "I really do have a lot to do, Marsh. If you don't mind, I'd really like to . . ."

He slid off the desk and raised his hands in surrender. "Okay, I'm leaving. But we'll talk again, Charlie Plato."

I stayed irritated for a good five minutes after Marsh was gone. Mostly with myself. I'd actually caught my breath when he leaned close. And he'd noticed.

Muttering to myself, I was nonetheless getting on with

my work when Zack came strolling in again. "What now?"
I demanded when he just stood there frowning.

"All of a sudden, that smell in my car stinks worse than
a road-killed skunk, Charlie," he said. "Car's been sittin' out
there in the heat of the day since I got here this mornin'.
Seems like maybe somethin's gone rotten."

I sat back and looked up at him. "Did you check the
trunk? Maybe you left some food in it. Did you take one of
your dollies on a picnic lately?"

He took a couple of minutes to think about that, then
shook his head. "I can't get the trunk open, the catch is
jammed."

"It's a new car, why would the catch be jammed?"

He took off his cowboy hat and looked in it, as if it would
provide some answers. After replacing it, he said slowly,
"The catch wasn't jammed when I brought the car home.
Leastways I don't think it was. First time I noticed it was
when I went fishin' yesterday with Winston and Angel and
Ted Ennis, over to Pillar Point. I had to put my fishin' gear
in the backseat. I meant to run the car over to the dealer,
but then I remembered him sayin' he was takin' his son to
visit his grandparents in Ashland, Oregon, so I thought I'd
wait until he came back."

His forehead was furrowed and he seemed a little pale.
"I wish you'd come take a sniff, Charlie. I'm sorta worried."

Angel was our worrier. Not Zack. "Worried about what?"
I asked.

"I just want you to come see what it smells like to you."

"What it smells like? How am I supposed to know what
it smells like?"

Zack was no longer among those present. I had no choice

but to save my file, shut down the computer, and follow him out.

There were still a few cars in the parking lot. When I went back in, I'd need to start clearing out the lingerers. The sun was really baking down, in spite of the shade of the ancient oak trees. I could feel heat bouncing back up from the plaza paving stones, making my jeans wilt.

Zack's gleaming new luxury car—a beautiful forest green—was parked well away from the other cars and the buildings. He wasn't taking any chances on another befuddled janitor.

A little breeze had come up, which seemed to promise a cooler evening. First breeze since the heat wave started a few days ago. It felt good wafting around my face. At least it felt good until we came close to the Lexus and I caught a whiff of the odor Zack had talked about. That wasn't new car smell. Nor was it mildew. Or BO.

My stomach did a double somersault. I stopped walking as suddenly as if I'd crashed into a brick wall. All the blood left my head.

Zack scanned my face. "That's what I thought," he said.

Once you've smelled death you don't ever forget it; you can't mistake it. We had both smelled death when I found that skeleton in our flowerbed.

Something or somebody dead was in the trunk of Zack's car.

CHAPTER 3

Taylor Bristow had already left CHAPS, Savanna said when we approached her in the main corral. Her eyes were big with questions, but we didn't want to get into explanations until our suspicions were confirmed. We went into the office and used the telephone.

Wherever Bristow had gone, it wasn't to the police station. After discovering he wasn't there, I explained our smell, and my interpretation of it, to Dispatch who said they'd have someone out there ASAP.

They sent a cheery, young, pink-cheeked officer who had surely graduated just this second from the police academy. "Something dead in the trunk?" Officer Calhoun echoed with an unmistakable note of skepticism in his voice. "You took a look?"

Zack shook his head. "The trunk's catch is jammed."

The cop pondered a moment, then went over to his patrol car, opened its trunk and removed a hefty crowbar from a toolbox.

"It's a *new* car," Zack reminded him.

"No problem," the officer said cheerfully.

Zack tensed, but the catch popped after a couple of minutes of pressure. Zack started breathing again. For a second or two. Then he stopped. So did I. With the trunk open, the smell was eyewatering, even upwind. The young officer backed up a step, no longer looking quite so cheerful, or so pink cheeked, then beckoned us forward.

There was a clear plastic tarp in the trunk. It was wrapped around a human form. At least the form had once been human. In movies death is nice and tidy, eyes and mouths are neatly closed. Death isn't really that neat. The body seemed to have collapsed in on itself. The man's eyes looked glassy, protuberant, glaring as if in his last moments he had thrown an apoplectic fit.

"But Gerald Senerac never lost his temper," I said, without intending to say anything at all. "He was a cold man."

"That's Senerac?" Zack exclaimed, reaching out a hand.

I slapped it back. "Don't touch anything," I yelled at him.

"Sorry, Charlie," he said. He looked stunned.

"Senerac?" the officer queried.

"The president of the Bellamy Park Bank," I explained, after a couple of convulsive swallows. I finally managed to look away from those bulging eyes. That pop-eyed stare had not been caused by apoplexy after all. A length of yellow rope was tied around the man's neck. Tightly. Nausea slithered into my throat and threatened to make me gag.

After sending us to stand under one of the huge live oaks that graced the plaza, near enough that he could keep an eye on us, the officer called in for a detective and a forensic crew.

I hoped Detective Sergeant Bristow would have arrived at the station in the meantime, but instead Bellamy Park PD sent out Detective Sergeant Reggie Timpkin. Timpkin immediately took charge, sending the patrol cars to surround Zack's Lexus like so many Westward-Ho wagons circling a camp. Once the forensic team started taking photographs, and hunting and gathering the necessary items that come under the heading of evidence, he came over to us. He was very nattily dressed in a white shirt and tie, dark slacks with a knife crease, shoes you could see your face in. He held a pocket-size tape recorder in one hand. I'd noticed him talking into it as he worked.

"Gerald Senerac," he repeated into it after Zack and I got through delivering our story. The three of us stood upwind of Zack's car. Timpkin had that cocky stance cops have—feet wide, chest out—maybe it's just a cop's body language, comes from always having to be prepared to repel all borders.

He was apparently devoid of facial expression. He had a solid build—maybe not quite so solid in the middle. His fair thinning hair was brushed carefully from a side parting. A skinny little mustache curled like a caterpillar over his upper lip. I hate that kind. Goatees too. If a man wants hair on his face, he ought to grow a Pancho Villa replica like Angel's or a full beard. Something that makes a definite statement.

"As I told the officer, the trunk catch was jammed," Zack said. "I don't know how come. I just brought the car home Monday. It's brand spankin'. I didn't notice anythin' wrong until yesterday mornin'."

"Yesterday." Timpkin mulled for a while, then asked, "You open the trunk at all since Monday?"

Zack took off his cowboy hat and worried his hair with his fingers. He does that to help himself think. Finally his lean face brightened and he nodded. "I put a suitcase in it on Tuesday when I drove a friend to the airport."

Melissa, I thought. The flight attendant with the searchlight smile. A fairly long-term, though sporadic, member of Zack's doll brigade. "Flyin' Missy," Savanna and I had named this one. "Comes complete with her own overnight bag and blow-dryer."

"Gerald Senerac's the guy who's running against Zack in the city-council race," I said. "*Was* running," I added. Saying his name had brought the image of his swollen dead eyes back into my mind. I thought it was entirely possible I was going to throw up right there in the parking lot.

"City council," Timpkin said, nodding to show he knew all about it.

He left us to greet Dr. Martin Trenckman, the county coroner/medical examiner, who had just arrived with Biff White, the coroner's investigator. Dr. Trenckman had been called in when we found the skeleton. He was as smartly suited now as he had been then. He frowned at Zack and me when he caught sight of us. I didn't blame him. Lightning isn't supposed to strike twice. Though I did read a recent story about a national park ranger who got struck seven times during his life. You'd think he'd have learned enough to stay in out of the rain.

During the ensuing police activity, Zack and I stood next to each other in the shade of the huge old oak tree and held hands. Tightly. Both our hands were sweaty. We watched, of course, but couldn't bring ourselves to comment for a while. A patrol officer had secured the crime scene with the usual yellow tape, wrapping it around a tree here, a vintage lamppost there. It soon became clear that Timpkin was fussy, and thorough. He talked into his little tape recorder constantly.

"I don't believe this is happening again," I said at last.

"Spooky," Zack agreed. "D'you suppose Watanabes had any bodies turn up when they owned the place?"

Before Zack transformed it into CHAPS, our building had housed a Japanese restaurant named Tomodachi. The Watanabes—Michiko and Joe, had owned it.

"I'm never goin' to get the smell out of the trunk," Zack went on. I'd have thought him heartless if I hadn't seen the darkness pooling in his eyes. We all have our ways of coping with horror.

"My fingerprints are goin' to be all over that car," he said in the next breath.

"The police will expect them to be," I assured him.

"Sheriff Lazarro would have impounded the car," he said.

"I expect Timpkin will, too. You probably won't get it back until after the trial."

"What trial?"

"Whoever did it. Whoever killed Senerac."

Zack sighed audibly. "Tell you the truth, Charlie, I didn't care for that car all that much *before* we found Senerac in it. I might just trade it in when the cops get through with it. Get me another pickup in the meantime."

Surprisingly enough, a lot of Zack's PR stuff was true. If he drank at all, he drank beer; pizza *was* his favorite food, and he really did feel more comfortable in a truck. Or else he was thinking that a pickup didn't have a trunk.

The coroner's van took Senerac's mortal remains away. The crew started working on the area the body had covered. Timpkin waved us over and gestured toward CHAPS' entryway. "Questions," he said.

A knot of spectators had shown up. They stood around staring, not yet knowing what had happened, but willing to stick around until someone told them. In the group closest to the entryway, I recognized P.J., the horsey-looking woman from the Granada apartment complex who was sweet on Angel, and pudgy Bernie Lightfoot from the minimart across the plaza.

"What's going on, Charlie?" P.J. called as we went by. She hadn't shown up at the campaign kickoff, she must have seen the activity from her apartment window.

I gave a noncommittal shrug and kept walking. "The media's arriving," I murmured to Zack as I caught sight of a van with a familiar logo on it just driving into the parking lot. "They'll have a wonderful time. A second murder at CHAPS."

Usually, any mention of the media affects Zack the way bells affected Pavlov's dogs—he straightens up and pays attention and almost salivates, at the same time settling his cowboy hat at its most fetching angle. But he was evidently still in shock and showed no reaction.

I waited for him to ask how I knew Senerac's death was murder, which is the sort of thing Zack is known to do, but again he surprised me. "Strangled," he said, his eyes shadowing up again. "What a helluva way to go."

He shuddered, then rallied. "Can you trace that rope?" he asked Timpkin. "I remember on an episode of *Prescott's Landin'*, Sheriff Lazarro recognized a piece of rope had been used to tie up a box as comin' from East Asia. Helped him solve the crime."

Timpkin's eyes were a very flat grey. Coupled with a way he had of bunching up his chin and lifting his jaw, they made him look suspicious of everything anyone said.

"Thought it might help," Zack said lamely.

"Uh-huh," Timpkin said. By now we'd reached the staircase that led to my private quarters. I thought of suggesting we go up there to talk, then decided I didn't want Timpkin in my loft, possibly poking around to see if there was anything incriminating in there, making Benny nervous.

For a couple of minutes the detective stood looking into the main corral where Angel, Savanna, and a few others were taking down the bunting and clearing stuff off the tables, which stood on raised platforms at either end of the dance floor.

"This particular ligature was a common-enough rope," he said after a minute or two. "Yellow nylon. Braided. Sort of rope used to tie up boats, or fasten Christmas trees on top of station wagons."

After a momentary pause, he passed on more information. "Only unusual feature is a loop tied each end with a bowline knot. To provide a handhold, I suppose." He darted a swift glance from Zack to me, as if hoping to catch us looking guilty. "That's not to be repeated," he added. "Especially not to the media."

"A *bowling* knot?" I queried, thinking he'd caught Zack's habit of dropping his g's.

"B-o-w-l-i-n-e," Zack volunteered. "It's used by boatin' or navy dudes." He was looking more like himself now that we were away from the actual scene—and smell.

Demonstrating with both hands, he said, "You learn how to tie it by rememberin' that the rabbit comes out of the hole, goes around the tree and goes back down in the hole."

Timpkin's flat grey gaze fixed itself on Zack's face. "I learned that on *Prescott's Landin'*," Zack said, belatedly becoming wary.

"Uh-huh," Timpkin said, his chin bunching.

Zack pointed left. "Our office is that way."

"Office," Timpkin said, and shepherded us ahead of him as if afraid we'd suddenly make a break for it.

He seated himself behind my desk and didn't invite us to take a chair. I hate power games, so I sat myself down. Zack followed suit. "Okay, Mr. Hunter, Ms. Plato," Timpkin said, placing his tape recorder on the desk between us. "Do you understand why you are being questioned?"

"Let me hazard a guess," I said. "Because we discovered a dead body?"

I'm not as unfeeling as I sound. Tragedy and horror always make me flippant. Which may be better than running through the streets screaming, but doesn't always make me appreciated.

Detective Sergeant Timpkin gave me his flat-eyed stare. "Tell me why you reached the conclusion the smell was a dead body," he said.

I did that. To the smallest detail.

Then Zack did the same.

Timpkin asked more questions, for which he required precise answers.

He knew about our association with last summer and fall's murder investigation, he said, though he hadn't been involved. I wished he weren't involved in this one.

"Sergeant Bristow appreciated our help," I noted.

Timpkin finally showed us a facial expression. It was skeptical.

"You and Senerac were rivals for the same city-council position?" he asked Zack.

Zack nodded.

"Friendly rivals?"

Anyone who'd read a local newspaper or watched TV in

the last couple of weeks had to know relations between Zack and Senerac had been unremittingly hostile.

"Not friendly, no," Zack said mildly.

The flat grey gaze moved to my face. "According to Officer Calhoun, you made the comment that Senerac was a cold man?"

He's certainly cold now, I wanted to say. "That was the impression he gave me," I managed instead. "He was a didactic, scholarly type. Gaunt. Apparently unfeeling. Like he'd been kissed by the Ice Maiden when he was a boy."

Timpkin's blank expression made it clear he had no idea what I was talking about. "The Ice Maiden," I repeated. "Andersen's fairy tales. The Ice Maiden kissed a boy while he was swimming, and he grew stiff with cold and sank. Senerac always made me think of that story." Timpkin was still looking at me. "Senerac said some pretty nasty things about Zack," I blurted out.

"Such as?"

I swallowed.

Zack jumped in to haul me out of the hole I'd dug for myself. "Such as accusin' me of havin' been an alcoholic. Also said I'd messed with drugs and knocked people around."

Timpkin had another expression in his repertoire. A smile. It was not a nice smile. It was an anticipatory smile. Think wolf gazing at Red Riding Hood.

"Those kind of accusations are often made during campaigns," I pointed out hurriedly.

"What's going on?" Angel asked from the doorway. "P.J. told us the police found another body. Was she joshing us?"

I swiveled my chair around. He and Savanna were both standing there, looking worried.

"These are our partners," I told Timpkin. "Angel Cervan-

tes and Savanna Seabrook. Detective Sergeant Timpkin. Is
it okay if I tell them. . . ."

He nodded.

I took a deep breath and looked from Angel to Savanna.
They looked somberly back. "Zack told me the catch of his
car trunk was jammed and he'd noticed a funny smell coming
from it. I went out to the parking lot with him to see if I
could figure out what it was. We decided it smelled like
someone died."

Angel crossed himself. I kept a wary eye on him. When
he first saw our skeleton's foot poking out of the ground last
August, he'd fainted. It had taken him a while to explain
about the dead body he'd found when he was a kid. So far,
he seemed more puzzled than upset.

"We called the police department and asked for Taylor
Bristow but he wasn't there," I went on.

Savanna looked dismayed. "Sorry, Charlie, if you'd said
you really needed him I could have told you he went to visit
his mom. She wanted to come to the meeting today, but she
had a cold. Taylor took her some posters to give her friends."

Along with her entire garden club, Taylor Bristow's mom
was a big fan of Zack's. She had never missed an episode
of *Prescott's Landing*.

"Bellamy Park PD sent out an officer," I went on. "He
opened Zack's trunk with a crowbar. There's a body in it
wrapped in a plastic tarp. It's Gerald Senerac. He's been
strangled."

"In *Zack's* car?" Angel said.

I nodded.

"Why would he be in Zack's car?" His eyes widened and
he stared at Timpkin. "You can't think that Zack . . ." he
broke off. "There's no doubt it's Senerac?"

"Ms. Plato identified him," Timpkin said. "We will of course seek confirmation."

Savanna sat down on one of the office chairs, wheeled it next to mine and reached over to give my hand a squeeze. Angel's eyes were hooded, but he seemed to be holding up okay. "Many people hated Gerald Senerac," he told Timpkin.

"Hated?"

"Like the entire membership of CFLC." It was obvious Angel was trying to take suspicion away from Zack.

Timpkin raised his eyebrows.

"Citizens for a Livable City," I explained, wondering if the guy ever watched TV news. CFLC was nothing if not vocal, and visible. Possibly he was pretending ignorance so we'd keep talking and incriminate ourselves. "CFLC's the group that asked Zack to run. They don't—didn't—like Senerac because he and a group of business people want to pave over the salt marsh where that small area of Bellamy Park meets San Francisco Bay. They want to build what they call an exclusive residential development. That translates into filling and dredging and driving pilings, building apartment complexes and streets, tennis courts, motels, a golf course, and all that good stuff. All of which activity will kill off the sensitive habitat of a lot of animals and birds and other wildlife."

We all heard voices out in the lobby. I recognized P.J.'s among them, and the familiar breathy articulation of a local, very perky, TV reporter. Discreetly, Angel pushed the door closed. Any one of us would have done the same, without thinking. "Senerac seems to think if he can get on the city council he'll be able to influence the city and whoever else has to get involved to let the group go ahead, regardless of the threat to the environment," I went on.

I'd lost Timpkin's attention. The air in the office had suddenly become charged.

His flat stare was fixed on the inside of the office door. Specifically on the dartboard, which you'll remember was covered with a poster of the now-deceased Senerac.

I swiveled my own chair around to look. Seeing that poster from a stranger's point of view made it look a lot more threatening. Especially considering the three darts that were sticking out of Senerac's rather prominent Adam's apple.

My digestive system coiled itself into a Gordian knot. Zack's face looked carved from granite, and about the same color.

"Darts," Timpkin said.

We all sort of nodded.

"Who threw 'em?" he asked.

"I did," Zack said.

"A lot of people have thrown darts at that poster," said Angel, who hadn't. "That doesn't mean . . ."

Timpkin was standing, looking at Zack. "Maybe we could continue this interview at the station," he suggested.

"Hey, wait a minute," I said, standing up. "There's no reason you can't talk here. You've no call to take Zack in just because it's his car. You surely don't think he's stupid enough to kill Senerac, his known enemy, then shut the body up in his own car."

The flat grey stare met my eyes, and I felt my soul shrivel like a punctured balloon. "This is just an interview, Ms. Plato," Timpkin said. "No need for you to be alarmed." He hesitated, his chin bunching. "Unless you have some reason to be."

"None at all," I said hastily. I looked at Zack. "I'll come with you," I said.

Before Zack could respond, Timpkin said, "Thank you, Ms. Plato, that won't be necessary. I'll be back to question you again later."

Zack had stood up when I did. He wrapped a big hand around my upper arm and looked directly into my face. "No problem, Charlie. I have to do whatever I can to straighten out this situation."

He was looking admirably macho, speaking lines that could have come out of Sheriff Lazarro's own mouth. Lazarro had better writers than Zack did, so he often quoted him. But the shadow was still deep in his eyes. Fear tightened my skin suddenly, so that my whole body felt constricted. I managed to swallow and gave him what I hoped was a reassuring smile.

Before opening the door, Timpkin removed the dart-board—holding it carefully by the handle—and carried it out with him.

CHAPTER 4

Savanna grabbed the phone as soon as the sound of the men's footsteps faded away. "I'm trying Taylor's mom," she said, glancing at me as she punched out numbers.

There was no answer.

She tried another set of numbers. A small part of my numbed brain noted with affectionate interest that she punched both sets of numbers from memory. "He's not at home either," she said as she hung up. "He must have taken his mom somewhere."

"Surely Sergeant Timpkin can't believe Zack killed Gerald Senerac," Angel blurted out.

"Don't you worry," Savanna soothed him. "Zack'll convince the police he's innocent."

I thought she was probably right. I *hoped* she was right.

Zack didn't turn up until nine P.M. By then, Angel and Savanna and I were sitting listlessly around one of the tables in the main corral. We'd cleared everyone out of CHAPS, explaining the reason only to Sundancer. He'd merely rubbed his hands together, blinked like an owl and said, "Hey, more publicity for CHAPS." I wanted to snap the stupid suspenders he always wore. As I said earlier, Sundancer is a great deejay, but certifiably eccentric. And heartless. Personally, I think he's spent so much time with a headset on he's become alienated from real people.

Once the place was empty, we'd put closed signs on CHAPS' plaza door and the entry from the lobby, and locked both doors. By then, the media had finished questioning both the crowd outside and the police officers who were trying to work. They turned their attention to us a fraction of a minute too late.

They banged on both doors, of course, then rang the doorbells until our ears were numb. We pretended we weren't around. For a while the phones also rang constantly, but eventually whichever TV or newspaper reporters were calling got tired of listening to the answering machine, which Sundancer had rigged up to play Travis Tritt's "A Hundred Years from Now."

For comfort, I'd brought Benny down. He was sitting on my left shoulder nibbling on my hair when Zack ambled in. I hadn't realized quite how anxious I was about our absent partner until I felt all the stuffing go out of me, leaving me draped over my chair like Raggedy Ann. Sensing the release of tension, Benny stuck his nose in my ear, which I've always taken as a sign of affection.

After Savanna got through hugging Zack, and Angel got through trading manly handshakes, Zack came over and sat down next to me and rubbed the spot between Benny's ears in the way that always makes the rabbit's fuzzy brown hair stand on end. "No hug from Charlie?" he asked, slanting his eyebrows up.

"Talk," I said.

The familiar bad-boy grin materialized. "You sound like Detective Sergeant Timpkin."

I punched his shoulder. He laughed and grabbed my hand and held on to it.

"I don't have the strength to hug you," I told him. "The minute you came in I went wobbly. I guess I was scared Timpkin would lock you up and throw away the key."

"Me too," Zack said. "He kept assurin' me I was free to leave, but he also mentioned from time to time that I might look guiltier than I already looked if I was to take him up on that."

He leaned over and kissed my cheek. "Thanks for worryin' 'bout me, Charlie."

He was still holding my hand and I noticed that my stuffing seemed to be reassembling itself. In fact, it was getting positively perky. Carefully, I removed my hand from Zack's.

"What happened?" Savanna asked, settling back on her seat.

Angel had already turned his chair around and straddled it. Why do men do that? It always looks hazardous.

Zack took off his cowboy hat, leaned back and set it down on the next table. One thing that amazes me when Zack takes his hat off—his black hair always looks perfect, casually shaggy, boyishly tousled, falling forward on his forehead in separate strands, just like his PR photo. I asked him once who cut his hair.

"Gemini," he said.

I might have known it would be the most expensive salon in town. "You think they could do anything with mine?" I asked.

He gravely studied my orange mane for a good two minutes, then his mouth formed itself into its bad-boy grin. "Nah," he said.

He was smiling a little on the wry side right now. "CHAPS out of beer?" he asked Angel.

Angel hopped up at once and brought a pitcher and four glasses to the table. Zack took a long swallow. "First off," he said, setting the glass down, "I want to tell y'all there's no way I could ever kill anyone, no matter how I felt about them. Senerac was a—well, shoot, y'all know he wasn't one of my favorite dudes. But nobody in this whole wide world deserves to die like that. I'm grieved that he got himself killed and I cannot for the life of me imagine how anyone could do that to a fellow human being. It's one thing to punch somebody out in a fit of temper—that I could understand—but to take a piece of rope and tie knots in it and . . ."

He shook his head, shuddering. "What I'm tryin' to say is that I did not kill Gerald Senerac."

Savanna patted his arm. "For heaven's sake, honey, we know that."

"Thought didn't cross our minds," Angel said firmly.

I have a peculiar memory. It stores bits of conversation I never even paid much attention to at the time, then pops them up like bread out of a toaster when I least expect them. Sometimes I don't remember who said these bits of dialogue. But in this case, I did. "Senerac's not going to get on that council, Charlie, you can count on it," Angel had said to me just a few hours earlier.

So what? I asked myself. This isn't *Murder, She Wrote*. That was a comforting comment, not a clue.

Zack was looking at me questioningly. "Don't be ridiculous," I said. "Of course I don't think you killed him."

It was not a good time for my memory to dredge up that missing sixteen months in Zack's life, and the magazine story

I'd once read about some knock-down-drag-out fight he'd had on the set.

"Timpkin's pretty well made up his mind I'm guilty," Zack said gloomily.

"Ridiculous," I said again, with a little more conviction this time. What possible proof could Timpkin have found in such a short time?

"Lab dude clipped some of my hair," Zack continued.

"They found hair at the scene?"

"I guess."

"Black hair?"

"Nobody's sayin'."

"Did it have roots?"

He squinted at me.

"It makes a difference, Zack. You can only get DNA from the root of a hair, not from the hair itself."

"How do you know ..." He held up a hand to stop me from replying. "I know—you read mysteries."

"Did you call Yoder?" I asked. If they were checking Zack's hair they were seriously considering him a suspect, and Nate Yoder was Zack's attorney. He represented a lot of well-known people. *Only* well-known people. He was a regular guest on a couple of TV programs—*You and The Law*, and another one I couldn't remember by name. Zack had picked him because his last name was so close to Yoda in *Star Wars*. He even looked like Yoda around the eyes. Pouchy. Yoder was pretty good with contracts. And he'd undertaken a lot of fairly famous lawsuits. Far as I knew he had little experience with murder.

Zack nodded. "He was in a meeting, accordin' to his wife. Knowing Nate, I expect it was more'n likely a party. She said she'd get a message to him. Last I heard. I decided to cooperate."

"Well, if the hair they found has roots and can be tested for DNA and doesn't match yours, then that's good that they took some. They'll have to go on looking to find out whose it is."

"Yeah. Right." Zack looked hopeful, then frowned. "You see them take away my car? They towed it up a ramp into a flatbed truck. D'you know what I *paid* for that car?"

That was evidently a rhetorical question. He didn't enlighten us. "The medical examiner's come up with an approximate time of death," he went on. "Seems Senerac was killed about three or four hours after the banquet."

"Thursday's banquet?" Angel asked.

Zack nodded and I winced. Senerac had been particularly vitriolic at the debate that preceded the banquet, directing insults at Zack in his chill, extremely high-pitched voice, which had always affected me like a kid rubbing a balloon with his fingernails. Zack, like the gentleman he was, or at least had been since I'd met him, had remained courteous, though his eyes had turned to flint. If he'd blinked, there would have been sparks.

A couple of times I'd wanted to kick Senerac on his bony shins, hard enough to make his eyes water; but fortunately I was sitting in the audience and couldn't get at him without making an exhibition of myself.

"So Timpkin reckons you had a motive," I said. "What about means and opportunity?"

"This is Timpkin's scenario, told to me as a hypothetical exercise." Zack held up one finger at a time. "Senerac threatens to dig up my unsavory past. I take him aside and strangle him, wrap him up in a tarp and stash him in my car until I can find a likely place to dispose of him. Trouble is, because of the heat wave the smell threatens to give me away before I can figure out what to do, so I confess to you, Charlie. We decide then to pretend we've just noticed the odor and hope nobody will believe I'd be dumb enough to put the body in my own car."

I blinked. "I'm an accessory?"

"In Timpkin's twisted mind, you bet."

I sat up straight, lifted Benny down from my shoulder and put him in his cage on the floor. He hunkered down comfortably and started chewing his way through his bowl of veggie-flavored bunny bites. "Timpkin's demented," I muttered.

"Demented's a good word." Zack took a deep swallow of his beer, sighed, then went on: "As for means and opportunity, Timpkin reckons anyone could get hold of a piece of rope like that. And I obviously knew all about bowline knots."

He grinned weakly. "Guess I did myself in on that one."

"You should never volunteer anything to a police officer," I told him. "Wait until you're asked a question, then answer it as briefly and truthfully as possible. Then shut up."

"Yes, ma'am, Ms. Plato. Why didn't you mention that to me before?" He shook his head. "Opportunity is somethin' else. I told Timpkin I was home alone after the banquet."

He rubbed his nose and stared morosely into his beer.

According to body-language manuals I've read, nose rubbing often indicates lying.

"Where were you?" I asked sharply.

He looked at an area about an inch above my right shoulder. "Home alone."

Avoiding eye contact is not a sign of a sterling character, either. I imitated his staring-into-a-dust-storm squint, keeping my gaze fixed on his face. After a minute or so, he blew out a breath, flicked a glance at me, then looked away again.

"No foolin' you, darlin'."

I kept right on looking at him.

"I can't talk about it," he said.

"A woman?" I asked.

"Charlie," Savanna said gently, touching my arm, evidently concerned about the hostility in my voice.

I shrugged her off.

Zack finally looked at me directly. "I *won't* talk about it," he said, his eyes hard as Alaskan jade.

I kept up the eye contact for a minute more, then let out my own breath. "Okay. We'll come back to it later. Given his suspicious nature, how come Timpkin let you go?"

Zack glanced at Savanna. "Taylor Bristow arrived. Said he'd left something in his desk, came in to collect it, heard I was on the premises." He looked back at me. "He made fun of Timpkin's theory, reminded him I'd played Sheriff Lazarro for seven years and learned enough about clues that if I'd killed Senerac I'd know at least to put him in the back of somebody else's car." He hesitated. "Got the impression there's some bad feelin' between those two."

"Can you imagine anyone having a good feeling about Timpkin?" I asked.

He gave a tired sigh. "Main thing, I guess, Timpkin didn't have any evidence to hold me on, so he let me go. Told me not to think of leavin' town." He shook his head. "Made me feel mighty peculiar, hearin' that, considerin' the number of times I said that on *Prescott's Landin'*. Didn't think real police officers said such a thing."

"I'm not sure Timpkin's real," I said.

Someone started beating on CHAPS' plaza door. Angel

got up and moseyed over there, looked through the peephole, then opened it up.

Detective Sergeant Taylor Bristow. Still wearing his yellow polo shirt.

His gaze found Savanna, gave her a smoldering look, then moved on to Zack. "Thought we should talk," he said, coming over.

He reversed Angel's chair to a normal position and sat down opposite Zack. Angel pulled up another and said flatly, "None of us believe Zack had anything to do with Mr. Senerac's death."

"I'm here to be convinced," Bristow said. "But it's going to take more than I've heard so far, no matter what I said to Timpkin." He fixed his brown eyes on Zack's face. "You want your partners to stay for this, or do we do it one on one?"

"You here officially?" Savanna asked before Zack could answer.

Bristow shook his head. "Timpkin took the call, he's the primary investigator. Which is not to say I won't be assisting, or interfering, according to your point of view, and depending upon my caseload." He looked at Zack. "Right now, I'm here as your friend."

Zack glanced at each of us in turn. "Charlie and Angel and Savanna are my friends, too. I'd like them to stay."

"So be it. Let's start by fleshing that story of yours out, okay? Gerald Senerac looked upon you with all the affection he'd give a rabid pit bull. He was spitting ice cubes every time he mentioned your name at that debate. Throwing out meaningful hints, too. Hints about drunkenness, drugs, mayhem. Didn't seem to have a whole lot to do with the issues under discussion. What did he have against you apart from his wanting to build apartments on the salt marsh and your being dead set against the idea?"

Zack took a moment to think. "He wanted to bring in a monster shoppin' mall next to the Proctor House grounds."

The Proctor House was a city-owned historic building that had stood in its extensive grounds since the turn of the century. It was not only a tourist mecca, it was a favorite place for local people to go on weekends. The tranquil gardens had been designed with an eye to attracting birds. Birders with binoculars were a common sight, as were photographers. The rose garden was outstanding and could be rented for weddings. There was a picnic area nearby.

"I was looking for something a little more personal," Bristow said.

Zack shrugged.

It was Bristow's turn to imitate Zack's squinting into a dust-storm stare.

Zack did it right back at him.

"You're saying that's all you had against each other?" Bristow asked.

Zack nodded.

Bristow wasn't buying.

Nor was I. Zack was now wearing his chivalrous expression. *Cherchez la femme,* I thought. Trouble was, there were so many femmes in Zack's life.

The two men were apparently trying to face each other down. If Sundancer was here he'd play the theme from *The Good, The Bad and The Ugly.*

"You lie in your throat," Bristow finally said.

One of the fascinating aspects of the character of Taylor Bristow, detective sergeant, is that he does Shakespeare in the Park. Quotes from the Bard's plays pop out of his mouth at the most surprising moments, all of them delivered in that smooth deep voice of his. That quote was from *Henry IV*. I've always liked it because it sounds more dastardly than just lying.

Zack didn't answer.

Normally, Bristow had the nicest eyes, a sort of amber brown, with a mild expression. All of a sudden they looked like rocks—agates maybe. "Let's try this from another angle," he said sternly. "I was asked to inform Gertie Tower-Senerac, the victim's widow, that her husband was deceased. At the same time I thought I might inquire as to why she hadn't reported him missing, Dr. Trenckman having determined that the man died Thursday night and this being Sunday night."

Zack swallowed.

"According to the Seneracs' housekeeper," Bristow continued, "Gertie Tower-Senerac left the house at eight forty-five P.M. the night of the banquet and didn't show up again until six A.M. the following morning. Evidently this had happened on several occasions in recent history."

"Gertie Senerac!" I said disbelievingly, staring at Zack.

One corner of his mouth twitched.

I'd seen Gertie around town a few times, enough to know she was a petite woman with classic features and champagne-blond, perfectly cut straight hair that swung like a curtain when she moved her head. I would give anything to have hair like that. I've been known to use an entire bottle of conditioner in one go, to try to have hair like that. I've ironed my hair. I've had it reverse-permed. It doesn't matter what I do, it kinks up like the cord that attaches a telephone handset to its base.

Gertie wore subdued makeup and a lot of gold jewelry

and owned a wonderful selection of designer suits and silk blouses. She worked as an office manager for a national insurance company headquartered in San Francisco. I'd always thought she was carved from the same block of ice as her husband. "Gertie Senerac?" I said again.

"'Gorgeous Gertie,'" Savanna murmured, evidently inducting the widow into Zack's doll brigade.

I raised my eyebrows at her. "I'm not sure she fits the pattern," I murmured back. "She's not young enough."

"Exceptions prove rules," Savanna said, looking wise.

The men weren't paying any attention to us. "Gerald's been threatening to leave Gertie," Bristow announced to the world at large, leaning his chair back on two legs. "Gertie says she didn't report Gerald missing because she figured he'd finally followed through on the threat."

He gazed at the ceiling. "Housekeeper says Senerac went out for a walk after returning from the banquet. A few minutes after nine P.M. Said he was too wound up to sleep. She thought maybe he went looking for his wife. House-keeper went to bed after her boss left, thought she heard him come in around midnight, but he wasn't there in the morning when Gertie came home. Gertie did not ask the housekeeper if she'd seen Senerac. Told me she didn't *care* where he was, so why *should* she ask?"

He slapped the chair down onto all fours, leaned forward and pinned Zack in his sights. "According to Sergeant Timp-kin, you stated you went home after the banquet and stayed there all night. You know anyone willing to vouch for that?"

Zack moved his head fractionally side to side.

"Zack," I said. "Taylor's trying to help you here. You *have* to come clean."

Zack's mouth tightened stubbornly.

Again the two men went into a face-off, then Bristow said, "I have no interest in your personal life, Zack. If your answers have nothing to do with this case, they will remain confidential. I might remind you that the legal consequences of homicide are far worse than for anything else you might have been doing."

Zack sighed, let his body slump, and averted his eyes. "We were at the Carson Motel in Dennison," he said.

"All night?" Bristow asked.

"From right after the banquet until midnight."

"You and Gertie?"

Zack sighed again.

"Anyone see you there?"

Zack shook his head. "She checked in. I called and got the cabin number from her, went directly to it."

"*Gertie* checked in?"

"Yeah."

"You left her at midnight?"

"Around then. I went to a couple bars in Condor after, then home."

"Anyone see you in the bars?"

Zack nodded. "Several people, I should think, the bartenders for sure—we talked." He mentioned the names of the bars. Bristow made a note on one of our bar napkins with a pen someone had left on the table.

I couldn't believe Zack was having an affair with Gertie Senerac. I knew he had the morals of an alley cat, and he'd never drawn the line at married women, but the wife of a man who already hated him—the wife of the man running *against* him!

Even Savanna seemed shaken out of her formerly joking mood. Angel looked more worried than usual. As well he might. Having an affair with the wife of a man who was subsequently murdered puts a person right up there on the list of suspects. The coroner had timed Senerac's death at three or four hours after the banquet. It wasn't likely the coroner could fix the time exactly, but it would certainly appear to coincide with the time at which Zack had left Gertie. I remembered something Dr. Trenckman had said in a TV interview once: "The body talks to me. It tells me what happened to it."

That particular body could be talking to Trenckman right now, telling him Zack killed it.

Bristow started talking again, almost conversationally. "The thing that made the Seneracs' housekeeper think Gerald might be going out looking for his wife that night was that he told her that very morning that he was planning on divorcing Gertie and asked if she'd remain in his employ rather than his wife's. She told him she'd think about it. Seems she didn't like Gerald a whole lot, but wasn't sure Gertie would keep her on if they did divorce."

"Will all of this have to come out?" Angel asked him.

"I'll try to keep a lid on it as long as I can," Bristow said.

Angel persisted. "Does Detective Sergeant Timpkin know about Zack and Mrs. Senerac?"

Bristow nodded.

Angel looked worried. "People in Bellamy Park are conservative. They aren't going to like it if word gets out Zack was playing around with Mrs. Senerac. Some won't vote for him because of it."

"They'll be a sight less likely to vote for him if word gets out he strangled her husband," Bristow said.

CHAPTER 5

"You don't believe that!" Savanna exclaimed, clenching both fists as though she'd hit him if he said he did. Savanna's so intensely loyal she'd have a terrible time choosing between two friends, even if she *was* well on the way to being in love with one of them.

I put in my two cents worth. "You really think Zack—your *friend* Zack—could strangle that man, wrap him up in plastic like a load of garbage, and stash him in the trunk of his car—his *new* car—then go on about his everyday life, which just happened to include boffing the dead man's wife?"

Bristow's gaze met mine directly, pained but sincere. "I've been a cop for a considerable number of years, Charlie. I believe anyone is capable of anything."

"Why would I kill him?" Zack said. "To be sure of winning the election? To get Gertie all to myself?"

"I have observed you to have a certain measure of self-esteem," Bristow said. "Senerac had spent considerable time hacking away at that. Wouldn't a man such as yourself become angry at such treatment, I wonder."

We all made pooh-poohing noises, and he waited until we subsided before going on. "Gerald Senerac was a rich man from a family with old money. If he'd divorced Gertie, she'd get half his assets. This way she'll get it all. Word around town's always been she was a big spender. Flies to New York every December to do her shopping, takes in a few shows. Vegas every couple months. South to Rodeo Drive fairly regularly. There's a double motive in your case," he added to Zack. "Sleeping with the guy's wife, rivalry in politics."

Zack's voice popped up in my mind, saying, a very short time ago, that he couldn't ever kill a human being. There had been a ring of truth in that statement. Okay, so he was an actor, used to conveying emotions he didn't necessarily feel. All the same, I was certain of his innocence, at least as far as murder was concerned. It was possible, of course, that because he was under attack, I was rooting for the underdog. Or else my hormones were doing my thinking for me.

"Just a minute," I said. "Let's not jump to any hasty conclusions here. Let's give Zack the benefit of *some* doubt."

Zack shot me a grateful glance. "Gertie let me know she was interested, not too long after I announced my candidacy. But there was never any thought or mention of disposing of her husband."

"Are you saying she didn't show any interest until you and her husband got into the race?" I asked.

He thought, then nodded.

"It didn't occur to you she might be wanting to get back at her husband for some reason?"

He shrugged. "She's a beautiful woman. I didn't do a whole lot of thinkin', darlin'."

I wanted to scream at him. But what's the use?

"That still doesn't mean I killed her husband," he went on. "There's no way in the world I would kill anyone, motive and means and opportunity notwithstanding."

The ring of truth was there again, clear as the sound of true crystal. Even Bristow seemed to hear it. His jawline became a little less tense.

"Well, Reggie Timpkin has you headed for a lethal injection," he said cheerfully. "Has you down as an identified suspect. Says all he has to do is come up with proof. He's out for your blood, Zack."

"Can't you influence him at all?" Savanna asked.

"Isn't any power on earth could influence Detective Sergeant Timpkin once he makes up his mind," Bristow said. "For one thing he's a former Marine. Note that I did not say ex-Marine. No such thing as an ex-Marine, according to Reggie."

"Do I get the impression you don't like him a whole lot?" I asked.

Bristow snorted. "He's a brother officer. I don't criticize brother officers." His sudden grin flashed across his face and had the effect of uncorking all the tension. The four of us let out breath simultaneously. "Between you and me," Bristow went on, "not meaning any disrespect, Reggie Timpkin is a mite gung ho. Sometimes a law-enforcement officer gets fixated in his mind—decides a certain individual is guilty—hates to let go of that belief, neglects to look for anyone else. Sometimes an officer like Reggie will get, well, you might even call it obsessed."

"But *you* don't believe it was Zack," Savanna said.

Bristow hesitated and tensed up again. Looking levelly across the table at Zack, he said, "One more question and I'll decide on the answer to that one."

Zack gave a half nod, his mouth tight.

"Did Gerald Senerac *know* you were sleeping with his wife?"

"It's possible, I guess," Zack said after a moment's hesitation. "I wondered about that myself on Thursday, way it seemed like he was really gunnin' for me. But Gertie said he hadn't said anything to her and he's not the type to keep quiet about his suspicions. Wasn't the type. That's all I know."

"Fair enough," Bristow said.

Zack breathed in and out, audibly.

"Isn't it possible *Gertie* killed her husband all by herself?" I asked.

Bristow gave me a fish-eyed look. "Now, now, Ms. Plato, let's not be taking over from the experts. Just because you have one case under your belt doesn't certify you as a sleuth."

I felt exhilarated suddenly. Maybe I *could* help solve this case. It was my probing and poking around that had solved the last one, whatever Taylor Bristow said.

"I just wondered," I said with all the innocence I could muster.

Bristow eyed me, then asked, "You think Gertie could strangle him? Stuff him in Zack's car?" I deduced he wasn't taken by the suggestion. "She's not what you'd call a large woman."

"Anger can lend strength. Besides, Gerald might have been tall, but he was all bones and no flesh."

"True, but ... strangling's not a woman's method." He hesitated. "ME says he was taken from behind, probably by surprise, not much evidence of a fight. Even if he was sitting down and she managed to cut off his breath before he realized what was happening, would she have the strength to lift him into Zack's car?"

"Maybe she hired someone."

"That's a possibility that's worth some consideration."
He raised his eyebrows at Zack. "You take any naps while
you were with Gertie Thursday night? Like, could she have
sneaked out the bathroom window, met her husband, fin-
gered him for someone else to kill?"

Zack shook his head. "No way. I was right there with
her the whole time, even in the bathroom."

I had a sudden mental image of Zack and Gertie going
at it in the bathtub. She was wearing one of her silk designer
suits. Evidently my subconscious didn't want to imagine her
naked.

Bristow tapped the table, making Benny scuttle around
in his cage. The sergeant leaned over to look at him. "Hey,
Ben, my man, didn't mean to alarm you."

Straightening, he said, " 'Stead of theorizing about a possible hit man, let's look at it this way—if Zack here did
not put Senerac's body in his car, and Gertie wasn't strong
enough to do it, who else had the opportunity to do so?"

"Which surely raises the question of whether the murderer chose Zack's car deliberately, or the Lexus was just
handy," I contributed, still trying to erase the image of Zack
cavorting with Gertie from my brain.

Bristow's amber eyes bestowed approval on me. "Ms.
Plato, you do indeed take after your philosopher ancestor,"
he said.

I'd told him some time ago that my father used to swear
we were descended from a relative of *that* Plato, the one
who sat at the feet of Socrates and went on to teach Aristotle.
Dad was Greek. His ancestors were Greek. I don't think he
had any more to go on than that. Plato's original name was
Aristocles but he was given the name Plato because of his
broad shoulders. So I was never sure how his relatives would

come by the name. But I didn't argue with my dad. If he wanted to believe we were related to a famous philosopher, where was the harm?

"If it *was* deliberate," Bristow said slowly, "if the murderer *chose* the Lexus *knowing* it was Zack's car, then he's not likely to be someone who's too fond of Zack. I'd say it's probable he holds a humongous grudge against Zack."

A shudder went through my body. Something much more frightening than a goose had walked over my . . . nope, that was not a good word to think of right now. I wasn't worried about danger to myself, you understand. I was worried about danger to Zack. Danger from Timpkin. Danger from whoever killed Gerald Senerac and made it look as if Zack did it.

"It would also seem likely our killer knew that Senerac and Zack were enemies," Bristow added.

"Everyone knew that," Angel said, obviously relieved Bristow's focus had shifted off Zack as murderer. "Their feuding was all over the local paper, and the debate was covered on TV. Mr. Senerac made it plain he hated Zack's guts."

"Nobody else has any reason to hate me," Zack said. Which was debatable considering the number of irate husbands or jealous boyfriends or wronged women there could be in his world. I shuddered again. "More'n'likely," Zack said easily, "my car just happened to be in the right place at the wrong time."

Possibly. Comforting if so. But the feeling of danger persisted.

"Okay. Let's look at that then," Bristow suggested, pulling over another couple of napkins and picking up the pen again. "Where exactly has the automobile in question been since that banquet/debate on Thursday?"

Zack's brow furrowed. "When I finally got away from the banquet, I parked in the alley at the side of the Carson Motel. After I left there, the car was in the lot behind The Irish Pub for an hour or so, followin' which I moved on to Paulie's Place, then home."

Bristow was having trouble making notes on the flimsy napkin. Savanna got up and brought him a yellow notepad from the office. His smile of thanks went way beyond gratitude for the small service. Savanna's answering radiance was something to see.

"What about Friday?" he asked after transcribing all of the above.

Zack's brow furrowed. "Friday mornin' I hung around home—swam for an hour or so in my pool, then went to Dandy Carr's for an hour-and-a-half workout. Ate lunch at home, again by the pool, then spent the rest of the day and part of the evenin' here."

"*Part* of the evening?"

Zack nodded. "I was fairly tuckered out after the debate Thursday and not getting a whole lot of sleep that night."

"Poor baby," I interjected. Sometimes I'm not nice.

Zack flicked a mournful glance at me and continued. "I must have left CHAPS around ten P.M. or so, I guess."

His eye caught mine again and I nodded. I'd been miffed at him for leaving so early. Much of the time Zack acted more like a sleeping partner than an active one. He seemed to think that was okay because he owned the lion's share of CHAPS.

Whenever anyone asked about the division of duties at CHAPS, I told them Angel and Savanna and I taught line-dancing, Angel also tended bar and bounced the occasional troublemaker, Savanna waited tables, I kept the books and subbed as security guard by occupying the loft apartment above the main corral and doing a walk through CHAPS a couple of times a day. In exchange for free rent, Zack always pointed out. Did he have any idea what it would cost to have a full-time accountant, I always retorted.

Zack spent most of his time at CHAPS simply being charming, something that required very little effort where he was concerned. To be fair, there's also the fact that it's his name that makes CHAPS such a draw. Nobody comes to CHAPS on the off-chance of dancing or standing shoulder to shoulder with Charlie Plato. Though if I keep discovering dead bodies, I suppose it could happen.

"You went straight home?" Bristow asked.

Zack didn't answer right away, and we all looked at him. He had a sheepish expression on his face.

"Gertie again?" I asked.

He shook his head. "I went to Paulie's Place," he said, then closed his mouth firmly.

"With whom?" I asked.

His dark eyebrows slanted up above his nose. "Thought Taylor here was the inquisitor in residence."

"With whom?" Taylor Bristow asked.

Zack sighed. "I went alone. Had a beer just to be sociable." He hesitated.

Bristow looked at him, waiting.

"Took a gal home," he finally said, with obvious reluctance. "She needed a ride. She invited me in for coffee."

"Coffee?" I asked. There may have been a note of disbelief in my voice.

"Coffee," he said.

"Someone you knew?" I asked. "Or somebody you happened across in a back alley?"

Bristow snorted.

Zack said, "Give me a break, darlin'."

"I need to know who she is," Bristow said. "I'm gonna need to check all this out if I'm going to attempt to get Timpkin off your back. Your choice."

Zack took the notepad and pen from him, shielded the page with his left hand, wrote on it and passed it back to Bristow. I'm pretty good at reading stuff upside down, but Zack hadn't used his best penmanship, and all I could manage to make out before Bristow turned the page over was: Apt. 4, something Poplar Street. Not too many apartments in that area; I might be able to track that down. Just out of interest, of course.

"So that brings us to yesterday, Saturday," Bristow said.

Zack nodded. "I was up with the birds—went salmon fishin' out of Pillar Point Harbor with Angel, Winston Jermaine, and Ted Ennis."

"Who?" Bristow asked.

"Ted Ennis is the cook at Dorscheimer's—the restaurant in the lobby," Angel told him.

"It was Ted's boat," Zack added. He thought for a while, doing his dust-storm squint. "Macintosh was supposed to go fishin' with us, but he begged off at the last minute."

"Why?" Bristow asked.

Zack shrugged. "Said he was tired. He moderated the debate Thursday night, taped some other CFLC meetin' that went on late Friday."

Bristow grunted and made some indecipherable squiggles on the pad, then looked at Zack again. "Where'd you park?"

"Right above the public boat launch, south end of the harbor."

"Crowded?"

"With vehicles and boat trailers, not many people around when we were there. It's away from the main part of the harbor."

Bristow made a note. "So you, Ennis, Angel, and Winston Jermaine were together all day?"

Zack hesitated and Angel spoke up. "Mr. Jermaine came down queasy around midmorning when the water turned rough. We had to come all the way back from the Farallon Islands to drop him at the fishing pier so he could walk to his car."

"He drove separately?" Bristow asked.

"We all did," Angel explained. "We all live in different towns." He thought for a minute. "Maybe Mr. Jermaine killed Mr. Senerac."

"Why?" Bristow asked.

Angel shrugged. "Maybe he just didn't like him."

"Maybe you just don't like Winny, Angel," Zack suggested. I wondered if he'd heard Angel's aura theory.

Angel shrugged again. "I'm not saying Mr. Jermaine's guilty for sure, I'm just putting out ideas. Brainstorming. If Mr. Jermaine had Mr. Senerac's body in his car, it wouldn't have been too hard for him to transfer it to the Lexus after we dropped him off. Maybe he wasn't really queasy. Maybe he was putting on an act."

Were his "ideas" part of some psychic insight, I wondered, or was he just trying to cloud the issue so Zack would look innocent? I'm never sure about Angel. Sometimes I think he's a simple cowboy, other times I suspect he has vast unplumbed depths.

"Time will tell," my mother used to say when I wondered about things.

Zack was shaking his head. "Winny turned *pea green*," he said. "I doubt anyone could fake that. Anyhow, the trunk of the Lexus was jammed when I went to put my fishin' gear in it that mornin'. I had to put the gear in the backseat."

"What time did you quit fishing?" Bristow asked.

Zack and Angel looked at each other. "Around three," Zack said, and Angel nodded. "Ted had to get dinner going at Dorscheimer's. Angel and I came on to work here."

"You leave here early last night, too?" Bristow asked.

"Nope. Left at closing time. Went straight home to bed. Alone." He looked virtuous. "Knew this was going to be a busy day, with the campaign kickoff and all."

It had surely been a *long* day.

"Okay, then," Bristow said, casting an eye over his notes. "What you're saying is some person, or persons unknown, could have placed that body in the trunk of your car anytime from approximately nine P.M. on Thursday, until you discovered the body on Sunday afternoon."

"He said there was a smell in the car earlier on Sunday," I pointed out.

"Noticed it first thing Sunday mornin'," Zack confirmed.

"So the body could have been placed while the car was outside the Carson Motel, The Irish Pub or Paulie's Place, your house . . ."

"It was in the garage."

"Burglar alarm?"

"Yes."

"Operating?"

"Yes."

Bristow scratched out a note. "Then CHAPS' parking lot and Paulie's again."

"Dandy Carr's gym in between," Zack reminded him.

"Many people there?"

"Packed."

Bristow considered for a moment. "CHAPS was during daylight, Dandy's and the parking lot at Pillar Point likewise."

"And the trunk was jammed by Saturday morning."

Bristow squinted into the middle distance. "Not significant enough to rule Pillar Point out just yet." He glanced back at his notes. "Pretty chancy transferring a body in broad daylight. Not impossible. But I'd say our first choices are the Carson Motel, The Irish Pub and Paulie's Place, because it's dark outside all three. Then the lady's apartment, CHAPS' parking lot and Pillar Point. I'll take a look around."

He did a complicated handshake thing with Zack, then stood up. "Thanks for leveling with me. I'll see what I can do." He gave Savanna his wide smile—the one Zack says makes him look like Michael Jordan. "This was supposed to be my day off. Not much left to rescue." He hesitated, his amber eyes glinting. "How about you allow me to escort you home, Ms. Seabrook?"

The expression on her face could have caused serious meltdown in the sternest heart. Off they went, the two of them. I wondered if Bristow would make it home to his own apartment before the night was over. I'd baby-sat Jacqueline enough to know she was a sound sleeper.

CHAPTER 6

It was an uneasy week. Every time I stuck my nose outside the door, someone shoved a microphone, or a camera, or both, in front of my face. Timpkin returned at least once a day with questions for Zack and me. Apparently, although the lab crew had turned up Zack's fingerprints all over the car, which was hardly surprising, they hadn't found any physical evidence, even after a careful vacuuming and microscopic inspection, that would tie Zack directly to the body or the plastic tarp that had covered it. It seemed to me that Timpkin was mainly making sure we hadn't skipped town.

CHAPS was crowded every night. A little scandal is always good for business, and the TV cameras kept hanging around. You'd be surprised what people will do to get on TV. Monday night I was caught returning from Lightfoot's minimart with a bag of critter litter by the same terminally perky reporter who had bugged me during our skeleton episode. She had just asked me how it felt to find a ligature-strangled body in a car trunk—("Not great," I said)—when a little old lady appeared from behind a nearby tree and started jumping up and down in front of the TV camera, as if her walker was a pogo stick.

My ex telephoned from Seattle on Tuesday morning. "I

can't believe you're involved with another murder," he said by way of greeting.

"Hi, Rob," I answered breezily—he always hated it when I was breezy. "How's it going? You operating on any famous ladies today?"

"Operating" was a double entendre where I was concerned. Whenever some Hollywood beauty decided her perfection had developed a slight hitch, she was likely to hie herself to a plastic surgeon. Rob was the surgeon of choice for many. Partly because Seattle was a little more private than L.A. or Beverly Hills, partly because Rob's reputation with a scalpel was only exceeded by his reputation as a swordsman, if you get my drift.

Having spent several years in blissful innocence as his fairly contented wife, I had finally seen the light when I walked in on him while he was examining Trudi—yes, *the* Trudi—"she who needs no other name." His pants were around his ankles; her skirt was around her neck. It had been apparent even to dumb old me that the examination was a trifle unorthodox. I had discovered after consulting the staff that it was, however, Rob's procedure of choice.

I could hear Rob swallowing his chagrin. He hated it when I put that kind of stress on "operating." "Who is this Senerac guy?" he asked.

"He was the president of our local independent bank," I told him. "He was also a candidate for city council. Zack's opponent."

"The guy you work for? He's running for city council?"

"I do not work for him, I'm his partner." I had told Rob this at least a zillion times. Well, four times anyway.

"The body was found in the hunk's trunk?"

"Is there a purpose to this inquisition?" I asked.

"I'm worried about you, Charlie."

There was a sudden sweetness in his voice, which brought back memories of shared experiences that had lifted my soul to the skies. In other words, major orgasms.

"You seem to keep getting in trouble," he went on, bringing me back to earth.

"I'm not in trouble," I said indignantly, hoping it was true. "I was the one who called the police."

"I'd say working for a boss who's as good as being accused of murder qualifies as trouble," he grumbled.

"Zack is not my boss." I don't know why I bother. I really don't.

"Whatever," he said, then sighed and hung up.

Tuesday afternoon, just about closing time, there was a bank robbery in East Dennison. Thursday, some guy shot his father-in-law in Condor. Interest in our murder began to fade.

By the following Saturday, my inner parts had settled down to normal, though my dreams were still on the lurid side; and I was going to be conscious of danger to Zack until whoever killed Senerac was caught.

It was a welcome distraction when Marsh Pollock showed up at CHAPS again.

P.J., the regular I mentioned earlier, zeroed in on Marsh the second he walked in and hauled him out on the dance floor. I watched them two-step. P.J. tended to throw in a few extra twirls, and he didn't seem to know how to control her. He had a good body but he wasn't too smooth a dancer. Maybe he needed a couple of lessons.

P.J. would probably be happy to teach him everything she knew, I thought. P.J. was divorced from her first husband. As her fortieth birthday approached, she was seriously, almost hysterically, looking for a second. As I also mentioned earlier, she'd already had a go at Angel. She'd worked on several others, as well, then settled in with Patrick, the young Stanford student who moonlighted behind the bar in the little corral. Patrick was probably seventeen or eighteen years younger than she was. I wished her well. If you're going to grab a man, it's better to grab him young and bend him to your will.

P.J. evidently knew Marsh. I'd heard she was another regular at Dandy Carr's. No western duds for this girl—she wore a black body stocking and tights instead, with a brief, gaudy, gauzy overskirt that made her look like a cocoon in the process of becoming a butterfly—but not quite making it. She did have very nice golden blond hair, which she wore tied back with a ribbon, but she was no beauty, and her personality around a man bordered on frantic.

I felt sorry for her. She'd had to put her father in a nursing home when his senility sent him wandering the neighborhood and he got hit by a car and almost killed. She felt guilty about putting him away, she'd told me, but she'd had no choice.

Marsh took her to her table after the dance was over. She sat down, smiling expectantly up at him. But just like Angel, he walked away. Acute disappointment showing on her horsey face, she got up and meandered disconsolately over to the little corral bar. Patrick set a bottle of mineral water in front of her, and she fluttered her lashes at him. You had to give the poor thing E for effort.

Marsh came over to where I was sitting with Savanna. Not too many people had arrived yet. I had a half hour before starting line-dancing lessons. Savanna smiled at him and then me with great fondness. It is one of Savanna's ambitions to see me matched up with a man. People in love have a tendency to want everyone else to see sparkly rainbows everywhere, just as they do.

"Hi, Charlie," Marsh said in his gravelly voice, without sitting down. "How about a dance?"

Usually I avoid slow-dancing one-on-one with the customers. I don't want complications in my life. The great thing about line-dancing is you don't *need* a partner, so you don't have to get intimate with anyone.

But Sundancer had a Patty Loveless album on and she was singing a song I liked, "When Fallen Angels Fly"—and my body was urging me to say yes. On top of which, Zack was hanging around young Lauren Deakins again and I wasn't yet over feeling disgusted with him for getting involved with his political rival's wife. It was pretty clear to me that Gertie had set Zack up deliberately because she didn't like her husband, but it enraged me that Zack had been dumb enough to fall for her little game.

Marsh had changed his boat shoes for ankle boots, his shorts and polo shirt for creamy chinos and a good-looking cotton sweater, the same shade of grey as his curly hair. No cowboy wanna-be clothes for him, either.

He looked good. Wholesome. Athletic. Intensely masculine. And I needed distraction. When I wasn't thinking about Zack making love to Gertie Senerac, I was remembering how her husband looked all done up in plastic wrap in the trunk of Zack's car, his eyes glaring up at the sky, his tongue. . . . Well, trust me, you don't want to hear about his tongue.

So I said okay. And we danced. Marsh's biceps felt like iron under my left hand. There was some chemistry, no doubt about it. Not quite nuclear fission but definitely some explosive potential.

"Zack's watching," Marsh murmured. "Think he's going to pop me for dancing with his lady?"

"I'm nobody's lady," I said, then laughed. "Let me rephrase that."

He laughed, too, his eyes crinkling up very nicely.

As I'd already observed, Marsh wasn't that great a dancer. But at least he didn't step on my toes. He didn't pull any touchy-feely stuff, either.

Afterward, he came back to the table and didn't walk away. He and Savanna and I talked about the body in Zack's car. Marsh swore he believed in Zack's innocence, and Savanna bestowed her killer smile on him. "I do admire a man with great instincts," she said.

He smiled back. "You ain't so bad yourself, lady," he said in his gravelly voice.

"You'd better watch it," I told him. "This particular lady's practically engaged to Taylor Bristow, who happens to be one of Bellamy Park's finest."

Savanna's eyes widened. "Don't you go talking about engagements in front of Taylor," she said. "You'll scare him away faster than a horse from a rattlesnake."

So. There was one question answered. Taylor Bristow still hadn't committed himself.

"Don't even *think* of talking to him about it," Savanna said. She knows me.

When the time came for Savanna and me to go to work, Marsh repeated his invitation to come to his gym and work out. Then he left. I felt mildly disappointed that he wasn't going to stick around, maybe dance with me again later when the live band got going. I know, I know, women are contrary, have I suggested otherwise?

"You ought to at least take a look at Dandy Carr's gym, girlfriend," Savanna said when she and Angel and I took a dinner break at Dorscheimer's later. She accompanied the statement with her Earth Mother smile. "That is one very attractive, intelligent man. And I just love his voice. It's like rough silk."

I made a face at her. "More like sandpaper, if you ask me."

She cocked her head sideways.

I held up my palms in surrender. "Okay—his voice is sexy. I'll grant you that. *He's* sexy. Very sexy. But I don't need the hassle of dating. I'm doing fine without it."

"Who said anything about dating?" she asked, her eyes widening as if her motivations could only be innocent. *Ha!*

"What do *you* think, Angel?" she asked.

He frowned. "I don't even know who you're talking about."

"The guy who took over Dandy Carr's gym," I explained. "He was dancing with me earlier. Marsh Pollock. He's one of Zack's poker buddies. He wants me to go work out at the gym. Savanna thinks I should."

Angel finished his coffee in one gulp, pushed his plate aside, and stood up. "Why ask me?" he said.

I watched him walk away. "What's gotten into Angel?" I asked. "That's the first time he's ever been rude to me. What did I do?"

"He likes you, Charlie," Savanna said gently. "I think maybe Angel likes you a lot."

I laughed shortly. "You've got to be kidding. Angel and I are friends, that's all. Besides, he's still interested in Gina from Buttons and Bows. Quit trying to match me up, Savanna."

"You matched me up with Taylor," she reminded me.

"No comparison. I do *good* matching. You and Taylor are crazy about each other. Jacqueline's crazy about both of you. You could be a happy family someday soon. I'm a whole other story. I can be dysfunctional all by myself."

"*You* could have a happy family," she said. "All you have to do is take down that stone wall you've built around yourself." She pointed a finger and thumb, cocked gun style, at me. "Don't give me that jeering look. I'm not suggesting you should get married again, for heaven's sake, I'm only suggesting you could do worse than go work out at Marsh Pollock's gym and see what happens."

I stood up. "Forget it, Savanna," I said.

And I really *didn't* have any intention of setting foot in Dandy Carr's gym, or of getting in any way involved with Marsh Pollock.

Which is why I was surprised to find myself walking into that same gym at eight A.M. Monday morning, wearing a new eye-catching neon-blue thong leotard over black lycra bicycle shorts, my willful orange hair done up in a kinky version of a Gibson Girl knot that had taken thirty-eight minutes to arrange.

Before anyone gets the wrong idea, I have to mention that I had a legitimate reason for going to the gym that Monday morning. I'd spent Sunday morning updating the address database I'd created for sending out campaign flyers, using county voting records as reference. I had discovered, because I'd looked, that Marsh wasn't registered to vote.

It was my civic duty, I had decided, to persuade Marsh

that his friend Zack needed every vote he could get, no matter what Marsh personally felt about politics. Especially as a very popular and personable TV personality called Janice Carmichael had just submitted candidacy papers in Senerac's place.

What the new eye-catching neon-blue thong leotard had to do with my civic duty is unclear.

To my surprise, Marsh was totally businesslike about showing me the exercise procedures. "Stretching tight muscles can cause injuries," he informed me, so we did a few slow laps around the upper track, side by side, until I felt warm and loose. (You can take that any way you like.)

He taught me a lot about stretching. I'd always done a few token stretches with one leg at a time up on one of the benches in my usual gym, but he had me on the floor stretching hamstrings and Achilles tendons, and all that arcane stuff.

I will also admit that the chemistry was still bubbling merrily away like dry ice in a beaker of water.

I was impressed that Marsh didn't take advantage, not even when he was pressing down on my knees and thighs to get them flat on the floor while the soles of my feet were pressed together. Yeah. Try that sometime. I was fairly worn-out even before he got me established on one of the monstrous pieces of high-tech equipment that looked like medieval torture instruments.

To mask my surprise at his restraint—no, I did *not* say my disappointment—I teased him a little about not being registered to vote.

He shook his head. "Not even for Zack," he said. "The democratic process doesn't work. What we need is a beneficent tyrant."

He was joking. I think.

"Who d'you have in mind?" I asked. "Idi Amin smiled a lot, did that make him beneficent? He probably qualified as a tyrant—a lot of former citizens washed up on shores of otherwise picturesque lakes while he was in power. You'd vote for someone like him?"

"Nobody votes for tyrants. You don't have to, that's the beauty of it." He was leaning over alongside me, making some adjustment to the machine, and that sexy little grin was hovering around his mouth. I thought about running my fingers through his curly grey hair. "You're not old enough to remember Idi Amin," he added.

"My dad introduced me to television at an early age." I looked at him curiously as he straightened. "You wouldn't really want a tyrant in charge, would you?"

He laughed. "I don't think the right guy's come along yet. I'll let you know what I think when he does." He eyed me critically as I attempted to pull down on something that looked like a yoke for a pair of oxen. "Straight down, Charlie," he ordered. "Don't lean forward."

Nothing moved.

He removed a couple of weights from the yoke's lower parts. The expression on his face said I was even punier than he'd thought. "Different people have different ways of looking at things, Charlie," he said. "Take poker. I can spend hours playing poker. Days. Do you play poker?"

I was still yanking downward. "Never," I managed.

"There you are, then," he said.

I gave up on the yoke. Mopping my brow with a hand towel he gave me, I waved him off when he wanted to demonstrate another part of the monster machine's anatomy. "Time out," I said. "I can't talk and gasp for breath at the same time." I drew in a couple of long breaths to illus-trate my point, then laughed. "When I was first married, my ex decided I should learn to play pinochle. So we'd go to friends' houses and have nice little foursomes. Only prob-lem—I was hopeless at pinochle. I could have lived with that, but Rob, my ex, was a terrific player with a photographic memory. On the way home, or in bed after the game, he'd tell me every single play I'd made and how I should have made it. I finally told him it was either cards or the marriage. So we gave up playing. The marriage went bust anyway."

I thought about that. "I think there's a moral in there somewhere, but I don't know what it is."

"What made the marriage go bust if it wasn't cards?" Marsh asked.

"My husband liked women."

"Me too," Marsh said.

While I wasn't paying attention, he'd got my feet hooked under some kind of bar and was adjusting weights on it. "Lift," he said.

I lifted.

"Very good," he said and I felt a glow.

Praise is such a turn-on.

"The trouble was," I said as I lifted again, "Rob liked women best when they were flat on their backs."

"I quite take to that idea myself," Marsh said. He stood back and I took my feet out from under the bar. "Does that offend you?"

"I don't know you well enough to let you offend me," I said. On reflection that sounded a trifle flirtatious, even arch, but I hadn't intended it that way.

He took it that way. "What do you want to know?" he said as he led me over to a pair of side-by-side treadmills.

A question like that is meat and drink to an inquiring mind like mine. "I don't even know where you're from," I said as he switched the equipment on and I began hiking.

"Minnesota," he said promptly. "I grew up on a farm. I got tired of the work and the snow, so I moved to California."

"You don't look like a farmer."

He showed me his hands. Lots of calluses. "I don't think there's any prototype, Charlie. But I never really felt like a farmer. I stayed on to please my father. When he died I sold the old homestead and moved on."

"No mother?"

"She died a long time ago."

Another orphan of the storm. "You've only been in California since you bought the gym?"

He nodded, adjusted the upward slant of the other treadmill, switched on, then stepped onto it and started jogging. "You're not married?" I asked.

"Do pigs fly?"

I glanced at him sideways. "Are you gay?"

"Nope."

"You don't mind me asking?"

"For you, Charlie, I'm an open book." He laughed shortly. "I have to tell you, I've had a lot of offers in my time. Curse of a pretty body. Maybe I'm missing a bet." He shook his head. "I'm totally into women, Charlie. I would have thought you could tell."

He ducked his head and turned it sideways as he made this remark, flirting with me.

He didn't agitate my hormones as much as Zack did, but he was the first man, other than Zack, to interest me in a while. And he sure looked great, jogging along next to me in blue gym shorts and a red tank top. The body was not just pretty, it was magnificent. He could do commercials for gym equipment. Moving right along as we both were, I could still feel vibrations in the air between us. Trouble was, I wasn't sure if I wanted to explore the chemistry, or let it alone. It was rather a delicious dilemma.

"*Why* haven't you married?" I asked, thinking at least I ought to get a few things straight before committing myself to anything.

"Circumstances beyond my control," he said with another sideways grin.

"You're about as much of an open book as Zack is," I grumbled. And decided to just wait and see how things looked to me as time went by.

I was pulling on a sweatshirt when I remembered there was something else I wanted to ask him about. By then a few more early risers were beginning to trickle in. "Zack told me Opal Quince is hassling you," I said. "I wondered if it might be something we could use against her."

Marsh laughed shortly. "It's not worth messing with, Charlie. The old lady objects to women going between the gym and the public parking lot in leotards or jogging bras and shorts. She's just as opposed to men in shorts, especially if the men are . . ." he lowered his voice to a husky whisper, ". . . bare chested."

We both laughed.

"She showed up in front of the gym with a picket sign a couple of days ago," he went on. "Something about indecent exposure. Members thought it was a hoot. It gave us all a good laugh. I wouldn't worry about her, Charlie. Poor old biddy's just looking for some attention."

"I don't want to underestimate her," I said.

He raised his eyebrows. They were darker than his hair,

well shaped. "You really want Zack to win, don't you? You think he can beat Janice?"

He might not want to get involved, but he was at least keeping up. Maybe before the campaign was over I could persuade him to help out or at least endorse Zack. "There are more women voters than men registered in Bellamy Park," I said. "I've counted."

He laughed. "Will any of the women vote for Winston Jermaine?"

"I can't imagine voting for him *or* Opal," I said, suddenly feeling gloomy. I groaned as another thought occurred to me. "If Zack does make it to city council, I'm no doubt going to be involved with Opal or Winston for some time to come."

"Give it all up," Marsh suggested. "Be like me. Stay out of the whole mess."

"Don't tempt me," I said.

Poor choice of words. The chemistry sizzled up again. "I'd better get going," I said hastily.

He gave me the kind of knowing smirk men give you when they know they've turned you on, then reached up a hand to tuck a twist of hair behind my ear. "I like the new hairstyle," he said.

Nobody ever says anything nice about my hair. Kind people just give it an amused look. Unkind people who think they are witty make remarks like, "How do you get a comb through it? I bet there's stuff in there you haven't seen in weeks." Or "What color is that, pumpkin number twenty-eight?"

For a heartbeat, Marsh held his palm against my cheek and ear, and neither one of us breathed.

And then Marsh dropped his hand and stepped away,

and I shot out of harm's way just like Benny charges out of his cage when I open it up in the morning.

"Come back tomorrow," Marsh called after me, and I waved vaguely without turning around, still not ready to commit myself to a thing. I'm such a coward.

CHAPTER 7

I'd volunteered to drive Zack to Gertie Senerac's house. Zack was in the process of acquiring a new pickup, but it hadn't been delivered yet.

He wasn't too enamored of my Jeep Wrangler, but I adored it. What was good enough for General MacArthur was good enough for me. Besides which, it had exactly the right jaunty image for a woman who was no longer materially minded, a woman who had no desire to settle down.

"I didn't know Gerald and Gertie Senerac lived in Paragon Hills," I said to Zack as I parked at number ten Willow Way. All the streets in Paragon Hills are named after trees, whether native or not. Willow Way was only a few blocks from Laburnum Street, which was where Zack lived. "Must have been very handy for you," I added.

"Gertie jogs," he said. "That's how we met. She turned her ankle just as she was joggin' past my house."

"Very handy," I reiterated.

Zack nodded. He doesn't always realize I'm waxing sarcastic.

Paragon Hills is only a mile or so from downtown Bellamy Park, but it is light years removed from the hustle and bustle of San Pablo Avenue. The residential area surrounds the golf course and country club. Need I say more? The streets are wider, shadier, quieter; the houses more upscale than anywhere else in upscale Bellamy Park. Flowers and shrubs flourish, lawns are weedless, hedges are always clipped. You get the idea.

My first thought when I saw Gertie Tower-Senerac's house was that I hoped she didn't have any baseball-playing munchkins in the neighborhood.

The widow lived in a glass house. Literally. There were whole walls of windows reflecting the morning light, and skylights glinting in every stepped-down roof. The entryway was a sunroom. All of the windows were double paned. White blinds with cunning micromini slats were sandwiched between the panes and could be opened and closed by a knob on the window frame. Amazing.

I had time for all this glass analysis while Gertie Tower-Senerac was sobbing her heart out in Zack's arms, whence she had hurled herself upon opening the door to find us on her threshold. To find *Zack* on her threshold, I should say. I didn't think she'd noticed me yet.

She hadn't been lounging around in grungy sweats the way I do when I'm home. She was dressed for company in a superbly tailored pink shirt of heavy silk, beige gabardine pants that clung to her curves as if she and they had been shrunk to fit. She also sported several pieces of gold jewelry, and four-inch beige heels that brought her up to a reasonably comfortable crying position on our man in black's chest. Her bobbed hair gleamed like champagne in the light from all those windows.

Gorgeous Gertie indeed! I suppressed a giggle. The name Savanna had blessed her with made her sound like a female wrestler. "Gorgeous Gert" would be even better. Maybe she belonged in Zack's doll brigade, after all—she could be outfitted with satin shorts and her own wrestling mat, which would be rolled up and ready to travel at a moment's notice.

Gertie had telephoned Zack and begged him to come see her. Showing a wisdom that was fairly rare, he had called CHAPS to consult me a few minutes after I returned from Dandy Carr's. I told him he'd be out of his mind to go anywhere within reach of the woman. He had then telephoned Gertie to tell her he couldn't make it. She became hysterical. He surrendered. I had insisted on accompanying him for safety's sake. I must admit that my inquiring mind was never averse to poking around in other people's business.

I had, of course, changed out of my neon-blue thong leotard, and had put on a striped western shirt and blue jeans instead.

As I turned from my minute examination of the entry windows, I saw that Zack was patting Gertie indiscriminately, his expression compassionate but mildly panicky. Peering around, I discovered a box of paper tissues in a glass box on a glass-topped table and thrust a wad of them into Gertie's hand. As she blew her nose and generally mopped up, Zack stepped back and politely removed his cowboy hat, setting it crown side down on the table.

"I'm sorry for your loss," I said awkwardly when Gertie emerged from behind the wad and regarded me suspiciously. I never know what to say to people whose nearest and dearest have died, much less people whose score on the grief scale you can't calculate. When my folks died, some well-meaning people told me to look on the bright side, Mom and Dad had been wonderful people and they had died together. Others said how fine it was that they died instantly. As far as I'm concerned there's no bright side to death, whether it comes fast or slow.

"Who're you?" Gertie asked, having looked me over thoroughly. Amazingly, her mascara hadn't run at all.

"This is Charlie Plato," Zack told her. "Charlie's one of my partners in CHAPS. She's also my campaign manager."

"That blasted campaign," Gertie muttered, without bothering to acknowledge the introduction with any murmurs of delight. She spoke with the kind of elongated vowels that always made me want to spit and cuss and say ain't, none of which I do as a rule.

Gertie touched the wad of tissues lightly to one eyelid. "If it wasn't for that stupid campaign, we wouldn't be in this mess."

"What mess is that?" I asked, knowing, but wanting her definition.

"That absolute *moron*, Sergeant Timpkin, is convinced Zack and I plotted to kill Gerald."

She seemed about to say more, but frowned suddenly. "I wasn't really prepared for visitors," she said to Zack. "I thought you and I agreed we should have a *private* talk."

On the word "private" her eyes shot me a glance that would have felled an ox, if there'd been one around. Her eyes were blue. Not nearly as blue as mine, I'm pleased to report. She was at least ten years older than me, I decided. Arbitrarily.

"Charlie knows everythin' there is to know about me," Zack said. Which was far from the truth, but earned me another death-dealing glance from "blue eyes." Zack continued, "she thought it would be best for us not to be alone, considerin'."

Gertie sniffed. Evidently she wasn't about to applaud

my wisdom. She led us into a sitting room that was filled with furniture of the kind designed by people with Dutch names. I'd seen chairs like that in magazines in dentists' offices, but I didn't know people actually sat in them.

Mirrors on all the walls reflected the glass windows and the bushes and the trees outside, as well as bits of sky and the contents of opposing mirrors. I began to feel dizzy.

As soon as we sat, gingerly in my case, a plump, mournful-looking woman, with dark circles under her eyes, appeared. She carried a tea tray, silver teapot, and three fluted bone-china cups and saucers, which showed she paid attention to the comings and goings. The housekeeper Bristow had mentioned, I deduced.

I smelled Darjeeling, and cheered up. Gertie had good taste in tea.

"Thank you, Melanie," Gertie said in a tone of voice that added, don't let the door hit you on your way out.

I was impressed. Having a housekeeper named Melanie seemed fittingly elegant. I thought I'd like to have a chat with Melanie, if it ever became possible.

"I wanted to tell you that a man entered this house in the middle of the night that Gerald was killed," Gertie said, twisting her body so that she faced Zack. Having provided me with a cup of tea, she evidently felt no further need to acknowledge my presence.

I remembered Bristow saying that the housekeeper had thought she'd heard Gerald coming home, but he hadn't been there when Gertie bopped in the next morning.

"Who?" Zack asked.

"I don't know," Gertie said; rather irritably, I thought. "I wasn't here."

"Oh, yeah."

"How do you know it was a man?" I asked.

Gertie gave a theatrical sigh.

"How *did* you know?" Zack asked.

She answered *him* immediately, putting me in my place. "When I came home the morning after the debate, I found a footprint on the rug in the foyer. Melanie told me she'd heard someone downstairs around midnight. She naturally assumed it was either me or Gerald."

"You found a *footprint?*" I queried. "How could you see it? Was there that much dust?"

She kept her eyes on Zack. "One of my neighbors has a large dog that escapes her fenced yard with alarming regularity. It's not a dangerous dog, but it has an unfortunate habit of doing its . . . business at the foot of my steps. I've complained to the police numerous times, but . . ." She broke off. "Our visitor, whoever he might have been, had evidently . . . stepped in one of Trigger's . . . accidents."

"Trigger?" Zack queried.

"The dog."

"That was the name of Roy Rogers's horse," Zack advised.

She had nothing to say to that. Me neither. After a moment, she continued, "My husband used to fly into a rage whenever he encountered Trigger's . . ."

"Poop," I suggested when she seemed at a loss.

"Melanie would no doubt have been rousted from her bed to deal with the mess if Gerald had been the person entering," she continued without acknowledging my helpfulness. "Besides which, the footprint was large and Gerald had rather narrow feet."

This was starting to get interesting. "Were there any signs of breaking and entering?" I asked.

It was really weird, the way she behaved. She wasn't going to answer me directly, it appeared, but she would answer my questions to Zack. Like she thought of me as some kind of ventriloquist's dummy. I wondered how she'd react if I sat on his lap. I wasn't sure how *I'd* react. I *knew* how Zack would react.

"It appeared our visitor used a key," she said. "It's possible of course that Gerald let him in and accompanied him, but didn't notice the footprint."

I took a sip of tea. Aromatic bliss. "Was anythin' missin'?" I asked, deliberately imitating Zack's drawl. If I was going to be his dummy, I might as well be in character.

She nodded, still facing Zack. I was beginning to think this was pretty amusing. Even Zack was straining to keep a grin from breaking through. "The person either stole Gerald's briefcase, which contained papers Gerald had been accumulating for several weeks, or Gerald gave them to him," Gertie said. "Melanie is sure Gerald brought the briefcase in with him when he came home from the debate. When he departed to take his walk, he left it beside his desk in the room he uses . . . *used* . . . as an office. She noticed it was missing soon after the police notified us that Gerald was . . . dead."

"Did you tell the police about the footprint and the missing briefcase?" Zack asked.

Yea, Zack! He was sitting at attention in the ladderbacked chair, his jaw clenched, his facial expression grim. I recognized that the persona of Sheriff Lazarro had taken over his body. He does that—like Superman used to take over from Clark Kent, but Zack doesn't have to go into a phone booth.

Gertie shook her head no. She even did that elegantly,

her bobbed hair swinging just so. Given an opportunity, I was going to ask to use the bathroom and see if I could find out the kind of shampoo and conditioner she used. On second thought, I nixed the idea—she'd never let me use her personal bathroom.

"Why didn't you tell the police?" I asked.

"Yeah," Zack said.

She leaned toward him, placing a dainty white hand on his knee. Her nails were long and perfectly manicured. Which shouldn't surprise anyone. "When I saw the footprint, I merely thought Gerald had brought someone home with him and hadn't noticed the ..."

"Poop," I supplied again.

"Naturally, I cleaned it up immediately," she told Zack, with a slight shiver of her shoulders, which rippled the pink silk of her blouse. "I didn't know then that Gerald had been ... murdered. When I *did* learn the truth, I was afraid if I mentioned the footprint, the police would think I was making it up to protect myself. I had in effect destroyed the only evidence of an intruder."

I didn't think Gertie would have made up anything to do with poop even if her life hung in the balance.

"Why didn't *Melanie* tell the police about the missing briefcase?" I asked.

This question finally brought her head around to me. "I imagine she wanted to keep her job," she said flatly. Her eyes were the shade of Arctic blue you see if you look into a hole in a snowdrift.

I decided I didn't ever want to make an enemy of this woman. I wanted to take Zack by the shoulders and shake the testosterone from his body. Why on earth had he slept with Gertie Senerac?

I knew the answer even as I posed the question. *Because she was there.*

"Why didn't *you* tell the police about the missing brief-case, Ms. Senerac?" I asked.

Her back was turned to me again. Her shoulders had assumed a ramrod position at my question. Looking straight at Zack, she said, "Most of the papers were about you."

Zack's eyebrows slanted up in his famous puckish way. It was a very endearing expression that always made my hormones cluster together and say, "Aw!"

"Gerald was figurin' to write my biography?"

Zack can be witty at times. Evidently Gertie hadn't known that. She looked surprised. "I don't imagine he was collecting the material for any good purpose," she said rather snappishly. "But he certainly didn't confide in me. The only reason I knew he *had* the papers was that I overheard him talking to one of his supporters on the phone, the day of the debate, about the dossiers he was putting together on Zack Hunter and Winston Jermaine. He said he didn't have much on Jermaine yet, but Hunter's portion was very interesting. After he hung up, I watched him put the file in his briefcase."

"What was in the dossier?" I asked after mulling for a while.

She finally turned to look at me. "I'm afraid I don't know," she said.

By the way the skin felt tight around my eyes, I figured I was probably giving her a fair copy of Zack's gazing into a dust-storm squint.

"You don't know," I said flatly. "You heard your husband talking on the phone about some information he was gathering on your lover, who happened to be running against said husband for the same position on the city council. Any thinking person might imagine this material to be damaging. You watched him put this possibly damaging file in his briefcase, but you didn't look in it?"

Her brief acknowledgment of my presence was over. "It was the day of the debate," she said to Zack. "Gerald took his briefcase with him to the banquet. When he brought it home, I was already gone. When *I* came home, *it* was nowhere in sight. Besides, Gerald always kept his briefcase locked. I had thought I'd wait for a chance to take his keys when he was asleep, but I never saw him, or the briefcase, again. I searched for it of course, but it wasn't in the house."

She took a breath. "That was probably just as well. At least it wasn't lying around when that dreadful Sergeant Timpkin showed up with a search warrant."

Zack looked shocked. "He searched your house?"

She nodded. "Yesterday. He brought a pair of officers with him. It was ... traumatic. Melanie was upset."

She looked at me directly again. "Do you really think I should have told Detective Sergeant Timpkin that up until the time he was murdered, my husband was happily collecting material with which to blacken Zack's name?"

Put that way, she had a point. So, if the person who killed Senerac was the same person who stole the briefcase, then Zack's car had not been a random choice. What then did that person intend to do with the contents of that briefcase?

"Did the police officers find anything?" I asked.

She shook her head, making that bell of hair swing again.

"Did Timpkin say what he was looking for?"

"It was on the search warrant. Yellow rope of the kind that was ..." She broke off. "He was also looking for some fabric that would match a fiber caught in the rope. It appeared to be from a cotton sweater, Sergeant Timpkin said. I assured him I rarely wore sweaters, and then only if they were cashmere."

But of course.

"He said he mainly wanted to establish that the fabric had not come from one of Gerald's garments. As he didn't take any of Gerald's clothing with him, I surmised that he hadn't found anything that matched. He also didn't find any yellow rope, which didn't surprise me. Why on earth would either Gerald or I have yellow rope on hand?"

"That yellow rope had to come from somewhere," I pointed out. "Though why Timpkin would think Gerald would carry rope with him on a walk is beyond me. Was he intending to offer it to his murderer and say, 'Here, strangle me'?"

"Maybe he was headin' out to strangle someone himself," Zack suggested. "I recall a couple episodes of *Prescott's Landin'* where someone was killed with their own gun that they took to kill someone else with."

Zack frequently called up memories of past *Prescott's Landing* episodes and equated them with real-life happenings. Laugh if you want to, but sometimes they worked out.

I tried to imagine Gerald Senerac walking downtown from Paragon Hills with a coil of yellow rope looped over one elegantly suited shoulder, but the image failed to jell.

"Well, if the police don't have a sweater they can compare that piece of fabric to," I suggested, "then they're no further along. They can hardly look in the closet of everyone who lives, or just happened to pass through, Bellamy Park."

Zack had fallen silent. I glanced his way just as he looked up. For a second, only a second, there was a little-scared-boy expression in his green eyes, then he called up the macho filter and put it on top.

I mulled some more, trying to come up with something that would make him feel better. "We haven't heard anything about that hair they took from you, Zack. It's been a week. Evidently your hair didn't match whatever they had on hand. Which is good, surely."

He brightened.

"As far as I can see," I went on, "we only have one road to go down. What do *you* think Gerald could have had on you?"

"My husband was quite capable of making something up," Gertie said before Zack could answer. "He had all kinds of dirty tricks planned."

"Like what?" Zack asked.

"A couple of ideas I heard bandied about involved sending out anonymous letters the week before the election saying you had spent time in jail for drug trafficking. Then Opal had the bright idea of calling registered voters at three A.M. on election day to tell them to vote for you and Winston."

Zack frowned.

"The theory being they'd be so hopping mad at being awakened they'd vote for Opal and Gerald," I offered.

"I know what it meant," Zack said patiently. "I just can't think people would be fooled by somethin' like that. And I've never spent a day in prison in my life."

That was good to know. Maybe I should add it to his campaign flyer. "By the time anyone thought to check for evidence, the election would be over," I pointed out. "All it takes is an accusation, and the majority of people take it for granted that you're guilty. Especially if you're running for office. A lot of people think there has to be some hidden motivation for doing something as insane as becoming a politician."

I looked at Gertie. "What did Gerald have against Winston? They weren't opponents."

She turned away, reverting to her previous behavior. I thought she wasn't going to answer, but after a minute or two she said, "Winston was Opal's opponent and Gerald had joined forces with her, even though he despised her. Who wouldn't?"

I was tempted to suggest that people who lived in glass houses shouldn't throw stones, but I managed to restrain myself.

"I think Gerald thought he might be able to control Opal more easily than Winston once he was on the council," Gertie continued. "He'd brought Opal around to his way of thinking about expansion, but he said Winston was a stubborn old no-growth coot."

"I have to debate Winston and Opal and Janice Carmichael, the new candidate, tonight," Zack said. "I can't say I'm lookin' forward to it, but I'm not worried about Winston. He's a weird kinda dude, but he's a stand-up guy."

Zack really was an altogether stand-up guy himself, in spite of his flaws. Such statements always made me feel very fond of him. Evidently they affected Gertie the same way. She flashed him a look that took me by surprise. Her classically beautiful features were imbued with a suddenly radiant expression that could not be mistaken for anything but what it was.

Love.

At first, I was totally taken aback. I had decided, with just cause, that the woman's sole motivation in seducing Zack was to humiliate her husband. Or to try to get him involved in getting rid of her husband.

As you've gathered by now, Gerald Senerac had been a

gaunt man who had emitted enough coldness to frost your
cheeks if you came within breathing distance. Imagine how
you'd feel if you'd been married to this statue carved from
ice for twenty years or so, and then you'd been exposed to
Zack Hunter—a rangy kinda guy whose inner warmth made
you want to hold out your hands as to a fire in the hearth;
a man whose wry but charming smile made your whole face
crinkle in response; a man whose mischievous green eyes
promised unlimited pleasure, if only you'd succumb; a man
who adored, admired, *appreciated* women. How could you
not love such a man?

Gertie Senerac loved him. There was no doubt in my
mind about that. How many murders, I wondered, had been
committed in the name of love?

CHAPTER 8

"Did you know Gertie Tower-Senerac's in love with you?"
I asked Zack the minute we were back in my Jeep and
heading for his house.

He winced. "Cut it out, Charlie. You know the L-word
makes me jumpy."

"You're sure she couldn't have sneaked out of the motel
that night?"

"Not while I was there."

"But you left at midnight?"

"Give or take."

"She could have left ten seconds after you did."

He turned his head and studied my face for several minutes. "You don't really believe Gertie strangled Gerald?"

"*Somebody* did. I'm just figuring out means, motivation,
and opportunity. We can't just sit around waiting for Reggie
Timpkin to arrest you, Zack. We have to find out who killed
Gerald."

"How?"

"I don't know yet. I'm working on it." I thought for a
minute. "At first glance Gertie would seem to have the most
reason to dispose of him. She's in love with you. According
to what she told Bristow, she *wasn't* in love with Gerald."

Zack frowned. "I think Gertie might have . . ." he trailed off, turned his head back to face the front, then resettled his cowboy hat at an angle that shaded his face. Zack's body language was always fairly obvious.

"What?" I asked.

"Stop the car," he said abruptly.

"Come on, Zack, this is no time to be getting grouchy."

"We're here, Charlie."

So we were. I had been driving on autopilot. I parked in his driveway.

"Lunch?" he asked.

I shook my head. "You never have anything but pizza in your refrigerator."

He got out of the Jeep, came around to my side. "I could order you in some rabbit food from Lenny's Market."

I was torn. On the one hand, I wanted to find out what he'd been about to say. On the other, I didn't trust myself alone with Zack. On a couple of previous occasions we'd come very close to getting too intimate. I don't suppose I need to explain why I was reluctant to get intimate with Zack Hunter, considering the number of women already in his life, and the fact that I still possessed some shreds of self-esteem.

"Speaking of rabbits," I said. "I have an appointment to take Benny for a checkup at the vet." This was true. It just happened that the appointment wasn't until four P.M., and it was now just going on noon.

"Last time I saw Ben he looked fat and sassy."

"I want to keep him that way. He has a mild case of diarrhea. Usually I give him orange Gatorade, but it doesn't seem to be doing the trick this time."

I thought up another excuse. "After I get back from the

vet, I have to get ready for the debate. I want to take flyers along, may need to print some more. Have you got your opening remarks memorized?"

"Yes, ma'am."

"You won't forget the bit about regretting Gerald's death and hoping the police make an arrest soon? I know that might not be easy for you to say, but . . ."

"No problem," he said. "I *do* regret it. And I do hope they catch the guy who did it. I didn't like Gerald Senerac, but nobody has the right to wipe somebody out."

"You're a good man, Zack Hunter," I said.

He displayed his wry grin and puckishly slanted eyebrows all at the same time. More than any girl could stand. "Come on in and I'll show you how good I can be," he said softly.

I shook my head at him. "I'll see how good you are at the convention hall. Seven o'clock sharp."

He stepped back and touched the brim of his cowboy hat in a minisalute. He looked so macho and devastatingly attractive that I berated myself for being a party-pooping idiot as I negotiated the hairpin bends that led down from Paragon Hills. What was I trying to prove with all this celibacy stuff?

That I wasn't insane, my brain said back at me.

We had a good turnout for the public debate. What with Gerald Senerac's murder, and the news that TV personality Janice Carmichael was taking his place, the local citizenry was agog. Besides, such events were always videotaped, and people—as I mentioned earlier—just loved seeing themselves on television.

I took a seat in the second row, the front one being

already filled with CFLC members. I sat on the aisle so I could mouth things at Zack if he floundered. I wondered if we should learn sign language. Angel sat beside me. Speeches made him restless, *sitting* made him restless, but he wanted to show support for Zack. Savanna would have been there, too, but Monday evening was the only night CHAPS didn't open, and she treasured the time with Jacqueline.

Lauren Deakins was seated farther along the row, I was sorry to see. She had on a ruffled green blouse and a tight thigh-high leather skirt with a zipper that opened from the bottom. Last time I saw a skirt like that it was on a hooker who wandered into CHAPS one night and wandered out again with Angel showing the way.

Lauren's gaze was fixed on Zack like a laser beam. I wanted to go over and talk to her like somebody's aunt, but I decided that probably wasn't such a hot idea. Sometimes I have to remind myself that I'm dedicated to the proposition that this is a free country. I might disapprove of a kitten dressing up like a febrile cat and looking at a king, but I'll defend to the death her right to do so. Well, maybe not to the death.

Macintosh moderated. He brought the meeting to order right on time and introduced each of the candidates rather tentatively, as was his style. His pleasant Scots accent made them all sound appealing.

I was glad to see that before letting the debate get under way, he reached over and removed the evening's program from Winston's nervous hands. During the first debate, Winston had systematically shredded the program right in front of his microphone, which had amplified the sound to irritating crackles.

Finally, after reminding the panelists they each had fifteen minutes for opening remarks, Macintosh gave the nod to Opal to begin. "I'm putting her on first, as part of my strategy," he'd told me before the meeting got started. "That way she'll maybe get stuff off her puny chest, and won't be panting to interrupt when the others are speaking."

I'll summarize here to avoid boredom. Opal's speech was pretty much a rehash of her previous offerings:

"Bellamy Park must grow, or die."

"Nobody has the right to tell anyone what they can or cannot build on their own property."

"People and jobs are more important than birds."

Her longest statement brought gasps of surprise from the audience. "The U.S. Supreme Court said that wetlands are the cause of malarial and malignant fevers. It said that police power is never more legitimately exercised than in removing such nuisances."

She didn't bother to mention that the Supreme Court she was referring to dated back to the last century. Luckily, having heard her deliver this speech before, I'd prepared a response for Zack.

Like Macintosh, Opal wore glasses, but hers had the effect of magnifying her eyes so much they looked parboiled. Her large teeth clicked at the end of every sentence, providing a sort of audible exclamation point, like something out of Victor Borge's comic routines. Subdued giggles erupted from the audience with increasing frequency. In spite of her eccentricity, however, Opal still managed to convey Senerac's message that without a thriving workforce, all of Bellamy Park's share of nature's bounty was not enough to feed all the people.

Well, of course not. Most of it has been paved over

already. And who says Bellamy Park has to be self-sustaining anyway? People commute to jobs all over the peninsula.

Angel emerged from his trance and nudged me. "You're muttering, Charlie," he whispered.

The most debatable point of Opal's whole position was, of course, whether maintaining a thriving workforce would be easier subsequent to the building of a huge housing development and a monster shopping mall. I made some notes to post into Zack's future speeches.

Winston Jermaine was seated at the next microphone. Neither he nor Zack joined in the laughter at Opal's expense. Winston probably had his hearing aid turned off.

Zack had remembered to take his cowboy hat off and to comb his hair, I was glad to see, and he appeared to be watching Opal with great attentiveness. A couple of times, though, I caught his eyes drifting to where the delectable Janice Carmichael was sitting sideways in her chair, her gaze on Opal, her profile and perky bosom showing to good effect.

Winston was up next. After passing a hand over his flattop and tweaking his bow tie into place, he launched into a speech that pretty well covered the same topics as Opal, except his views were diametric to hers.

Unfortunately he weakened his whole speech by saying, "This country is going to hell in a handbasket," several times. I've never been quite sure what a handbasket is, and how a whole country could fit in it, or why a nation should choose that method of transportation. Nights when I can't sleep, I ponder such imponderables.

Both Winston and Opal were droners. I was beginning to miss Gerald Senerac's high-pitched patrician voice. At least it had had some variation to it. Angel's breathing had become so regular, I thought maybe he'd gone to sleep, but if he had he'd done it with his eyes open. I wondered if he was into self-hypnosis as well as auras.

Zack followed Winston. You could almost feel people settling back in their chairs as he started off in his relaxed drawly voice. They warmly applauded his sentiments with regard to his dearly departed rival. Opal interrupted to say in a voice of outrage that, of course, she was sorry, too, and if she hadn't been rushed into speaking first, instead of in last place, which was what she'd requested, she would have said so. Her grief was much deeper, she insisted, because Gerald had been her friend, whereas he had been Zack's enemy. And justifiably so.

I got to wondering if maybe Opal had seen the contents of Gerald's briefcase. I was still very worried about that briefcase floating around.

A few people in the audience were booing, but Opal went right on harassing Zack. Macintosh's strategy was a failure, and chagrin showed on his bearded face. After his scowling at Opal failed to have any effect, Macintosh had to resort to gaveling her to silence.

Applause rang out at the end of Zack's speech, but I had the feeling most of it was because he was a celebrity. People had developed a great fondness for Sheriff Lazarro in the seven years he was visiting their living rooms via their television sets. I hoped Lazarro's popularity would carry over into votes for Zack, but I knew a lot of the businesspeople were not inclined to favor ecology over economy; and as much as they might like Zack, the bottom line is a potent factor in "the U.S. of A.," as Zack always called it.

Janice Carmichael had a lot to say about the bottom line

as it affected the mall Senerac's group of citizens wanted to build. She was all for it, "born to shop," she said, which got her a round of applause and good-natured laughter. I thought she'd echo Senerac all the way, but to my amazement she went on to say she didn't like the site Mr. Senerac had wanted to build the mall on—the site he had just happened to own—because it was too close to the Proctor House and would disturb its tranquility. She was quite sure another site could be found.

She went on to talk about experiencing the solitude of the marsh Senerac and his group had wanted to turn into an "exclusive residential development." She had obviously made the acquaintance of the salt-marsh flora and fauna. And she'd read up on biosystems and realized how important they were to the bay. She talked lovingly of California gulls and brown pelicans, American kestrels, rails, and hawks, and told how she'd seen a great blue heron taking off with a *whoosh* of its huge wings, at the same time scolding her with its hoarse prehistoric squawk.

I felt so strongly about the survival of the marsh in question that I'd written some similar experiences of my own into Zack's first speech. A lot of his fans had been visibly moved. Senerac had responded, "If you've seen one heron you've seen them all," which of course paraphrased something said by a well-known California governor several years ago. Opal had thought Senerac's remark was funny. Even Winston had neighed.

There was obviously no comparison between Janice and Senerac. She even mentioned a similar proposed development of Palo Alto's Baylands nature preserve that had been attempted in the fifties and had been roundly defeated by outraged citizens.

All of this was great, but meant my job was going to be a lot harder. If Janice had a similar agenda to our side, it was going to be difficult to present a clear choice to the voters. There wasn't as much divisiveness about the mall. And with a change of site, even that would fade.

Personality would probably be the deciding quality, and Janice and Zack both had more than their fair share.

Janice wasn't a beautiful woman, but she had an interesting face and a good figure, if a little pointy in the upper reaches. Her voice—low, throaty, sexy—was her next best feature. It certainly held our man in black's attention.

She made some good points, well thought out and intelligent. Several times she used the word "balance," which had not been in Senerac's vocabulary. She stood a good chance of beating Zack.

Nah. What was I thinking of? I'd still bet on Zack and the women of Bellamy Park.

The question-and-answer segment was lively and fairly polite. Opal, of course, had a few acidic comments to make, including the tired one about Zack being a TV actor and thus one of the devil's disciples committed to corrupting the morals of our youth. She didn't have anything to say about Janice's TV career.

Macintosh handled the session well. His charmingly reticent manner and soft voice had a soothing effect on the members of the audience, just as it did on the children who watched his programs, making them much more inclined toward good manners.

I told him so when he climbed down from the stage and sat next to me after the crowd began to disperse.

"Some kind of regional Mr. Rogers, you mean, lassie?" he

asked, rolling every r. "Perhaps I should buy a few cardigan sweaters?"

I stretched my legs out, now that people had stopped shuffling past. "I thought I was paying you a compliment," I protested.

He gave me his shy smile. "You think *you'd* feel complimented if some sexy person you admired told you your personality was soothing to children?"

It took me a minute to get over the fact he was indirectly calling me sexy. Which thrilled me to no end. My ex, Rob Whittaker, the noted plastic surgeon and compulsive adulterer, used to say my figure was too boyish, that I should allow him to do some breast enhancement.

"Boyish," somehow, never sounded sexy. Nor did "soothing," I had to agree. "Point taken," I said with a grin. "I apologize."

"You're forgiven, lassie. I've no doubt I'm the cardigan type at that." He quirked an eyebrow. "Are you keeping your hard drive optimized?"

Macintosh was a tidy person. He wanted my computer files to be as neatly lined up as his own. "You ask the most personal questions," I said, to make him blush. Which he did.

I grinned at him. "I'm using the defrag program. I like it better than the other one I bought. It's quicker, too."

"Just so you're cleaning up the drive regularly." He pushed himself to his feet. "I'm off for a puff," he said, waving toward the door. "I'll be back in two shakes of a lamb's tail. There's something I'd like to share with you."

I looked back up at the stage as he headed at a fast

clip for the door. Zack was surrounded, mostly by women. Surprisingly, this wasn't always the case. Sometimes women were shy around him, because of his sex-symbol reputation I supposed. Perhaps they figured now that he was a politician, they could approach him without losing intellectual face.

Winston was sticking close to him—probably enjoying the fallout. Janice was hovering, too. And so was Lauren, leaning over so her cleavage showed. Opal had already left. As had Angel. He wasn't one to hang around places. Once the job was done—off he went. I often wondered what he did in his spare time. Once in a while, I'd ask him if he'd watched a certain TV show, gone to a certain movie, enjoyed the sunshine. He usually just tugged on his mustache and shook his head, making his ponytail wag.

I decided to wait for Zack so he couldn't get taken over by Lauren or Janice. It would never occur to him that he shouldn't fraternize with his opponent, and he'd driven over in his newly purchased pickup so he was free to disappear with one woman or the other unless closely observed.

At the same time I wondered what it was Macintosh had to share with me, and if it was connected to Senerac's killing. As he eased himself sideways between the rows of chairs on the way back from his smoke break, it occurred to me this was a good chance to question him. "Who do *you* think might have killed Gerald Senerac?" I asked as he sat down, permeating the air with the not unpleasant smell of burnt tobacco.

"Mrs. Gerald Senerac, maybe," he suggested.

"You've met our Gertie?"

"I have."

"I wouldn't be surprised myself if she did it," I told

him. "Taylor Bristow doubts she'd be strong enough, but Sergeant Timpkin doesn't seem worried by that little detail."

Under his breath Macintosh said a word I'd never heard him use on his children's program. It didn't sound at all Scottish.

I looked at him with interest. "I take it you've met Reggie. Did he ask you how come you didn't go fishing with Zack and the guys the way you planned?"

He nodded, grimacing. "He made it sound as if I bowed out so I could finish off Gerald."

"Did he come up with a motive for you?"

"I'm Zack's friend. We play poker together so I must be. And I was at that banquet. I spoke sharply to Gerald when he went into overtime on his speech. Made me so angry that after the banquet I killed the guy, then put him in Zack's car so it would look as if it couldn't have anything to do with Zack because Zack wouldn't be stupid enough to put the body in his own car."

I laughed. So, after a moment, did Macintosh. Then he sobered. "I told Sergeant Timpkin there was no particular reason I changed my mind about going on the fishing trip. He didn't like my answer, but I stuck to it, even though it wasn't true."

Taking a handkerchief from his inside suit-jacket pocket, he removed his glasses and cleaned them carefully. I was afraid he wasn't going to continue.

Eventually, he put the spectacles back on, tipped his head back and peered at me through the lower part of the lenses. He must have read the question on my face. I've been told I have a transparent face. I need to practice guile. No—actually, I'm guileful enough, I need to practice hiding it. "I decided to stay home and entertain a friend," he said.

Have you noticed that when people mention a "friend," there are a bunch of different meanings that can be inferred from the way they do or do not stress the word?

Macintosh stressed it. Meaningfully. With double quotation marks around it. This was what he'd wanted to share with me.

He nodded. Again, my face must have shown what I was thinking. Of course, it wasn't a surprise to me. I'd told Savanna at the campaign kickoff that I suspected Macintosh was gay.

"Zack started out trying to protect someone who could give him an alibi," I told him. "Bristow pointed out the repercussions of an indictment for homicide could be far worse than from anything personal."

"Not in my case, Charlie," Macintosh said.

I've always understood how difficult it must be for someone to feel they can't admit they're gay, no matter how much he or she might want to. The psychological pressure of a secret that embodies all a person is, or ever will be, would have to be horrendous. But Macintosh produced and starred in a children's TV show, remember. That show was his life. Children loved him. Their parents loved him. Teachers loved him. Librarians thought the world of him and frequently invited him to take part in events.

I probably don't need to explain that there are uptight people everywhere, and that sometimes uptight people cause trouble for people who don't conform to standards they consider proper. *Of course* Macintosh didn't want the world to know.

I grinned at him and nudged him with an elbow. He

smiled, looking suddenly ten years younger. Just telling *someone* helped, I guess.

"You think I ought to have a tea or something for Zack's campaign?" he asked. "I make splendid scones. My grandmother taught me. We could have it in my garden, hire somebody to play the bagpipes. I could make up some invitations in Print Shop."

"A tea would be great. We have several coffees lined up. And a couple of fund-raising dinners. Tea would make a nice change."

I found myself remembering what Savanna had said about Macintosh maybe having a crush on Zack. If he had a *friend*, surely he wouldn't be interested . . . Oh sure, Charlie, like you've never felt an interest in two men at the same time. I decided to believe Macintosh's motives were purely political. After all, he played poker with Zack every Sunday night, why should he host a party just to get him to his house?

"Just don't invite any bonny lassies," I told him. "Zack's turning over a new leaf—no women for the duration of the campaign."

Macintosh's tentative smile dimpled his cheeks above his fuzzy beard. "Does Zack know about his new leaf?"

I grinned. "Not yet."

We sat in companionable silence for a minute or two, but then I couldn't resist asking, "I take it you don't think Zack murdered Gerald."

He lifted his left hand and smoothed his fuzzy beard with the backs of his fingers. "I certainly *hope* he didn't, Charlie."

I pulled my legs off the chair in front and sat up straight. "Macintosh! You can't seriously . . . you play poker with Zack, have you ever seen him lose his temper? He's always good-natured, easygoing. . . ."

"I keep recollecting that dartboard," he said.

"Well, you can't blame Zack for disliking the man, after all the awful things Senerac said. But that doesn't mean he killed him."

"I certainly hope he didn't," he said again.

CHAPTER 9

I did a good job of cutting Zack loose from the crowd. "I need to talk to you, right now, at CHAPS," I told him the minute the mob around him showed signs of breaking up. Then I walked out, without giving him a chance to argue prior commitments.

He showed up in CHAPS' parking lot right behind me. We admired the sunset for a few minutes. Working nights, I didn't often get to see a sunset, and this was a fairly spectacular one with mauve and apricot layers trailing purple-black ribbons. Zack put his hand on my shoulder. It felt warm. I moved out from under it, which made him look sadly at me, but then I invited him up to my loft, and he perked up a whole lot.

While I opened him a beer and poured myself a glass of Kendall Jackson chardonnay, he lifted Benny out of his cage and sat down in my wobbly rocker, gently cradling the little rabbit in his big hands, a sight that never failed to move me.

The best you could say for my loft is that it's eclectic. It's one long wide room, directly above the main corral, with lots of windows and miniblinds, which are usually in need of dusting. I've arbitrarily divided it into kitchen, dining,

sitting and sleeping areas with thrift-store furniture. When
I failed to leave my ex-marriage as soon as I should have, I
realized I was sticking around because of treasured "things,"
like antique furniture, my blue-willow dishes, and the house
itself—a wonderful Tudor semimansion on Puget Sound.

I'd vowed then that I'd never again let myself get
attached to "things." I'd already vowed not to get attached
to people.

"After we left Gertie's this morning," I said as I handed
Zack his beer and sat down on the overstuffed and partly
sprung sofa opposite, "I commented that she was in love
with you, and you started to say something. 'I think Gertie
might have . . . ' What was the rest of it?"

He took a swallow of beer direct from the bottle, his free
hand still supporting Benny against his chest. Benny doesn't
show a lot of facial expression. Well, none at all, really,
except his eyes are either open or closed. But he has an air
of contentment around him when Zack holds him. Other
people, he tends to hip-hop out of reach when they let him
go.

Having lowered the bottle, Zack assumed the gently
puzzled expression he'd perfected as Sheriff Lazarro when
Lazarro was at his most devious.

I narrowed my baby blues and fixed them on his face.
That always makes him feel guilty. "Timpkin thinks it's
entirely possible you and Gertie are both lying to establish
alibis for each other," I said. "If you *are* lying and he finds
it out, you're going to be in deep . . . trouble."

"We're both tellin' the truth," he said.

"So what was it you stopped yourself from saying?" I
asked.

He set down the beer and began rubbing Benny's cheeks,

which made the bunny quiver and push his nose into Zack's hand, begging for more.

"Zack?"

Deep sigh. Then he handed Benny over to me and I put him on my shoulder, where he could burrow into my hair.

"What makes you think Gertie's in love with me?" he asked.

"I saw her face when she looked at you."

He shook his head. "You're wrong, Charlie. I've an idea Gertie's been seein' someone else right along. That's what I started to say, but I didn't want you goin' after Gertie to find out who it is."

"Well, she was seeing Gerald, I should think," I pointed out amiably, reserving the right to go after Gertie any old time I wanted. "Even if they weren't getting along, she probably ran into him at the dinner table, or going in and out of the house."

"Besides Gerald, Charlie."

I frowned at him. "If Gertie's been doing it with someone else, you'd better let the police know. The guy might have had reason to do away with Gerald. Maybe Gerald came after him and he defended himself. Though it's hard to imagine Gerald showing that much passion. Maybe this other man's the one who stole Gerald's briefcase. Why didn't you mention him before?" I sat up straighter to consider this new angle, almost unseating Benny. Extricating him from my hair, I lifted him down to my knee and stroked him back to somnolence. He yawned, showing his cute little buckteeth.

Zack squirmed on the rocker, drank some more beer, then heaved a sigh for all the nagging women there were in the world. "I don't know *who* the dude is, Charlie. I just know that a month or so ago, Gertie went to a company dinner. There were pictures in the *Gazette* the next day. One showed Gertie by herself, but her hand was touchin' a man's arm."

He worried his hair. "You could see the jacket sleeve and a French cuff and a cuff link. It had a horse's head on it."

"Wait a minute." Something had buzzed faintly in my memory. Hadn't I seen something similar? The thought was gone as quickly as it had appeared. Probably wasn't important. "Gerald always wore suits," I pointed out. "He was the type who would wear French cuffs."

"I asked Gertie if she took Gerald to the dinner and she said, 'God, no—I never let him get around people I work with. He'd probably go off into one of his monologues against treehuggers.' A good number of the people she works with are liberals, she said."

"Maybe the man with the French cuff was a liberal she worked with," I suggested.

"Could be." He reached over to pet Benny. There was a look of embarrassment on his lean face.

"What?" I demanded.

"A couple of times Gertie was sorta frayed because I couldn't be with her when she wanted me to be." He stroked Benny some more.

"I'm listening," I said with an edge of sarcasm even Zack couldn't miss.

"Both times she said I wasn't the only man in her life and she'd just call this other dude she knew."

To my relief, he leaned back in the rocker again. "I thought she was just tryin' to make me jealous, you know, the way women do."

I let the sexist comment pass.

"But then I saw that photograph," he continued.

"You kept on sleeping with her even though you thought she might be sleeping with someone else?" I asked.

"It's very difficult for me to say no to a lady," he said with a suggestive glance from under his eyelids. Then he shrugged. "I'm not an exclusive-kinda guy, Charlie. I don't expect a woman to be any different."

I sighed at this bit of outdated and misguided philosophy. "Don't you ever worry about AIDS?"

"I'm careful," he protested. "I'm always prepared."

"No protection is one hundred percent certain."

"But what's the alternative, darlin'?"

"Abstinence."

I swear he blanched under his tan. The jagged scar on his left cheek, usually faint, showed up appreciably darker. And he definitely shuddered. "Bite your tongue, Charlie."

The man was hopeless. I was suddenly furious with him. And not for the first time. And when I was this furious, there was only one thing to do. "It's time for you to go," I said sharply.

"Charlie . . ."

"Out!"

Standing up, I put Benny carefully into his cage, fetched him a lettuce leaf from the refrigerator, then stood with my arms in a washerwoman position, glaring at the infuriating man while he sucked down the rest of his beer, reached for his hat and put it on, shook his head at me and grinned his wonderfully attractive thin-lipped grin and walked out of the door, which I kicked shut behind him with all the force I could get out of my Code Wests.

Five minutes later, after realizing it was only 9:15 P.M.,

I was on the phone to Marsh Pollock's apartment. Which only goes to show how mature I am.

After some banter, Marsh invited me over, but I wasn't mad enough at Zack to forget all caution, so finally we settled on a nightclub that featured a good mix of music, and I met him there a quarter of an hour later. With a dress on, yet, a long loose black silky number that sort of floated around my ankles and made me feel like an unnatural woman.

We slow-danced. I drank a glass of wine. A dumb thing to do. I was still angry with Zack for his indiscriminate love for womankind, and mixing wine with anger inevitably leads me into a total disregard for common sense.

I was beginning to get a pleasant buzz on as I sashayed around the floor in Marsh's muscular arms. The cause might have been the wine, or the chemistry. Marsh was only a couple of inches taller than my 5'10" and I had flats on, so we fitted nicely together. When the band took a break we sat down fairly close together and began to talk.

"Tell me about farming in Minnesota," I said, rather archly, I must admit.

"I'd rather talk about you," he answered in his sexy gravelly voice.

"I'm serious," I said. "I'm interested."

He leaned an elbow on the very small round table and took hold of my hand, as if he were going to arm wrestle me, but instead he brushed my knuckles very lightly with his lips.

Zack Hunter? Who ever even *heard* of Zack Hunter? Recklessly, I gulped another jolt of chardonnay.

"Wouldn't you rather hear about the Minnesota Twins?" Marsh asked.

I shook my head. "Farming," I insisted.

Farming, I thought, would be safe. There was also that little niggling need-to-know area of my brain that wanted to be quite sure this hunk, with the muscles and the curly grey hair and sailor-blue eyes and gorgeous face, was the former farmer he claimed to be.

"We had about three hundred thirty-three acres," he said.

"How can you have *about* three hundred thirty-three acres?" I asked. Wine also makes me argumentative. "You can have *about* three hundred acres, or even *about* three hundred fifty acres, but three hundred thirty-three is pretty precise."

He nipped my knuckles with his teeth. "Okay," I said, extricating my hand, "I'll accept *about* three hundred thirty-three acres. What was in them?"

"Soybeans."

"Healthy," I said.

He nodded. "You can get thirty-seven bushels of soybeans out of an acre."

"You're beginning to sound like an encyclopedia."

"We also had a few milk cows," he said. He went on to tell me *about* how many farms there were in Minnesota— though he also wanted me to understand that the state was highly industrialized, with many giant business enterprises operating within its borders. From there he segued into what other principal crops were grown, and why his father chose soybeans instead of wheat farming, and how Minnesota does more dairy farming than wheat growing nowadays. He also imparted a bunch of information about the Saint Lawrence Seaway.

My eyes began to fog over. Who'd have thought a man

who looked like Marsh Pollock would generate yawns? He knew about farming, all right. Yes sirree, Bob.

So what had I expected? Every man I was attracted to had a fatal flaw. My ex took celebrity worship (female) to the nth degree. Zack couldn't discriminate between women so he simply bedded them all. Marsh was boring.

We slow-danced again. Marsh kept inching me closer and breathing into my hair. I kept inching back and babbling about Zack's campaign, which Marsh obviously found as boring as I'd found his dissertation on farming. I decided I wasn't having fun and it had been pretty dumb of me to try to distract myself by getting Marsh's hopes up. It was time to tuck myself into bed. Alone.

Carefully, I explained that it had been a long, full day and I had an appointment with my gynecologist early the next morning.

Marsh didn't argue. I like that in a man. We walked outside together and stopped to look at the moon, which was full and appeared larger than life. It lit the parking lot almost as if it were daylight. There had been a full moon last August on the night Zack and I found the skeleton in CHAPS' flower bed.

I shivered.

Marsh put his arm around my shoulders. I thought he was just being chivalrous, but then he increased the pressure slightly, and I found myself flat up against his hard body before I knew what was happening. Well, I *knew* what was happening, I'm not that dumb a cluck. But it happened so fast I wasn't sure if he'd yanked me around, or I'd done a hop, skip, and a jump into place all by myself. A combination of both maybe.

He buried one hand in my hair and touched my right

breast very, very lightly with the other, then kissed me a lot more intimately than I'd ever been kissed by my ex-husband. To tell you the truth, I never did see what was so great about tongues until that very moment, but his felt pretty good. Also, though normally I hated having my head held, it didn't seem to matter. Not to mention the hold he had on more significant parts. All of a sudden, Marsh Pollock didn't seem at all boring.

Maybe it wouldn't be such a bad idea to just go ahead and have sex with someone, I thought. It might be therapeutic. I'd left Rob more than two years ago. I'd stopped having sex with him several months before that. My hormones hadn't gone into hibernation, however; witness my knee-jerk response every time Zack heaved into view.

It probably wouldn't hurt those hormones to have a lube job. We could stop at a drugstore on the way to Marsh's place.

Then again, I had decided I wanted a life free of complications. This sort of thing could get very complicated.

I heaved myself free. Easily. Points for Marsh for realizing that any signs of struggle on the part of a female means no. Not all the fellas know that yet.

He was breathing hard. I was a little short on oxygen myself. But I really didn't want to proceed. I'd got myself into this situation to distract myself from my anger with Zack, and that wasn't fair to any man.

"Are you going to slap my face?" Marsh asked, his eyes twinkling in the moonlight. I realized I'd raised a hand, but it was more as a protest than a promise of violence.

"I don't slap faces," I said. "This is the nineties. Real women kick shins." He took a step backward, smiling his knowing little smile. "I'm not going to kick you," I added hastily. "I can't accuse you of forcing me. I went into that clinch willingly enough."

"But?" he asked.

"But I'm not ready for anything at this stage."

He studied my face. And I have to admit it did my heart good to see that he looked disappointed. You'd hate to have a guy not care one way or the other after an outstanding kiss like that.

"Look, Marsh," I said carefully. "I called you because I was in a bad mood and needed cheering up. I shouldn't have done that. It's not a good way to start—a relationship. And all of . . . this . . . happened just a little too fast for me. I was looking for distraction, but it's really not a good time for me to get distracted from the stuff I have to do."

"Like getting Zack elected?" he asked.

"That's one of the things on my itinerary, yes. Keeping him out of prison's another. Finding out who killed Senerac, if I can. You're not involved in any of those tasks, so it sort of comes down to not being able to spare the time."

Now, how come I hadn't thought of that before I called him? Heat of the moment? Or were all these excuses the equivalent of backpedaling because I was scared spitless at the thought of intimacy? Life was certainly much, much easier without it.

Marsh cocked an eyebrow. "Aren't the police working on the Senerac case?"

"Detective Sergeant Timpkin has convinced himself that Zack did it. He's not looking for anyone else."

"So who do *you* have in mind for the role?"

I shook my head. "No one yet." It wasn't fair to share my suspicions of Gertie when I had nothing solid to back them up.

He touched my cheek lightly. "How are you going to go about this investigation, Charlie? Maybe I could give you a hand. I've never tried to solve a murder before. Except reading Agatha Christie and Sue Grafton, and whoever. We could go on a stakeout together. Do you have a suspect whose house we could park outside? At night? It's always best at night. We might have another major bonding experience."

That gravelly voice of his could sound *so* suggestive. "I don't have *any* suspects. I just know Zack didn't do it."

"Are you sure?"

"That's not funny, Marsh, of course I'm sure."

Well, 99% sure. If I could just get Zack to open up about those missing months . . .

"You don't look sure," Marsh said.

I forced a shrug. "I'm still just looking around, that's all, talking to people, thinking about things."

"I can talk to people," he said, smiling.

He tucked my hair behind both ears, exerting enough pressure to bring my head forward. I resisted. "You have a gym to run. And I can't take on anything else right now, Marsh. The timing's incredibly bad. Let's just ease back into being friendly acquaintances and give it some time, okay?"

Looking suitably chastened, he let go of me and held out both hands, palms up. "I'm sorry I came on board with all guns blazing, Charlie. It's—well, it's been a while for me."

He really was a nice guy. I already knew I was going to be kicking my own shins, if such a thing were possible, for letting such a rare find get away. But then again, if he didn't want to wait until my life was uncluttered, he'd hardly be someone I wanted to get involved with.

Taking a breath, I held out my right hand, "Friends?" I asked.

He looked for a second as if he really wanted to argue, then he shrugged, but looked regretful as he took my hand. "Sure," he said. "If we can maybe date once in a while. Talk on the phone? Have a drink?"

Marsh Pollock was a lot less dangerous to my peace of mind than Zack Hunter, I rationalized. And I was getting tired of saying no. "Okay," I said.

CHAPTER 10

A gynecological exam is not the activity of choice for most women. I arrived early at Dr. Hanssen's clinic the next morning, so I could get it over with, but found I had to wait anyway, as he hadn't yet left the hospital after delivering a baby. I really think the medical profession ought to consider splitting up OB and GYN. Babies always arrive just ahead of my appointments, which is very inconsiderate of them.

Okay, I was cranky. I'd jumped out of the proverbial frying pan into the even more proverbial fire the previous night, and now I had to work on not going to bed with *two* men. I don't mean that in the kinky way it sounds. I'd woken up thinking about Marsh and the kiss, and telling myself there was no damn reason I couldn't just have a fling with the man. He might be on the boring side, conversationally, but he had a gorgeous body. Men went for a combination like that all the time. Zack made a specialty of it. Witness his doll brigade. *Zack.* Everything always came back to Zack.

I'd gritted my teeth and taken a cold shower. There is no stupidity I get more annoyed at than my own.

Besides being cranky, I was also nervous. This was my second exam this month. My regular checkup pap smear had been designated Class III, which according to the local library's medical encyclopedia did not bode well for our side. The receptionist had told me on the phone, in that reverent voice people use when they convey potentially bad news, that it was probably nothing serious, but it might be a good idea to get in here ASAP and have another checkup.

The only bright spot on my personal horizon was that I had a good excuse to sit and read. I was trying to figure out what to do next in my ongoing attempt to find out who killed Gerald Senerac, and reading often triggers the more creative areas of my brain. As a bonus, I found my favorite tabloid hidden behind a *New Yorker*. I was disappointed that it was nine months old but I hadn't read that particular issue, so at least it kept me occupied until Dr. Hanssen—a young, fair-haired, Scandinavian, athletic type—showed up, looking worn but proud. "Twins," he announced.

There is nothing good to say about lying on your back with your knees up and your feet in stirrups, gazing up at the ceiling while someone probes your vulnerable inner areas with inquisitive fingers. Dr. Hanssen not being much of a conversationalist, I let my mind play idly with some of the stories I'd been reading, hoping one of them might trigger some ideas. Sure enough, my brain suddenly popped up the memory of the story about Zack I'd read in that magazine long before I ever met the man, or had any idea I'd one day work with him. Along with the memory came the thought that maybe Gerald Senerac had come across that article, too.

It was at least a place to start. I felt energized, all worries forgotten. For the moment, anyway.

After the doc muttered something about calling me in a week or so with the results, I leaped off the table, pulled my clothes back on, and tracked down Matilda, the elderly receptionist. "You have any older copies of this magazine?" I demanded, waving it at her.

She blinked and I apologized. "How far back you wanna go?" she asked.

"Two or three years."

She scrunched her eyes almost closed. "It's possible, Charlie. I've been working for Doc Hanssen for three, and I've taken 'em all home sooner or later. Doc said I could," she added defensively.

"I'm looking for an issue that dealt with stars of TV dramas," I told her. "Zack Hunter was on the cover along with a couple of other television hotshots."

"I could check," she offered. "How about if I find it I bring it in tomorrow and you can stop by and pick it up."

"Terrific. Thank you. I owe you one." I turned to go.

"Don't you work for Zack Hunter? At CHAPS?" she asked.

I let out a long-suffering sigh. "I'm his *partner*," I said. Feeling some explanation might be called for, I added, "I'm planning a sort of surprise for him."

"Like on *This Is Your Life?*" she asked. "The old TV show?"

It sounded vaguely familiar, and close enough to the truth, which I always *try* to adhere to, so I nodded. "You're so lucky," she said. Which I took to be a yearning reference to our man in black. "Could you get me his autograph?" she asked. "Not for me, of course, for my niece. She's such a fan of his."

I figured if she came up with the magazine I wanted, I

was getting off light. "It's a deal," I agreed, and she beamed with such obvious joy my doubts about the niece story were validated.

Marsh Pollock sent me a basket of yellow daisies with one of those foil balloons attached and a message written in a loopy scrawl on the accompanying gift card: "I'm biding my soul in patience. Is virtue a point-getter? Can we do lunch tomorrow? Nothing threatening about lunch, is there?"

The man had imagination, I had to give him that. Yellow daisies pleased me a lot more than hothouse roses would have. I called the gym at a time when I thought he'd probably be busy and left a message on his voice mail. "Not tomorrow. Maybe the next day. *Maybe*. I'm thinking it over. Don't call us, we'll call you."

The following day Matilda delivered as promised. She was thrilled beyond measure with Zack's flamboyant autograph, which he'd gladly written for me without questioning its ultimate destination. She gave me a funny look, though, as I took the magazine from her and expressed my gratitude. I understood why when I sat down a half hour later at my flea-market dining table with my usual turkey and lettuce and nonfat mayo sandwich, and pulled the magazine out of the shopping bag she'd put it in.

"TV's bad boys," the blurb on the front cover stated, along with photographs of the three actors. "The Shocking Story of Zack Hunter's Hair-trigger Temper," the first inside headline read, followed by, "Zack Hunter walks off set after fight with director."

"What causes Zack Hunter to constantly play macho

pick-a-fight?" the article began. "He has top billing on today's most popular television drama, he has every woman in the country, perhaps in the world, panting for him—(a slight exaggeration, I might add)—he's pulling down one of the biggest salaries in TV history. Why, then, does he continue to get into violent arguments with his directors? The show's been successful for more than six years—they have to be doing something right. Why does he keep getting arrested (though no one ever presses charges) for taking part in drunken brawls, subsequently showing up on the set with a black eye or swollen jaw the cameramen have to shoot around?"

"It's not true that I'm a fallin'-down drunk," Zack was quoted as saying. "Sometimes I just feel like takin' a nap on the floor."

This sort of statement was Zack's idea of humor.

Just as I'd remembered, the article told about a knock-down-drag-out fight with one of the directors of *Prescott's Landing*, after which Zack had walked off the set and disappeared for a month. Writers had to scramble to account for his absence. What they did was work up a story of Sheriff Lazarro going off into the woods on a manhunt (filming his double from behind) and coming down with Lyme disease, caught from a tick, which gave him arthritis. Lazarro's deputy took over for a couple of episodes, then when Zack showed up again, the writers presented him with a script in which Lazarro couldn't walk very well, and he was hit and killed by a runaway bus. Exit Sheriff Lazarro. Exit Zack Hunter.

I finished the article and the sandwich at the same time.

"And there it is," I said to Benny, who was hip-hopping around the loft. He sat back on his haunches and twitched his whiskers at me.

"The trouble is," I went on as I put my plate and water glass in the dishwasher, "none of this matches up with the Zack we know, does it?"

Benny had lost interest and was gnawing on a "natural chew stick" that looked like a carrot. He has a low attention span.

I had never, in fourteen months, seen Zack lose his temper. I had never known him to drink more than a beer or two. What had happened between then and now to change his personality and habits? Always supposing the story was true. After all, some of the tabloids occasionally reported stories of babies born with bats' heads, or men who got pregnant. Though this particular magazine didn't usually engage in such blatant fabrications.

Somewhere, sometime after the story appeared, I had seen a query in a magazine about Zack and where he had gone. Nobody had seemed to know. There had been various rumors, I remembered. He had been seen hobnobbing with one of the English royals. He was down and out in Seattle's Pioneer Square. I couldn't recall if that was before or after he'd supposedly checked into Betty Ford's clinic. He had been seen in a wheelchair in Vancouver's Stanley Park. Elvis Presley had probably been sighted in most of those places, too.

By the time I'd answered Zack's ad for a partner, I'd forgotten the details of this story, or at least put them at the back of my mind. I'd had a life to live, after all. And problems of my own at the time. A compulsively adulterous husband. Stepchildren bent on making my life miserable.

I hadn't thought about the story again until last year when the skeleton turned up in CHAPS' flower bed, and I was looking for signs of guilt anywhere and everywhere.

I reached for the telephone on the end table and punched Zack's number. It didn't ring, but I heard someone breathing. "Hello," I said.

"Is that you, Charlie?" Zack asked. "I just picked up the phone to call . . . someone else."

Otherwise known as a female person, I was willing to bet. Flyin' Missy? Adorin' Lauren? Gorgeous Gertie? Or the mystery lady I had almost forgotten about, the one I had yet to track down, the one who'd given Zack coffee after meeting him at Paulie's Place the night after Senerac was killed.

"Your phone call was going to be a terrible mistake," I said. "Trust me, I'm psychic." I was fairly safe saying that, I felt sure. "It also comes to me that something's troubling your mind, though I'm not sure what it is. Do you want to confess?"

"Wild horses wouldn't get it out of me," he said, either entering into the spirit or pulling the wool.

"I called because I got to wondering about something," I said. "We know from Gertie that Gerald was digging up stuff on you to put in his dossier. So where was he likely to get stuff from?"

"I don't . . ." he broke off. The airwaves sang with his breathing, which sounded a little agitated all of a sudden.

"Zack?"

"Hold on." Evidently he was thinking. "Dang," he said finally.

"What?" I asked.

"Maybe you should drive over here so we can talk about it in private?" he asked. "Appears I have the afternoon unexpectedly free."

He *had* been about to call a woman. Which one? Ah, what did it matter.

Whatever he'd suddenly thought of, it had to be something important if he didn't want to tell me about it on the telephone. "Why don't you come here," I suggested, ever alert for ways to get Zack involved in the day-to-day running of CHAPS. "Angel and Savanna will be showing up in an hour or so. We have to do bar inventory, remember?"

He evidently hadn't remembered, but couldn't think up an excuse now that I'd trapped him so neatly.

"I'm relying on you to protect my honor," I told Benny after I hung up. He was nibbling on the toe of my Minnetonka moccasin. "Don't let me do anything dumb. If Zack makes a pass, fasten your front teeth in his ankle and hang on. No, wait a minute, his cowboy boots might be too tough for you. How about you hop onto his knee and . . ."

Benny skedaddled behind the sofa, obviously not wanting to take responsibility for my safety.

I hid the magazine under the sofa cushions, not sure if I was ready to reveal what I was up to. At least until I found out a few more details.

"What it is," Zack said, after I'd settled him in the rocker, with a mug of coffee, and seated myself at a safe distance. "When you asked me who was most likely to know stuff, I remembered this phone call I had from Rudy DeSilva a couple months back. Didn't seem all that important at the time, but thinkin' on it I wonder if it might have some bearin' on Gerald Senerac's so-called dossier."

Rudy DeSilva sounded vaguely familiar, but I couldn't place the name.

Zack enlightened me. "Rudy was one of the directors of *Prescott's Landin'*."

The director he'd had that last fight with.

"He said some dude had come around askin' questions about me. Why I got written out of the show." He swallowed some coffee.

"Why did you?" I asked, seizing the moment.

He was looking at the basket of daisies Marsh had sent. "Nice posies," he said. "You got an admirer, Charlie?"

"Marsh Pollock sent them," I said, setting a standard of honesty for him to meet or surpass.

He rocked and nodded a few times. "Figured Marsh was sweet on you. Kept askin' if we had somethin' goin'. Had to tell him no, though it wasn't for want of tryin'."

He gave me a sideways glance. "You datin' him, Charlie?"

"We've had one date. Night before last."

I watched him think that over. "After you kicked me out?"

"Somewhere around that time, yes."

He kept his gaze on the flowers while he thought some more. "She got irate with me," he said, as if talking to the basket. "*Then* she went out with Marsh Pollock. Cause. And effect."

Every once in a while Zack surprises me with an insight.

"You goin' to see him again?" he asked.

"Maybe," I said. "I haven't decided yet."

"How come—he make a pass at you?" He squinted. "You're blushin', Charlie." His eyebrows went up in puckish humor. "You and Marsh . . . ?"

He didn't finish the question, but the question mark was clearly there.

"That's none of your business," I pointed out.

He nodded. "None of your business what *I* do for a love life either, but you sure get your orange feathers ruffled when it's mentioned."

"You were going to tell me why you left the show," I said hastily.

He gave me his bad-boy grin, but didn't pursue the matter. "Writers just got tired of old Sheriff Lazarro and wrote him right out of the series, darlin', didn't leave me a whole lotta choice."

"Oh, I see," I said, my voice heavy with sarcasm. "They got tired of making money hand over fist. Screenwriters do that regularly, I understand. They got tired of winning all those Emmys, too, I'm sure. Got tired of keeping everyone in the nation at home on a Thursday night."

He nodded, his face as smoothly blank as someone pleading the Fifth Amendment in a courtroom drama. "That about sums it up, darlin'." He finished his coffee, set the cup down on the end table next to his chair, and rocked a couple of times. "Anyway, Rudy didn't tell the stranger anythin'. Like I said, I didn't pay a whole lot of attention. Heck, there's never any shortage of weird people gettin' off on actors and actors' doins. Used to be a woman worked at the studio, security, pulled down the zipper on her jumpsuit and flashed her breasts at me every time I went by."

"I shall sleep well tonight, for you telling me that," I said.

He eyed me sideways. "It's like they don't have a life of their own, you know?"

Like Adorin' Lauren Deakins, I thought, but didn't say.

She was still showing up nightly at CHAPS. She never danced, unless Zack took pity on her; never drank anything but water; mostly just hovered somewhere close to Zack, watching his every move; blushing if he spoke to her, which, being Zack, he often did.

"Dude told Rudy he was a reporter, but he didn't have any credentials and got to soundin' pretty vague when Rudy asked who he wrote for."

"Did Rudy give you a name? Description?"

Zack shrugged. "Not that I recall."

I pondered for a few minutes. Benny showed up and sniffed around Zack's Tony Lamas until Zack picked him up and held him. Maybe the rabbit *had* understood what I'd told him about protecting my virtue.

"Well, this guy may not have anything to do with our current problem," I said at last. "But it's worth checking out. A couple of months ago would be around the time you told the *Gazette* you were planning to run for city council. Why don't you give Rudy a call? Find out if this so-called reporter had a name."

Taking Benny from him, I handed him my cordless phone. "Have you had lunch?" I asked as he started punching numbers. He shook his head, and I went into the kitchen area, put Benny in his cage, and got out the makings for another turkey sandwich.

It took several calls, but Zack finally tracked Rudy down on location in Monterey. "See if we can talk to him in person," I suggested as Zack waited for someone to bring Rudy to the phone.

Five minutes later we had a date for the following day. Lunch at Il Mare, a seafood restaurant on Monterey's Fisherman's Wharf. Marsh was out of luck again. Maybe fate was taking a hand.

"An out-of-town date, darlin'," Zack said after he hung up. "Maybe we should figure on spendin' the night." He squinted at me with that wicked glint in his green eyes.

I shot to my feet. "Eat your sandwich," I said. "We have an inventory to do."

CHAPTER 11

The name Rudy DeSilva and the title of director had led me to expect a distinguished man with silvery hair. The reality was a slightly built juvenile wearing blue jeans with an obligatory ragged tear across the knee, a flannel shirt, a gold earring in the shape of a cross, and a baseball cap with lank brown hair hanging out of it. He looked about seventeen years old.

He and Zack did a round of shadowboxing, pounded each other's shoulders a couple of times, and did some complicated handshaking. Male bonding is always interesting to watch.

According to the story on the front of the enormous menu, Il Mare was famous for its seafood and its view of frolicking seals. The interior was all tricked out in Italy's national colors and cute lanterns made out of candles in Chianti bottles. "Come back to Sorrento" played softly on the PA system. The maître d' was surly.

Zack and Rudy went for the "steak and fried calamari platter." I shuddered and ordered the "flame-broiled snapper with fresh vegetable medley."

Zack and Rudy sawed away at their rare meat and reminisced about *Prescott's Landing* and Zack's portrayal of

Sheriff Lazarro. "Subtle, powerful," Rudy said. "All that inner turmoil."

I hadn't noticed any inner turmoil. It must have been too subtle for me.

While the two men talked I savored my snapper and watched a dozen brown pelicans hurling themselves from sky to water like kamikazes, barely missing a pair of the promised frolicking seals. Actually the seals weren't noticeably frolicking. They were lurking, lounging, hanging out, on a huge buoy to which a large but fairly ancient fishing boat was tied. Occasionally they clasped their front flippers in a prayerful attitude, hoping perhaps that some kind soul would open a window and chuck out a fish. Nobody did.

The Pacific was living up to its name—its peaceful swells barely lifting the bosom of the water, wavelets lazily splashing against the pilings the restaurant was built on. A glass-bottomed boat slowly circled the bay with a full load of tourists on board. Sailboats tacked here and there. Kayakers in yellow life jackets paddled. Seagulls swooped.

Even inside the restaurant, the air smelled salty. I was reminded of my dad. On the rare occasions he took time out from the Greek restaurant he and Mom owned in Sacramento, he used to love to go to San Francisco or Monterey or Carmel, where he'd walk by the sea and smell the "ozone." That's what he called the sea air. He died before people gave much thought to the ozone *layer*, never mind that it might develop a hole big enough so the sun could burn us all up.

"Your friend looks unhappy," Rudy said.

"Low blood sugar," Zack said. "Charlie doesn't eat red meat or anything fried. What d'you expect?"

"I am *not* unhappy," I told them. "I'm merely waiting

politely for you to get through with your nostalgia-fest so we can talk about this so-called reporter who came visiting."

A trio of horizontal creases showed up above Rudy's nose, making him look at least twenty. "Reporter?" he asked.

"Dude you called me about," Zack said. "Couple months back. Askin' questions."

Rudy corrugated his forehead some more and advanced to age twenty-five or so. He tugged on his earring for a minute, which made me wince. I've never understood how people can willingly poke holes in their ears or noses or any of the other vulnerable places they put them. "Weird guy," he said finally. "Tall, thin. What's the word?" He snapped his fingers a couple of times to stimulate his thinking processes. Our pretty waitress, who had been lingering next to a faux-marble pillar, came rushing over, and he apologized for sending unwarranted signals. She looked disappointed. She was probably a hopeful actress. California's full of them.

"Cadaverous," Rudy said triumphantly.

My heart threw in a couple of surplus beats. "What kind of voice did he have?" I asked.

He meditated. "Screechy."

I picked my purse up off the floor and took out the *Bellamy Park Gazette* clipping I'd brought along, just in case. "That's the guy," Rudy said, pointing his forkful of calamari tentacles at Gerald Senerac's photo.

"Dang," Zack said.

"You *know* him?" Rudy asked.

Zack nodded. His lean face had paled. The perpetual wry smile he was famous for was noticeably absent. "I *knew* him. He's dead."

"Murdered," I said.

"Strangled," Zack added.

Rudy took off his baseball cap and scratched his head. His pate. His hairline had receded some years before. Which led me to believe he might possibly be even older than my revised estimate. Replacing the cap, he pulled the bill low on his forehead, at the same time pursing his mouth in a soundless whistle.

I filled him in on the details, Zack having lapsed into glum silence.

"Didn't you get mixed up with a corpse a year or so ago?" Rudy asked him.

"Last August," I said, Zack apparently remaining mentally absent. "The earthquake uncovered a skeleton in CHAPS' flower bed."

Rudy grinned, his cheeks swelling like a chipmunk's. He was so cute it was hard to take him seriously. "I read about your skeleton, saw you on the news," he said to Zack. "You too," he said, with a sudden brightening of his eyes in my direction. "It's all coming back to me."

He laughed, glancing at Zack. "I figured you might have offed the guy yourself. Didn't call the cops with my suspicions, though. Old times' sake."

"Thanks," Zack said gloomily.

"So where'd you find *this* body?" Rudy asked.

Zack sighed. "In the trunk of my car."

Rudy thought that was hilarious. "I made a movie like that, I'd get all kinds of static," he said when he calmed down. "Two bodies a year apart? Too much of a coincidence. Too much to *be* a coincidence. If I was the Bellamy Park Police Force, I'd lock you both up and lose the key."

"Not funny," Zack said. "Detective sergeant in charge of the case thinks I might have killed the dude."

"What exactly did Senerac want to know?" I asked to get us back on track.

"That's the weird guy's name? Told me he was Bill Robinson." Rudy selected a toothpick from a holder on the table, slumped back in his seat and began to dig out beef and tentacle debris. I decided I'd had enough snapper.

He held up a finger. "Asked how come Zack here got written out of the show. I told him to go read the tabloids, take his pick of the stories—one of them just might happen to be true. He asked where Zack had disappeared to after he left. Told him I didn't know." He wriggled his eyebrows at Zack. "Just like we agreed."

My ears perked up. "What does that mean?"

Rudy and Zack exchanged a loaded glance. I might have imagined the slight negative movement of Zack's head, but I didn't think so.

"It means I didn't know," Rudy said.

Which wasn't what he'd implied.

"I saw this guy Senerac talking to a couple other people later the same day," Rudy went on. "Nobody I knew. But he might have talked to some of the old gang. Might have got some answers, too." He pulled himself upright abruptly. "Was he blackmailing you?" he asked Zack.

Which would seem to imply there was something Zack could have been blackmailed *for*.

"Nah," Zack said. "He kept throwin' out teasers to people, sayin' he knew for a fact I'd been a drinker and a whorer, done drugs, got in fights, that kinda garbage."

"Well, he got part of that right," Rudy said. "The whoring's a given, and you sure knocked 'em back for a while, but far as I know you never did drugs." His eyebrows wagged a question mark.

"Never did," Zack agreed.

So what about the fighting, I wanted to know.

"How come Senerac was trying to besmirch your reputation?" Rudy asked.

Zack had sunk back into his gloomy silence, so I explained about the city-council race. "Zack's getting a lot of help from his fan club," I added snidely, still irritated by the "whoring's a given" comment. "But we may get him elected in spite of that."

Rudy's eyebrows went up again. He'd noticed I was sounding a little hostile, maybe.

Zack surfaced. "Charlie's irked because one of my fans keeps hangin' around," he explained. "She's jealous but she'd never admit it in a thousand years."

I managed not to roll my eyes. "Zack failed to mention the fan is barely twenty-one years old," I said.

Rudy's eyebrows did their thing. "So?"

"So she's fairly naive. Starstruck."

"The best kind," Rudy said. He gave a boys-will-be-boys grin to Zack. Zack didn't grin back. Something Rudy had told him was obviously worrying him badly. He kept absenting himself from the assembled company.

"Here's a funny thing," Rudy went on. "Soon's I get through with this Monterey deal I'm working on, we're gonna be casting a new miniseries. *The Honorable Mr. Scott.* It's about a politician. Now there's a coincidence, huh?"

Too much of one to *be* a coincidence? I wondered, echoing Rudy's former statement. Had Zack heard about Rudy's forthcoming project and decided to run for Bellamy Park City Council so he'd have some credentials to offer? Would he be *that* devious?

Maybe.

I remembered the two actors who'd shown up at Zack's campaign kickoff—the two who'd been in San Francisco for summer theater. Had one of them mentioned Rudy DeSilva's miniseries?

"Saw John Donatelli, few days ago," Rudy said, flicking a hand at the waitress and making a pouring motion. She raced over with a carafe of coffee. Her hands shook as she poured. I couldn't decide whether she was anxious to impress Rudy, or affected by the sight of Zack.

Rudy looked at Zack over his coffee cup as he drank, his eyes suddenly shrewdly assessing. "John said you'd mellowed out. Is that right?"

A shadow of Zack's bad-boy grin flickered at the corners of his mouth. "Mellow as an old yellow dog lyin' in the sun," he said.

John Donatelli. His name I knew. He'd produced the musical country-western murder-mystery pilot Zack had starred in the previous winter.

Setting his cup in his saucer, Rudy rubbed his nose and laughed. "I'm glad to hear that." There was a rueful note in his voice. "Maybe I'll be in touch once I get this *Scott* thing rolling."

"Great," Zack said, but his heart didn't seem to be in it.

We drove back to Bellamy Park with the pickup truck's windows open. The air-conditioning wasn't functioning. My hair was going to be a fright.

Traffic was heavy. "What do you think?" I asked, once we were well under way.

Zack blew air out noisily. "We did real good, Charlie," he said with a slightly bitter note in his voice. "We're supposed to be finding out who killed Gerald Senerac and we come up with evidence that points to me."

I mulled that in silence for a while and conceded he was right. "Did you know Rudy was planning a series about a politician?" I asked.

"I may have heard a rumor to that effect," Zack said.

"Is that why you decided to run for city council?"

He looked puzzled. I didn't think he was acting, but how can you ever tell with an actor?

I let that particular question ride and decided to give Zack time to come up voluntarily with answers to the other questions which were whirring through my brain like hummingbirds looking for nectar. Instead he tuned the pickup's radio to 93.3—"Young Country"—and began singing along in his croony, catch-in-the-throat tenor with the likes of Alan Jackson and John Anderson.

About the time we passed through Castroville—artichoke center of the world, according to the billboards—it became apparent he wasn't going to volunteer anything. I switched off the radio. "What could Gerald Senerac have found out about you from Rudy or anyone else at the studio?" I demanded.

Zack took a few minutes to formulate an answer. "Accordin' to Rudy, he didn't find out much," he said finally.

"That's not what I asked."

When Zack zipped his lip he did it literally.

"Look, Zack," I said wearily, which was the way I often talked to him. "I'm trying to help you stay out of prison and you're not cooperating at all. I can't do a thing for you if I'm not acquainted with all the facts. I *know* you had a big fight with Rudy DeSilva and walked off the set of *Prescott's Landing*."

He turned a shocked expression toward me.

"I *know* that it wasn't long after that you were fired," I continued. "Then you disappeared. All of that is in the public domain. If I could find it out, so could Senerac or anyone else. What I'm asking is—what *else* could he have found out? What else *is* there? What Did Rudy DeSilva agree to keep quiet about? And is it connected to that period just before you got going with CHAPS, when nobody seems to have known where you were?"

Lines I hadn't noticed before had shown up at either side of his mouth. His beautifully chiseled jaw had lifted noticeably, and a small muscle in front of his right ear twitched a couple of times from the strain.

"Let's *start* with the fight you had with Rudy," I suggested. "What was the fight *about?*"

He frowned. "Damned if I remember, darlin'."

"Come on, Zack, give me something. A crumb."

He shook his head. "I'm not funnin', Charlie. I really don't remember. I'd been drinkin', I suspect."

"Okay. Let's explore *that* avenue. You used to drink a lot, I take it?"

"More than was good for me, but not enough to get me into AA meetings. Just enough to dull the . . ." He pretended to cough.

"Enough to dull *what?*"

"The senses. The sense. Common sense, that is." After this minor witticism, his mouth zipped itself shut again. He'd realized he'd made a slip, didn't intend doing it again. Tread wary, Charlie. *Enough to dull the pain?* Was that what he'd been about to say?

"You don't drink heavily now," I said casually. "Haven't as long as I've known you."

He pretended to be concentrating on the traffic. "Saw the error of my ways." He looked a mite more at ease.

"Because of the fight you got in with Rudy, the one that lost you your job?"

He cocked his head slightly. "Could be. In a way."

This was like trying to open the cap on a childproof pill bottle. It didn't matter how hard you pressed, you couldn't get it to uncover its contents.

I kept my gaze fixed on Zack's profile while I tried to think of a question that would somehow unlock the part of his stubborn brain where he'd sealed the information I wanted.

"Are you goin' to Senerac's funeral tomorrow?" he blurted out suddenly.

Obviously he was trying to distract me. All the same, this wasn't something I could ignore. "I didn't even know about it."

"Gertie's tryin' to keep it quiet. She doesn't want it to turn into a circus."

I had a sinking feeling. "Don't tell me you went to see Gertie?"

"Okay, I won't."

"Zack!" It came out more like a wail than a protest.

The glint in his green eyes as he glanced my way meant he'd been teasing. "I didn't go to the house, Charlie. Gertie *called* me to ask if I'd go to the funeral."

"What did you tell her?"

He shot me a virtuous look. "Told her I'd talk to you about it, see what you thought. Seemed to me on the one hand, it would be a nice thing to do, not just for Gertie, but because Gerald was runnin' against me, and runnin' me down. Show there's no hard feelins. On the other hand, maybe it would just cause talk if I was to go."

"Let's go with the other hand," I said promptly. "It might look more innocent if you *did* show up, but it might also lead to more media types attending. If Gertie was to collapse on your chest again, you'd really be sunk."

He winced.

"It's really not a good idea to see Gertie right now, Zack," I said in the most reasonable voice I could manage.

"I realize that," he said, surprising me. He cogitated for a couple of minutes, hunching forward over the steering wheel. In the middle distance, the sun-dried California hills were dotted with trees, which looked like green French knots on a brown tapestry. The sky was overcast.

"Tell you the truth, Charlie, I wasn't too much in favor of gettin' somethin' goin' with Gertie in the first place. Just didn't hardly seem any way for a gentleman to refuse."

I sighed. I do a lot of sighing around Zack. "Does it never occur to you to just say no?"

He shook his head, looking perfectly serious.

"Let's get back to the subject at hand," I suggested, before I could give in to my impulse to punch him in his perfectly formed abdominals. "You were going to explain what the fight with Rudy was about and where you vanished to after it."

"I'm not goin' to talk about that, Charlie," he said after several minutes of tense silence. "That period of my life has nothin' to do with you or anyone else."

"You *want* to go to prison, Zack?" I asked.

He ignored that question as we drove through Gilroy. The truck filled with the scent of garlic—the town even advertises a garlic wine—then he said, "If that period of my life got known, I'd be *more* likely to go to prison."

As if knowing that would silence me, he turned on the radio again, listened intently for a while, then started singing along with Mary Chapin Carpenter—"Stones In the Road."

Something about the expression on his face, the stiff attitude of his usually relaxed shoulders, made me think his singing was more closely related to a kid whistling in the dark than an outpouring of joy.

CHAPTER 12

Thursday's not one of our busier nights at CHAPS—maybe people stay home resting up for the weekend push. But as long as there are customers, we give our dancing lessons and serve the drinks and put on happy faces.

To my surprise, Zack stuck around most of the evening. He even slow-danced with P.J., who plastered herself and her gauzy miniskirt against him like cling-wrap. Maybe she'd mistaken the meaning of the "Zack Hunter for Position 2" button he was wearing on his black western shirt. I'd already been questioned by several of our urban cowboys about which position *I* preferred.

After returning P.J. to the main bar, which Patrick, her current love interest, was tending, Zack two-stepped with Adorin' Lauren Deakins, which didn't please me *or* P.J. Neither dance seemed to please Zack—I'd never seen his lean face look so morose.

"What's happening, Charlie?" Angel asked, sliding into the booth where I was hiding out while trying to think through today's meeting with Rudy DeSilva. As usual, he looked as if he'd just come out of a shower and picked up his clothes fresh from the cleaners. Wherever he was having his whiter than white shirts laundered, they were doing a grand job.

Angel was closely followed by Savanna and Gina from Buttons & Bows, whose hair was now uniformly green and fitted her head like a cap, making her look decidedly elfin.

"Not a whole lot," I said, trying to extricate myself from the brown study I'd been roaming around in.

"Jacqueline sends hello," Savanna said. "She says you've not been to see her in 'this much long.'" She stretched her arms wide, then smiled her killer smile—the one that made her look more beautiful than any one woman had a right to look. She was wearing one of her red fringed cowboy shirts. Her black cowboy hat sat on the back of her head, framing her gorgeous face and cascade of thick black curls. Incredible.

"You been seeing Marsh Pollock?" she asked.

I shook my head.

The smile acquired a teasing edge. "Macintosh?"

Angel frowned at me and tugged at his Pancho Villa mustache. "You're dating *Macintosh?*"

"I'm not dating anyone," I said flatly. "I've just been busy." I turned to Gina. "It's nice to see you," I said. "Your hair is really ... green. You're getting pretty good at the line-dancing," I added, to save me from having to make any further comment. Gina had started closing her store earlier a couple of nights a week so that she could join us. Make that so she could join Angel.

"Angel's a great teacher," she said, beaming up at him. He beamed back, which surprised Savanna and me into exchanging a startled but meaningful glance.

"I guess I should mention that Savanna and I were in there teaching, too," I said kindly. "You may not have noticed."

Gina blushed brighter than the blusher that served her for cheekbones. So did Angel. Except that he *had* the cheekbones.

"Angel's been teaching me stuff in the back of my shop," Gina explained, which earned Angel a teasing "I'll bet," from Savanna.

"Angel is a very kind person," I said gravely.

Angel narrowed his eyes at me, but Gina took me literally. "He sure is. He comes and helps me tidy up my store every night before I close. He even hung some shelves for me, and he's helped me with several displays. That rodeo window this month—that was almost all Angel's doing."

Angel shifted a little on the bench. "Yeah, he's a great guy all right," I said. "Savanna and I think so, too."

Savanna nodded seriously. So did Gina. "He's wonderful," she said. "I don't know how I ever managed without him. And he's so sexy-looking, too, don't you think? I just can't get enough of staring at him." She smiled blissfully, a reminiscent gleam in her eye. Savanna and I exchanged another look that meant stand by, Gina's about to throw out one of her startling statements. "I'm here to tell you, this guy's looks don't lie," she went on. "He's really, really—"

Angel shot her a thunderous look, and she blushed again and closed her mouth.

"Clean?" I supplied, and we all laughed except for Angel.

Savanna and I raised eyebrows at each other. It looked as if Angel had finally been seduced. Or else we were just finally finding out about it.

"I think I'd better go do my final walk around the store,"

Gina said, gazing at Angel in a winsome way that no man could surely resist.

"I want to talk to Charlie," he said.

"I'll come with you, Gina," Savanna said.

Gina looked gratefully at Savanna, and with disappointment at Angel. He gave her his rare smile, his wonderfully even teeth gleaming against the black of his droopy mustache. "Hurry back," he said, and she lit up to the roots of her green hair and went off happily with Savanna.

"I really do want to know what's happening," Angel said as soon as the two women were out of earshot. "Zack's acting like a hound with a thorn in its paw. You looked like a robot doing those line-dances tonight. And the Honky Tonk Stomp starts with two *fans*, not heelstands. You don't usually make mistakes, Charlie."

"Got a lot on my mind," I muttered.

He wasn't done with me. "You and Zack came in together. You were late for the usual three o'clock meeting. The way you were, I thought you must have been wrestling with a cactus."

"The air-conditioning's malfunctioning in Zack's new pickup. We had to keep the windows open."

"I'm not talking about your hair, Charlie. There's not a whole lot you can do about that. I'm talking about your prickly attitude."

He was leaning forward on the table, the skin tight over his high bronze cheekbones. That always means he's serious.

I said the first thing that occurred to me. "It's Gerald Senerac's funeral tomorrow."

Angel's expression softened, and his big warm hand covered mine where it lay on the table. "You're not thinking of going?"

I shook my head. "Zack was, but I talked him out of it."

"Good." His eyes held mine. When Angel's eyes darken, they look black. They are always direct. I wondered if he was scoping out my aura, and if it was giving away the fact that I was being less than straightforward.

"I'm worried about Zack," I conceded.

"Good," he repeated. "Someone *needs* to worry about Zack. How could he be dumb enough to think of going to that man's funeral? There're already rumors about him and Mrs. Senerac."

I perked up. "You ever hear any rumors about Gertie Senerac and anyone else?" I asked.

He shook his head without hesitating. "You?"

I nodded, but didn't tell him I'd heard it from Zack himself. "Trouble is, I don't know *who.*"

He was successfully distracted. Resettling his straw cowboy hat lower on his forehead, he gave me a squinting look that was worthy of Zack. "You sleuthing again, Charlie?"

"In a very minor way."

"Want me to ask around?"

"If you can do it discreetly."

His now-you-see-it-now-you-don't smile appeared under the mustache and disappeared again. "Gina knows a lot of people. She might have heard something."

"Speaking of Gina," I said.

He shook his head. "Subject closed, Charlie."

I was going to object, but I saw that the worried look had returned to his eyes. "That funeral's not all that's on your mind, is it, Charlie?"

I came clean. "Our man in black is not always forthcoming. He's keeping things from me. I'm worried that Detective Sergeant Timpkin will find out what his secrets are, before I can."

"Most people have secrets, Charlie."

It was a perfect opportunity for my inquiring mind to set *him* up for some answers, but it hardly seemed sporting when he was trying to comfort me. In any case, Zack chose that moment to straighten up from the post he'd been leaning against and dart a really shifty-looking glance around the room, as though checking on where everyone was, including me. A moment later he strode toward the lobby door.

"I think maybe Zack's looking for me," I told Angel. I didn't think that for one moment. Zack had seen me, I was pretty sure. But it seemed imperative that I follow him and find out what he was up to.

Bernie Lightfoot, the owner of the minimart across the plaza—the pudgy dude, Zack always called him—waylaid me before I got past the little-corral bar. He'd been sitting on the long bench next to the railing, where guys sat to watch girls go by. Except that Bernie watched guys. "You going to teach any more line-dancing tonight?" he asked.

I shook my head. "Lessons are seven-thirty to nine. Just like always. There'll be more tomorrow."

He moved slightly as I tried to edge around him. "Is Angel off duty now?"

I glanced over my shoulder. Gina had returned and was just approaching Angel, who was still sitting where I'd left him. His face was brighter than I'd ever seen it.

"You leave Angel alone," I said fiercely.

Bernie's doughy face flushed. "I was just wanting a beer," he said.

I wasn't sure I believed him, but I pointed him in Patrick's direction and hustled on out.

Opening the heavy outer door, I peered around the parking lot. Zack's rented pickup was still where he'd parked it.

The way the streetlights were placed, I couldn't see into it, but I didn't think anyone was inside.

Which meant Zack was either in Dorscheimer's or the office, since Buttons & Bows was closed. I glanced in the windows of the restaurant. A dozen or so people were enjoying snacks, but Zack wasn't one of them.

As I entered the office he was just hanging up the telephone on my desk.

My mom had a photo of me that was taken when I was about two and a half. I was standing by a kitchen cabinet with a box of Lucky Charms in one hand. My other hand was plunged halfway into the box. I had obviously just swung around and noticed the camera. The furtive expression on my face was duplicated by Zack, when he caught sight of me.

"What's up?" I said breezily.

He stood up and offered a grin, which looked weak around the edges. "What's wrong, Zack?" I said soberly.

It was his turn to be breezy. "Not a thing, darlin'." Reaching for his cowboy hat, which he'd placed on his own desk, he stood up and stretched a little. "Guess I'll mosey on home. Not much happenin' tonight."

Normally I would have argued that we had to stay, so he should, too. I was also half tempted to tell him to put his butt down on that chair and answer my questions, but I had a feeling he'd had enough for one day, and I didn't have the heart to go after him again.

Which all sounds tremendously compassionate and kind, as long as you don't know about this other little sneaky cluster of brain cells that was telling me to just let him go before he or anyone else could pick up that phone and punch in new numbers.

"I'll see you tomorrow," Zack said, hesitating in the doorway.

I nodded as I bustled over to the filing cabinet, as if that was what I'd come in for. When I felt the change in air that meant the big outer door had opened and closed, I sat down and looked at the telephone.

Trust is an important part of friendship, of course. Without trust, you can never be truly close to anyone. And I didn't exactly distrust Zack in a way that meant I thought he was a criminal. I certainly didn't believe he'd tied knots in a piece of yellow rope and slung it around Gerald Senerac's neck.

I just felt I needed to know what he was doing. For his own good.

With all my rationalizations firmly in place, I picked up the telephone and punched the redial button.

The phone rang six times. I hung on, hoping at least for an answering machine.

But it was a real person who answered; a woman, a little out of breath. "Jaenicke Institute," she said.

The name sounded familiar. I'd seen it on a signboard somewhere.

"Hello?" the woman said, and I muttered, "sorry, wrong number." I needed to know more about the place before I started talking.

Pulling the hefty Pacific Bell phone book out of the bookcase, I thumbed through the business listings. I found the Jaenicke Institute for Problem Solving Therapy right away, but it took me a while to track it down in the Yellow Pages. It was listed with physicians and surgeons under psychiatry.

"California Board Certified Mental Health Center," the entry said.

CHAPTER 13

The Jaenicke Institute—an attractive complex with soaring roofs—was on the road to Half-Moon Bay. That was why I'd remembered seeing the name on a signboard. Half-Moon Bay was one of my favorite places. I'd even gone there with Zack once, when we were involved in our previous investigation, last September. He'd described the Halloween festival the area celebrated every year, though he'd supposedly not arrived in the region until the previous January. Another of those little anomalies that I'd tucked away in a corner of my brain.

The office manager was in a room off the main lobby. She was possibly pushing twenty-two, petite and personable—with round blue eyes and long straight auburn hair I would have loved to fish out of my mom's genetic pool, instead of the orange crinkly stuff I was fobbed off with.

According to the little wooden plaque on her desk, the office manager's name was Mary Grace Nolan. The name echoed in my memory, and I thought she looked sort of familiar as we shook hands over the top of her computer terminal. Maybe she'd shown up with Zack sometime or other—she was the right type to join the doll brigade.

"I've met you before, Ms. Plato," she said as she waved me to a chair.

"I recognize you," I admitted, "but I'm not sure . . ."

"There were a lot of people around." Her lower lip stretched into a comical grimace. "It was at that get-together you had for the neighbors. At CHAPS. Last year. After that awful skeleton was found in the flower bed. I live in one of the Granada apartments."

Her expression switched to one of grave sympathy. "You found the skeleton, didn't you? Did you wish to make an appointment with one of our therapists?"

The implication being that anyone who found a skeleton in a flower bed was in need of therapy? Which was probably true. I still had nightmares about that skeleton. Joined now by bad dreams about Gerald Senerac's bulging eyes.

"I'm interested in some information," I said.

It was interesting the way her face changed to suit the occasion. Now she was all formal and businesslike as she handed me a slick-looking brochure. "This will tell you all about the Jaenicke Institute. Our therapists specialize in anxiety, panic attacks, depression, and of course physical, emotional, sexual, and substance abuse." Her voice throbbed with understanding.

"That's not quite the kind of information I need," I said.

Mary Grace switched into a polite listening mode while I tried to phrase my first question in a way that wouldn't get me kicked out by the nearest orderly.

"I owe you a big thank-you, Ms. Plato," she said after a few seconds, apropos of nothing that I could think of. "I kept promising myself I'd tell you so, but I was afraid you'd think I was weird."

She noticed my confusion. "Another girl and I went to that party at CHAPS because we were curious to see Zack Hunter in the flesh." Her eyes grew very round. "I got to shake his hand. I was totally thrilled. That way he has of looking at a person from under his eyelashes! Totally awesome."

Tell me about it.

"He's even more majorly sexy than he looked on TV, isn't he?" She didn't wait for an answer. "I heard at your get-together that this job was open. I'd just come through a totally grotty sexual-harassment thing with the dentist I used to work for—you wouldn't believe the nerve of that jerk—and I was desperate to change jobs. The very next day I applied for this position and got it."

She flushed prettily. "A few months later, I got this." She flashed a sizable sapphire at me. It was situated on the third finger, left hand. "Sugar says it's the exact same color as my eyes," she said, then bit her lower lip and looked coy. "I'm engaged to the senior doctor, Dr. Barry Sugarman." Her face appeared more wistful than joyous, I thought. "Didn't seem likely anyone like Zack Hunter was ever going to show up in my life, so I thought I might as well look to my future."

I wasn't too sure I understood that last comment, but it didn't seem to have any bearing on my problem, so I let it pass.

She owed me. That was the best part.

"Well, I have to admit Zack is pretty special to me, too," I said, lowering my eyes modestly. "We're sort of—well, I guess you could say we're going together."

Well, we'd gone together to Monterey the previous day.

"Totally awesome," Mary Grace breathed.

I nodded. "He's a wonderful guy." I looked up. "He's the reason I'm here. We have a situation that's really very worrying."

"The body in his car?"

Damn. I'd hoped I could convince her I had an ex-husband who was raging with jealousy and trying to turn up dirt on Zack. That way I could ask legitimately, or semilegitimately, if anyone had been around asking questions about our man in black, and if so, what the answers might have been.

"Yes," I said, rapidly ditching the story I'd prepared during my sleepless night. I leaned forward. "This is really hush-hush, so I'd appreciate it if you'd keep it to yourself."

Her expression had switched to that of a thrilled and eminently trustworthy listener. "Of course. Nothing between these walls ever goes outside, Ms. Plato. I'm totally trustworthy."

Damn. I'd reminded her of doctor-patient confidentiality. That wouldn't do at all. "Call me Charlie," I said, then went on hurriedly. "It seems to me, and certain members of the police department, that someone, probably the murderer, is attempting to frame Zack for that murder."

Her eyes looked like Betty Boop's, the character you see on a lot of T-shirts nowadays. Totally circular, as she might have said herself.

"Whoever the guilty party is, he appears to have uncovered certain information that could only have been given to him by this institute."

She gasped and covered her mouth with her hand. "You know, it's a funny thing," she said after a minute's thought. "I understand Zack himself called here last evening. The night receptionist told me. She was all aflutter about it. He wanted to know if anyone had been around here asking questions about him in the last couple of months."

Pay dirt!

"What did she tell him?" I asked.

"She told him she didn't know. She put him on to my fiancé. Dr. Sugarman. Naturally, she doesn't have any idea what Barry ... Dr. Sugarman told Zack." She looked from side to side as if expecting eavesdroppers to be hiding behind the file cabinets, then lowered her voice. "I thought I'd ask Sugar—I'm sorry—Dr. Sugarman what it was all about when I see him tonight. Just out of curiosity, you understand."

"Do you suppose you could let me know what he says?"

She looked a little troubled.

"I'm very much afraid Zack's life may be in danger," I said. Well, if he went to prison, it would kill him. No women. No adoration. Possibly too much adoration. "We think we know who the person is, but we have to have proof that he's at least shown an interest in Zack."

"Wow!" she said softly, and I knew I had her.

"I also need to know what Zack was treated for here," I added briskly. Sometimes you just have to plunge in, and hope there's some water in the pool. "I'm not only worried about the threat to his life—but for my own sake. If we were to have children ..." I let my voice trail away.

Envy showed up in the round eyes. "Oh, Zack Hunter would make beautiful babies," she said. "But I know what you mean—sometimes there are things that can be passed on, you wouldn't believe ..."

She shook her head. "I do owe you, Ms. Plato, Charlie, and I'd love to do anything I can for Zack Hunter, but it would be more than my job's worth to talk about one of our patients." She sat up very straight in her chair. "You're asking me to do something that's totally against the rules of this institute."

I nodded my understanding, but didn't try to hide my disappointment.

"There's no way I can tell you what you want to know," she continued. "Oh, I can probably ask Dr. Sugarman if someone came looking for information on Zack Hunter, and let you know that, but to reveal the details of a patient's treatment . . ."

She broke off, maybe realizing she'd just revealed that he *had* been a patient. I was that much ahead. And I couldn't really blame her for refusing to go further. I suppose if I'd been one of the hard-boiled male detectives in the mysteries I read with such avidity, I would have slipped her fifty bucks and hinted I might get rough if she didn't cooperate, but I was just a struggling amateur. Yeah, I know, you'd already worked that out.

She stood up and nodded, as if to confirm her decision. "I have to go do some copying," she said. "I've been putting it off far too long. It's too confidential to entrust to the receptionist."

I was going to be evicted. About to stand up, I hesitated when she began punching keys on her computer keyboard. "The screen saver on this computer is set to come on after a minute if there's no movement," she said. "Jiggling the mouse makes it go away. If the mouse doesn't work right— sometimes it gets sticky—you can use the arrows to scroll. There's not much here, it's just the summary, but it'll give you an idea. . . ." She glanced up, blue eyes stern. "You hear anyone coming, get back in your chair and look innocent. If you get caught, I went out just for a minute, never suspecting you'd crack my password and get into my computer. Right?"

Stunned, I managed to nod.

She put on an expression she might have learned from the spy who came in out of the cold and walked out. "I'll be back in ten to fifteen minutes," she said sotto voce from the doorway.

I remained stunned for all of ten seconds, then I scurried around the desk and started scanning the computer screen.

I'm not really up on medical terminology, especially when it comes to psychology, but I was able to figure out from the doctor's notes that Zack had most certainly suffered from some kind of mental problem. There was apparently a great deal of additional information on other files, and I fiddled with a few keys for a while, but got a bunch of error messages.

This summary dealt mostly with the treatment Zack had undergone for some unspecified problem. Tranquilizers had been prescribed. Hypnosis was used. There were sessions of analysis. Suppressed memories were mentioned, but not detailed. I scrolled beginning to end, and found that the period covered an initial couple of weeks of inpatient care, a gap of a month, then fourteen months of outpatient visits. All of which coincided neatly with the time line in the tabloid stories I'd read. I now knew for sure that Zack's missing months had been spent in this area, while he received treatment on first a daily, then much, much later, a weekly basis.

I heard footsteps.

I was sitting in the chair on the other side of the desk, my nose in *House & Garden* magazine when the owner of the feet came in.

"Are you waiting for Mary Grace?" a well-modulated voice asked.

I nodded, hoping my face wasn't showing how rapidly my heart was beating.

He was a handsome man of about sixty, with silvery hair that complemented the white coat he had on over his shirt and tie and dark trousers. As a matter of fact, he looked a lot like I'd expected Rudy DeSilva to look. Prosperous and successful—the sort of person you would instinctively trust. I immediately understood Mary Grace's cryptic remark about looking to her future.

According to his name tag he was Dr. Barry Sugarman. Sugar. Very fitting. I've nothing against May-December marriages, but Mary Grace hadn't struck me as a giant in the intellect department. Wouldn't she seem boring to a man with such an intellectual occupation as psychiatry? Totally?

"Mary Grace said she'd be right back," I told him helpfully. "Shall I give her a message?"

"Thank you, that won't be necessary. I'll return later."

I hate to admit it, but I was too chicken to go look in the computer again after he left. Scribbling a note to Mary Grace that I'd call her later, ending with a thank-you, I hightailed it out of there.

CHAPTER 14

Zack's house in Paragon Hills was a single-story, Spanish-style, red-roofed adobe built around a central courtyard, complete with a swimming pool and a hot tub, which glittered like blue topaz under the sun.

After calling Marsh one more time to leave excuses on his answering machine, I'd brought lunch with me—sandwiches made with tuna canned in spring water, nonfat mayo and chopped onions, sliced tomatoes and olives, with mango chutney and a salad on the side, peaches and nonfat yogurt for dessert. We ate on the patio, each equipped with a luxuriously cushioned chaise longue. Even though Zack had considerately moved the chaises into the shade cast by the house, I kept on the long-sleeved shirt I'd put on over a tank top and shorts. Redheads burn; people with orange hair char.

At home in the summer Zack dressed in short shorts or swim trunks, and nothing else. Swim trunks today. The kind that look like paper. Multicolored, in a stained-glass pattern. Out of consideration for me he'd put on a white Dandy Carr polo shirt, which reminded me of Marsh Pollock.

Zack's body was just right, muscular but not overly bulky, tanned, smooth. I tried not to look at him.

He ate two thirds of everything I'd brought, complaining the whole time about its healthfulness.

When I told him I was there to get some answers, and I wasn't going to leave until he came across, he looked as if the food had turned bitter in his mouth. His chaise was the other way around from mine, so that we could face each other—my idea, I wanted to watch his body language.

I saw his bare feet tense. "Don't even think of going anywhere," I said sternly.

I've probably mentioned that Zack's eyes are perpetually narrowed as if he's squinting into a dust storm. When he's really suspicious of someone they squinch almost closed. Right now all I could see of his eyes was a green gleam.

I'd rehearsed how I was going to open this discussion before I'd called Zack to suggest lunch, but now the words didn't seem adequate. I decided to slide into it sideways.

"I saw a murder mystery on TV once where the detective who'd been called in went straight to the telephone after finding the body and pressed the redial button. That was how he found out who the victim had called just before he was killed. I'm not sure if it helped his investigation along, all that stayed in my mind was the punching of the redial button."

Zack's dark eyebrows slanted up above his nose in the way that usually made him look puckish, but right now indicated confusion. I let him think about it for a couple of minutes and watched his face clear as he understood, then close up tight.

"I went to the Jaenicke Institute this morning," I told him. I'd decided I'd tell the truth, except for the part that might get Mary Grace into trouble. "I talked to the office manager, but she wouldn't tell me anything. I'm hoping you will."

His mouth stayed stern.

I leaned forward. "You have to tell me all of it, Zack," I said. "Starting with whatever led up to your fight with Rudy and getting fired from *Prescott's Landing*, and where the Jaenicke Institute fitted in. For your own sake. It seems apparent to me that whatever it is you're holding back, that's what Gerald Senerac found out. If the police learn that he had something on you—and they will—you'll be up in a tree house without a ladder. I can't help you unless you're willing to come clean."

He rose from the chaise in one fluid motion. Trust me, he could do fluid real well. I was momentarily dazzled, and not by the sun. Next thing I knew he'd hauled off his polo shirt and was executing a flawless shallow dive from the end of the pool, entering the water with barely a ripple.

He swam several very athletic laps, which started me worrying like a mother because he hadn't allowed an hour to pass since eating. Women worry about the damndest things.

My next worry was where to look while he toweled himself off. All that tanned and muscled flesh, and wet tousled black hair shining in the sun, made my stomach go *whomp!* Not to mention that the very thin, very wet swim trunks were now plastered against his lower parts.

So I pretended to be napping until I heard his chaise creak as he sat down on it.

"I wasn't fired from *Prescott's Landin'*," he said.

My eyes flew open. I was so surprised by this statement I whipped off my sunglasses, the better to gape at him. "The tabloids made it up?"

"Nope. They wrote it the way they were told, for once. Rudy and I made it up. True story was—I quit. If word had got out about that, people would have been lookin' me up, seein' if I wanted to do this or that. This way, thinkin' I was a troublemaker, they were more likely to leave me in peace."

After putting his shirt and sunglasses back on, he rearranged his chaise so he could lean back in it. Maybe the position put him in mind of his psychiatrist, maybe I'd finally convinced him it was time to let it all hang out. Whatever the reason, he seemed ready to go on, and I sat very quietly, not wanting to discourage him in any way.

"I know you read the tabloids, Charlie, so I expect you saw some of the stories about me fightin' on the set. The fight with Rudy wasn't the first by a long shot."

"The magazine I read said it was a regular practice." I used as little inflection as possible.

He nodded. "I was always a fighter, since I was a kid, where I lived I had to be to survive."

"In Beverly Hills?" I queried. There may have been an edge of disbelief in my voice.

Zack ignored the interruption. "My aunt Sophie used to say I'd grow out of it, but I didn't. Dr. Sugarman—the head honcho at the Jaenicke Institute—said it was as if there was this dormant volcano inside of me and every once in a while somethin' would trigger an explosion. He used to joke that in my case the volcano was like Stromboli, which'd been continually active since the time of Homer, whatever that is."

"Homer was an epic poet. Lived in ancient Greece." I should have been a teacher—I have this impulse to educate all the time.

"Like your grandpa? The philosopher?"

"He wasn't my *grandfather* . . ." I broke off, recognizing that Zack was automatically using delaying tactics.

"I really *don't* remember what started the fight with Rudy," he went on when he saw I wasn't going to be distracted. "Except that the storyline on *Prescott's Landin'*, a subplot about a little kid who was always in trouble, had been triggerin' a lot of miniexplosions. For some time I'd been seein' these pictures in my head, like outtakes from a movie—the parts that aren't used in the final version? They seemed like bad dreams, but I was awake. I didn't recognize anything in the dreams but they seemed to be of me when *I* was a kid. When the pictures came, a kind of black fog would well up inside me and block out everythin' but the need to hit out at someone, anyone. One day the need was real bad, and I got in the fight with Rudy and knocked him to the ground. Gave him a nosebleed that wouldn't quit. He was sure he was going to bleed to death."

He moved his head slowly from side to side, looking dazed. Obviously he was still amazed at what he had done. "Rudy was my *friend*, Charlie. The other directors I attacked, the producers, other actors—they were all my friends. I had no reason to want to hurt them, no reason at all. After the fight with Rudy, I got in my old pickup and started drivin'. I didn't care where I was goin', I just wanted to keep on truckin'. The pictures in my head kept flashin' by so fast I couldn't make them out, but I knew they were all of me, and by now I knew for damn sure that they weren't dreams and I wanted to get away from them. I didn't stop for food or water or anything except gas. That's when I discovered I was on Highway 1 headin' north. I thought maybe I'd just keep goin' and drive off the end of the world. Couple times comin' through Big Sur I came close to swingin' the wheel over and goin' off the cliff. But each time traffic was comin' the other way, and I didn't wanna take anyone out but myself."

He was speaking in a flat monotone, as if the experience had been horrible enough without adding the drama of inflection to it. I wasn't about to interrupt.

"When I returned to myself I was at Half-Moon Bay. We'd been shootin' in the studio in L.A., so I'd driven a few hundred miles. Luckily, that old truck of mine was a gas hog and I had to stop a second time to fill up. By then, I'd calmed down enough to realize the bad shape I was in. I decided to take Highway ninety-two and cross over the San Mateo Bridge and ride the I-five back to L.A."

He paused. "It was on Highway ninety-two I saw the sign for the Jaenicke Institute. There was somethin' on it about treatment for anxiety and depression, and I figured they had me pegged, so I turned in. Took me a long time to get up the courage to get out of the pickup. Toughest thing I ever did, goin' in that clinic and sayin' I needed help. I was shakin' head to toe—couldn't hold still."

"You saw the doctor you mentioned—Dr. Sugarman?" I asked, careful not to give away too much prior knowledge, for Mary Grace's sake.

He nodded. "He fed me, then gave me some kind of medicine to make me sleep. When I was rested up, he got me talkin'. Wasn't easy. Toughest role I ever played. Didn't want to do it. But Dr. Sugarman kept proddin', and all of a sudden somethin' he said hit a weak spot and I opened up like a faucet. Seemed like I wasn't ever goin' to stop. Sugarman finally told me there was no way we could go through it all quickly. It would take months, he said, maybe a couple of years, maybe more."

He took in a deep breath, let it out and paused again. "Can I get you a beer, Charlie?"

I shook my head. "Water, maybe."

He got up and brought two glasses and a pitcher with ice cubes in it.

"I stayed at the Institute three weeks," he said as he poured. "I let Rudy know where I was and he promised he wouldn't tell anyone. People have sympathy for you if you're sick with somethin' like appendicitis, or gall bladder, or even Lyme disease, but you talk about mental institutes and they find somethin' to do in the other direction. Fast. So Rudy said they'd write around me for a while. And that's what they did. We brainstormed on the phone, me and Rudy and the writers, and worked out that dumb story about the tick gettin' old Lazarro in the neck and him gettin' Lyme disease and arthritis. Thinkin' was, we could go either way with the story. Lazarro'd either recover or turn up dead."

"And he chose death," I said.

He nodded, looking somber. "Dr. Sugarman came back with me to the studio, so's we could be sure I'd be okay. We filmed my part in that one last episode—where Lazarro got run over by a bus—then the doc and I closed up my house and arranged for a caretaker. Then I came right back to the Institute and checked in. Dr. Sugarman worked with me for over a year. I see him off and on still, mostly sociable stuff— he's a nice guy."

He came up with a shadow of his wry grin. "The doc even hypnotized me. I always thought that kind of stuff was pretty hokey, but it's just like you're feelin' real relaxed and what the doc calls the censors are missin'. So you talk and talk and talk, and the doc catches it all on a tape recorder and asks a question now and then to push you along."

His mouth twisted. "I spilled my whole insides on those tapes, Charlie. I cried, hell, I cried gallons. Sobbed. Cussed. Shouted. Screamed. You can imagine how stirred up I was when we found out Senerac had been pokin' around in my past. If the tabloids got hold of those tapes, they'd tell the world I was a nutcase."

My blood ran cold at the very thought.

He reached across and patted my foot. "It's okay, darlin'. When I called Dr. Sugarman last night, he said nobody had been around asking *him* questions. And they'd have to ask *him*, because he'd destroyed the tapes as soon as he was sure I'd recovered. Said he usually hangs on to the tapes for educational or research purposes, but me bein' in the public eye, he didn't want to risk them gettin' stolen."

"What about transcripts?" I asked.

"He burned those, too. Said all he has on the computer is a bare record of my treatment, no details. Felt he had to keep that much."

I didn't tell him I'd looked at that record. I hoped Mary Grace wouldn't split on me. I didn't think she would, because she'd be splitting on herself. At the same time, it was easy to imagine that Gerald Senerac might have conned someone *else* into letting *him* take a peek. He wouldn't have needed details, it would have been enough for his purposes just to know Zack had been a patient there.

"I'm goin' to get a beer," Zack said abruptly. "You change your mind, darlin'?"

I shook my head. I must have looked worried. He smiled much more naturally than he had before and said, "Cold beer on a hot day tastes good, Charlie, that's my only reason for drinkin' one. Never did get to where alcohol was an illness. Don't ever seem to need it now."

He came back with a foam-topped glass and poured me some more water. "Not sayin' much, darlin'," he said.

"I expect I will. I'm worried that this is painful for you."

"Not anymore, darlin'. Once Dr. Sugarman made me bring all the monsters out of the basement and face them, I began to improve in a hurry."

"I can see that for myself. I mean, I wondered about the tabloid stories because they didn't seem like the Zack I knew. But I'm still not clear on what problem actually brought you to the Institute. The fighting, the drinking . . . ?"

"The anger." He sat down on the edge of his chaise and took a long swig of beer. Then he set it down on the nearby table and leaned back again, his hands behind his head. It was a relaxed pose, but his body looked taut, and his face was strained again.

"I'm gettin' to the bad stuff now, darlin'," he said.

"I wonder if maybe we should have Bristow sit in if he's available," I suggested. "He's sympathetic, he's your friend, if he knew the full story he might be able to head off Timpkin and—"

Zack was holding up his right hand in a stop-the-traffic signal. "No way, Charlie. I tell this story to you, it goes no further. You and Dr. Sugarman. Nobody else. Word gets out I'm deranged, or at least used to be, my career's over. Hard enough to get anyone to work with me now, because of my reputation for fightin'."

"You don't trust Bristow?"

"He's a friend, yeah. He's a police officer first."

I couldn't argue with that.

"I get through talkin' and you still think Bristow should hear any of it, we'll talk about it," he added.

"Okay," I said.

He took another swallow of beer, set the glass down. "First off, you have to know I didn't grow up in Beverly Hills like my press kit says."

While I was still trying to digest this bit of unexpected information, he named a part of L.A. that had been notorious for its high crime rate for several decades. That was where he'd spent his childhood years, he said.

"We lived in an old house that had once been nice, but had gone downhill," he said. "Me and these two other people. They were my mother and father, but I never use those words for them because those words imply warm and lovin' hearts, and they had none of that. Their names were Jake and Tess, okay? Tess was a whore, Jake was her pimp. Jake was usually crocked. Tess preferred to space out on methamphetamine. You may not know that speed addicts develop a voracious sexual appetite. That's why Jake kept Tess poppin' pills, so she'd keep right on lookin' for business. She specialized in orgies. There was a kinda crawl space under the house, so when Tess had her little tea parties, Jake would dump me down there and put an iron bar over the board that sealed the entry hole. Didn't want a cryin' kid upsettin' the party-goers. Problem was they'd start bingein' and forget I was underground. Amazin' I didn't starve to death early."

Somewhere in here I had closed my eyes. The pictures Zack was painting were coming through very clearly. I could see the little boy he must have been, with his black hair all over the place, his ribs showing through his skinny torso, his feet perpetually bare and dirty. I'd seen such children in the parts of cities tourists didn't go to. My parents had taken me with them every evening when they delivered leftover restaurant food to people who needed it. My mom and dad had also regularly bought shirts and pants and skirts by the bundle from thrift shops, washed them and mended them and ironed them, and delivered them along with the food. As Zack talked I kept contrasting my mom and dad and their kindness and generosity with Zack's monstrous parents.

Those pictures that had come into his mind years later were horrifying. His father had not only dumped him in the cellar, he'd whipped him with his belt if he cried. Sometimes he'd whipped him to *make* him cry so he'd have reason to whip him again. Usually, after those episodes, he'd leave him in the cellar until he was so weak from hunger he didn't have the strength to cry.

Here was another picture. Tess—his *mother*—decided that at seven he was old enough to watch her entertain her visitors, as a special bonus to her guests. Jake didn't approve of that, so whenever he found Zack in the room, he beat both of them, then put the boy back in the crawl space.

It was no wonder that Zack, as he grew older, had escaped whenever he had the opportunity. He'd lived a hand-to-mouth existence on the streets, running with a pack of kids who begged and stole and fought without provocation. He was a gang leader before gangs were fashionable, he said, running wild and angry day and night. "It was safer out there than at home," he said. "Especially when Tess had visitors."

And then his life changed.

He was sitting up on the edge of the chaise again, hands gripping the edge of it. "It was a cruel thing that happened, but it saved me," he said. "One day . . ." He swallowed and started again. "One day, I saw a man shoot a fourteen-year-old girl. I had seen guns before. Once in a while a kid would

pring one out and brag about how he was goin' to blast
somebody's brains out, but most kids didn't have guns then,
not like now."

He swallowed some more beer and I drank some water,
and I thought how this story seemed impossible in this beautiful courtyard with its planters full of cool green shrubs
and bright flowers, the border of trees for privacy, the pool
and hot tub shining blue.

In such a place as Zack was describing, the sun never
truly shone.

"It was a weird sort of night," he continued . "Burn-
your-eyes smog sittin' right overhead. No breeze. So hot
there wasn't much action on the street. It was after dark,
but there were a couple of streetlights functionin'. I saw the
whole thing. Nobody else there, except the girl, me, and the
guy who shot her. Lucky for me, he didn't see me."

He sighed. "I knew the girl. She wasn't tough and rude
like the rest. Black girl. Name was Carrie. Had a real soft
voice. Kids used to tease her. She didn't mind. She'd just
grin. Easygoin'. Always had a smile for me. Not too many
smiles in that neighborhood. She was no better off than the
rest of us, though. Ten kids in that family. Carrie had to
sell drugs to eat. No other way to make it."

He sat in silence for a minute, remembering. His face
was open now, his expression softened. "I was seventeen
years old. A man, I thought. But when that girl got shot, I
cried like a baby. She was lyin' in the street on her back,
blood pumpin' out from under her, making a puddle alongside. Nothin' I could do but watch the life go out of her eyes.
They were open, her eyes, lookin' up at the sky, but not
seein'."

He was silent for several minutes, his own eyes focused on that long-ago scene.

"I got scared after she died. I ran, and I kept runnin', and all I could see was that guy shootin' her down and her fallin' and the blood and the life goin' out of her. It kept happenin' in my head, like a movie that got stuck somehow and kept repeatin' and repeatin'."

"Did you know the man who shot her?" I asked.

He nodded. "I knew who he was, but I didn't really know him. Dude named Eugene Everard. White guy. Not much older than me. He was the *man*. Drug dealer. Carrie was one of the kids doin' the runnin' for him. Prosecutor said at his trial she kept back $25 from him. So he shot her. Had to teach the others a lesson not to do the same. Emptied his gun into her back as she ran from him. She didn't stand a chance."

"He was caught then?"

"Sure. Someone passin' through saw me runnin' away and described me to the cops. They picked me up and I told them what I'd seen. Hadn't occurred to me to tell them without being asked. You didn't talk to cops. Nobody talked to cops. But I did. And I picked the guy out in a lineup. Wasn't hard to do. Couldn't miss him. I'd been seein' him around for a year or more. Big nose he had, a real honker. Long stringy brown hair. Skinny as a broomstick, chain-smoker. I wanted to see him get a death sentence for killin' Carrie but it didn't happen. He did go to prison, though, not just on my testimony. When the cops caught up with him, he still had the gun, and the bullets matched up. Judge put him away for life, but it turned out he didn't stick around that long. A couple years later I ran into one of the kids from the neighborhood. He told me Eugene got shot in a prison riot."

"You said *your* life changed," I prompted when he seemed to have finished.

He sat very still for a few minutes, thinking. "Seein' that girl get murdered was like a turnin' point," he said finally. "In a way I owe somethin' to Eugene Everard, though I wish he could have taught me the lesson without taking it out on Carrie. What he did got me thinkin' about life. And death. I knew I wasn't ever goin' to have much of a life the way I was doin'. So I called my aunt Sophie."

"You've mentioned her a couple of times."

He nodded. "Great lady, Aunt Sophie. Tough. Smart. She was Tess's aunt on her mother's side. In her fifties then. Tess kept away from the whole family, but I'd met Sophie once when Tess's mother died. Sophie thought it was her duty to come and tell Tess and me. Pretty appalled at what she saw, and she didn't see half of it. Reported Tess and Jake and got a social worker all stirred up, but it didn't come to anythin'. Tess and Jake cleaned up their act for a while until the social worker quit comin', then went back to partyin'. Aunt Sophie tried to get them to let me stay with her, but by this time I was startin' to be useful to Tess. Leastways that was the way she put it."

He looked bleak, staring ahead without apparently seeing anything.

"You called your aunt after you saw the girl shot," I prompted him.

He took a breath and nodded. "Aunt Sophie came right over, picked me up and drove me off to her house in Beverly Hills. Changed my last name to hers, made me go back to school. Sent me to actin' lessons with a friend of hers who owned a school. Somethin' like Lee Strasberg who ran the Actors Studio with his wife Paula? Coached Marilyn Monroe? Aunt Sophie thought actin' would help channel my anger. She saved my life."

"She sounds great," I said. "I've noticed you like old ladies. No wonder." He looked far less tense as he nodded. "Is she still alive?"

He shook his head. "She died goin' on three years ago. Seventy-seven years old. Didn't live long enough to see me come through the anger, but long enough to watch every episode of *Prescott's Landin'*. Way she told it, it was the greatest show in the history of television."

I could almost see her smile, though I'd no idea what she'd looked like. "The acting did help, then?" I asked.

He nodded. "Trouble was, I loved it so much I managed to suppress everythin' so it wouldn't interfere. Not just the anger. All of the memories. Livin' with Aunt Sophie was like I'd died and gone to heaven. Why would I want to remember what my life had been like before? I just put all those memories away in that crawl space and put a hunk of iron against the door, the way Jake had. I did well at actin', got a few parts in TV dramas, stupid parts, but what the heck, I made money and I could pay Aunt Sophie back some. After a while the memories went away, the bad dreams went away. Sometimes an image from that time would show up in my mind—that board Jake used to keep me shut in for days would open up a little crack and I'd see things I didn't want to see. So I would slam it shut and put the iron bar back in place."

"But the memories kept resurfacing?"

"I guess I hadn't managed to forget completely. Doc said it was like a computer when somebody deletes files. They don't seem to be there, but they're still on the hard drive somewhere. Somethin' would trigger a memory and I'd blow without knowin' why. But once Dr. Sugarman got me to give in, and let everything out of the basement—I was okay. Not right away, but over that year and a couple months. But about the time Dr. Sugarman was decidin' it'd be safe to let me go, I was findin' out from my agent there wasn't any work available for me. I'd got the reputation for being unreliable and hard to work with, and I was stuck with it. Then I heard about the Watanabes wantin' to sell their restaurant, and I got the idea about CHAPS. The rest you know about."

He laughed shortly. "At first, after it was all out in the open and I'd dealt with the monsters one by one the way Dr. Sugarman taught me, I felt light-headed and silly. Like I'd had one of those operations Jack Nicholson had in *One Flew Over the Cuckoo's Nest*."

"A lobotomy," I said.

He nodded. "Happy all the time. Gradually, it was like a miracle, the peace that came over me. Like after a war and there's no more fightin' and everyone lays down their arms and there's dancin' in the streets. Then later, there's just day-to-day livin', with only the wonder that it's possible to enjoy that."

I stood up and moved over to his chaise and sat down beside him and put my arms around him. His face was still a little tight around the edges, but it didn't take him long to return the hug. We just sat there like that, holding on to each other, for the longest time, listening to a little breeze that had come up and was rustling in the trees, listening to the sound of our own breathing, listening to the world turning on its axis.

CHAPTER 15

The next day was Saturday, and Mary Grace Nolan was not on duty, which made our visit a little less awkward for me. Dr. Sugarman was in, which Zack had determined before we drove to the Institute.

After shaking hands warmly with Zack, and giving me a curious glance that told me he remembered seeing me in Mary Grace's office, the doctor gestured us into comfortable, leather-covered chairs in a sitting area at one end of his immaculate, high-tech office. He sat facing us, smiling at Zack, looking every bit as prosperous and trustworthy as when I'd last seen him. His silver hair glittered in the light from the high windows.

It had been my idea for us to make doubly sure there hadn't been any leaks. Sleeping fitfully, I'd kept remembering Zack saying that Dr. Sugarman hadn't known of anyone coming around to ask questions. But what about the rest of the staff? I'd wondered when I was drinking my first cup of coffee this morning. I'd managed to con Mary Grace fairly easily. Might someone else not have been gulled the same way by Gerald Senerac, even if he did lack my devastating charm?

Leaving Mary Grace out of it, I put this last possibility

to the doctor. At first he was completely negative, unwilling to believe anyone in his establishment could betray the sanctified doctor-patient relationship, but then he hesitated. "When might this have taken place?" he asked, running a hand over his lovely hair in an embarrassed way.

"About two months ago," Zack said. "That's when Senerac looked up Rudy DeSilva."

"Hmm." The doctor put on a pair of glasses and peered at a large week-at-a-glance organizer on his desk, shuffled back several pages, then picked up the telephone receiver and asked for Alice Waters to come to his office.

"A couple of months ago," he said when he hung up. "I became engaged."

"To Mary Grace," Zack said with a knowing grin.

The doctor nodded gravely.

I wondered if they'd double-dated. Adorin' Lauren was of an age to fit right in with Mary Grace. So was Flying Missy.

"Mary Grace and I took a little trip, to celebrate," Dr. Sugarman said. "We spent a long weekend in Las Vegas."

I may be in the minority but Las Vegas, though a great place to visit, is not my idea of a romantic hideaway. You want to play the slots? Okay. You want to see colorful shows? Go for it. Watch the ship sink outside the Treasure Island Hotel. Shop your heart out in Caesar's Forum. But all the heart-shaped bathtubs in the world wouldn't convince me to take a lover there.

Hey, you've guessed it. My ex, Rob Whittaker, took me to Vegas for our honeymoon. I learned later he'd stopped off a couple of times at the room of a certain well-known starlet whose bosom he'd amplified the previous year. And

I thought he was engaged in an innocent game of blackjack.
Ha!

"Las Vegas. That's cool," Zack said.

I sat up straight as I realized what the good doctor was
actually telling us. "You and Mary Grace were both away
from the Institute," I said, sounding more accusing than I'd
intended. "Someone could have come during your absence
and—"

He held up a hand as a slender woman in a neat skirt
and blouse came in. She had grey hair cut in a no-nonsense
style, no makeup. "Miss Waters, our accountant," he said.
"Mr. Hunter, Ms. Plato."

Miss Waters may not have heard the introduction. She
was too busy gazing at our man in black with worshipful
exophthalmic eyes. It wasn't amazing to me that so many
women were smitten with Zack, it was the fact that the age
range was so broad. Eight to eighty, they all responded.
Most of it, of course, was his celebrity status. Though he
did have a lot going for him in the lean-and-hungry-looks
department. But then, I thought, Marsh Pollock was just as
good-looking, maybe more so, yet he didn't have that . . .
whatever it is . . . the quality the French call *Je ne sais
quoi.* Was it Zack's mantle of celebrity that kept turning *my*
erogenous zones into minefields? Was I really that shallow?

"Miss Waters?" Dr. Sugarman said gently.

With obvious reluctance, the woman swiveled her head
away from Zack and toward her employer. "You remember
when Mary Grace and I went to that conference in Las
Vegas, leaving you in charge of the office?" the doctor asked.

Ah, a conference, that was even more romantic.

Alice nodded, then looked puzzled for all of ten seconds, following which she flushed and glanced sideways at Zack. My inner parts wound themselves into a giant pretzel.

"To your knowledge, during that time, did anyone come to the clinic asking questions about Mr. Hunter?" Sugarman asked.

For one second she seemed about to shake her head, then she caught my eye. As I said earlier, I have the kind of face that shows what I'm thinking. One look and she knew that I had seen her glance guiltily at Zack.

Red blotches stained her neck and face, and tears sprang to her eyes. Swaying as if she was about to collapse in a puddle on the floor, she moaned, "Oh dear, oh dear."

Zack, wonderful gentleman that he is, jumped up and guided her quaking body into his chair.

"He seemed like a perfectly nice man," she said after a few more groans. "And he was a movie producer. He seemed to want only the best for Zack ... Mr. Hunter."

"Did he have a name?" I asked.

"Bill Robinson," she said and moaned again. "I knew right after he left that I shouldn't have told him anything, but he seemed so ... sincere."

"What did he look like?" I demanded.

"Well, he was tall. Quite handsome. Receding hair, but I've never let that ... he was a bit on the thin side, I'd say."

"Voice?" I snapped.

She gaped at me.

"What did his voice sound like?"

"Oh. Well, that wasn't his best feature, I guess. It was quite high-pitched and nasal. But he had a nice way of *talking*," she added. "Real well-mannered." She leaned forward.

"He looked a lot like the man who was running for city council. I saw his picture in the *Gazette* after that, but I've forgotten his name—he was the man who was found ..." She broke off, her mouth making a round o.

"What did you tell Mr. Robinson?" Dr. Sugarman asked with a hint of steel in his voice.

Her lips trembled and he softened his voice. "Just tell us what happened, Alice. It's very important."

She nodded, looking tearful again. "He asked me about Mr. Hunter. He said he was going to produce this really big movie and he wanted Mr. Hunter to star in it, but he had to know if he was okay to work now. Zack, Mr. Hunter, had given his word, he said, but the money men insisted on confirmation."

"And you told him what?" Dr. Sugarman asked gently.

"Well, you know that I really like Zack—Mr. Hunter. When he was staying here, he treated me—well, he was so kind, always, and I knew he felt bad about losing his place on *Prescott's Landing*, which was a wonderful show, but nothing, nothing without Sheriff Lazarro, which they should have known if they'd had ..."

She seemed to have lost her thread. Maybe she was missing several threads. Working in a place like this might do that to a person.

"What did you tell the man?" Dr. Sugarman persisted.

"Well, we talked, and—"

"What about!" I exclaimed, then apologized when Dr. Sugarman looked at me reproachfully. Rob used to look at me that way. It's an effect I have on a lot of people.

"I told him Zack had problems when he was a little boy— that he was abused by his family." Alice's face was the color of buttermilk now, her large protuberant eyes fixed on her employer's face. The words were coming out one at a time, slowly, as if she thought by stretching them out she could make them seem less important. "I told him Dr. Sugarman had helped Zack get beyond his anger, and he hadn't had any problems at all since he left the Institute."

She turned to Zack. "I'm so sorry if I spoke out of turn, Zack—Mr. Hunter. I thought I was being helpful. The man seemed so set on wanting to get you back on television, and I knew you wanted that, too, so . . ." her voice trailed away. "I'm sorry," she added in a whisper.

It was a moment before Dr. Sugarman spoke. When he did, his voice was still controlled. "I'll talk to you later, Alice. You can go back to work now."

"Yes, Doctor. Thank you."

She looked scared. And evidently she'd gauged the doctor's reaction correctly. "It's going to be very difficult to replace Alice," he said with a sigh as soon as Alice had left the room. "She's been with us a long time. An excellent accountant."

"D'you have to fire her?" Zack asked. One of the great things about Zack, one of his most redeeming traits, is his compassion for every living creature. Well, for women, anyway. "Seems like Senerac really meant to get some goods on me, come hell or high water," he went on. "Someone must've told him I was a patient here. Someone at the studio would be my best guess. Rudy saw him talking to other people. If Alice hadn't told him the story, someone else might have."

"And if someone else had, he or she would be the one being fired," Dr. Sugarman said flatly. "We promise our patients confidentiality. There is no excuse for breaching it."

Pity poor Mary Grace if he ever found out what I'd talked her into. I hoped she had sense enough not to confess. Remembering the look in her round blue eyes when she'd talked about looking to her future, I rather thought she knew how to keep quiet.

"I think we'd better go do some damage control," I said to Zack. Standing up, I held out a hand to the doctor, who shook it warmly, still looking deeply apologetic.

We tooled out of the Institute's parking lot and headed east on Highway 92, a narrow winding road that had been cut out of the scrub-covered hillside. Traffic was steady but not heavy. "What damage control?" Zack asked.

I shook my head. "I've no idea. I just wanted to get us out of there so we could talk. I don't think Dr. Sugarman entirely realized the significance of what Alice had done."

Zack nodded wisely. Which meant he hadn't a clue, either.

I took in a deep breath and let it out. I'm a believer in breathing right. Most people don't. A proper intake of air helps the brain function. "With all that talk about Alice," I said after I'd aired myself out, "the good doctor missed the *conclusions* to be drawn from what Alice did." I turned slightly in my seat, so I could watch Zack's face as he drove. He was frowning slightly, but appeared to be following the conversation.

"Getting you to tell me about your stay at the Jaenicke Institute was like pulling teeth," I reminded him. "I tried for a year to get you to tell me where you disappeared to for all that time. You really, really, really didn't want *anyone* to know about it, right?" I said.

"My career . . ." he began.

"Yeah. I know why Zack. I understand now. What I'm

trying to point out is that *Senerac* knew. Bristow said you had a double motive for killing him—political rivalry and the fact you were sleeping with his wife. Senerac's knowing about the Jaenicke Institute gives you yet another motive. If Timpkin was to find out you'd spent time in an institute, he'd make a case out of it. If he finds out that Senerac *knew* you'd spent time in an institute and was keeping a *dossier*— he probably wouldn't even bother with a trial. He already knows you and Senerac weren't bosom buddies."

"But I didn't *know* Senerac had that information," Zack said. He was keeping up very well.

"Try proving that," I suggested.

He swallowed visibly, his hands gripping the steering wheel like a lifeline. "So what do we do now?" he asked after negotiating a steep curve.

I took in a couple more deep breaths and did some cogitating of my own. We passed a flower farm with miles of greenhouses, a Christmas-tree farm with neat ranks of beautifully trimmed evergreens. "First, I think we need to find out exactly what Senerac had collected in his so-called dossier. Then we'll know how dangerous it would be if whoever stole it decides to go public with it."

Zack's eyebrows slanted up over his nose. "If he went public, he'd have to admit he was a murderer, wouldn't he?" he said.

"He could just send the dossier anonymously to the police," I pointed out.

"So how do we find out what he's got, when we don't even know who he is?"

"We go see Gertie again. See if there could possibly be any copies in existence. Senerac was a banker, Zack. He probably had a safety-deposit box. He might even have had a spare vault, for all we know."

"Gertie's not around today," Zack said.

My inner parts dragged themselves down to the pickup's floor. "You're still communicating with Gertie?"

"She called me, Charlie."

I should buy him a Caller ID. Program it to block all calls from women. One thing Dr. Sugarman hadn't taught him was how to say no. Maybe I could get the doctor to devise another course of treatment. *Female-aversion therapy. Touch a woman and your fingers, or other parts, turn green and fall off.*

"Gertie went to visit her sister in Los Gatos," Zack said. "Said she'd be back tomorrow evenin'."

"She didn't invite you to go with her?" Sarcasm was one of my highly honed skills. Or flaws, depending on your point of view.

There was silence.

"Good grief," I said. "The woman has no sense at all. She's suspected of murdering her husband for God's sake, with your connivance."

I kept my gaze on him. His mouth had a hurt droop to it. He was watching the road very carefully. Well, it *did* wind, and it *was* hilly. And hey, he hadn't gone with her.

"Okay, let's give Gertie a call after CHAPS closes tomorrow and see if we can go talk to her then," I suggested.

"Okay," Zack agreed, brightening up.

Because he'd get to see Gorgeous Gert? Or because I was working at trying to get him out of the mess he was in. Who knew?

I wasn't relishing seeing Gertie Senerac again, or watching her look at Zack with love radiating from all her classic features. But as it happened, our visit to her house had to be postponed, because the next morning Opal Quince was found dead in her Cadillac Seville.

Strangled.

CHAPTER 16

Opal Quince's old white Cadillac had been parked at the base of a one-hundred-foot eucalyptus tree at the edge of the parking lot that served Lenny's Market. A store employee named Dwayne Camitz noticed it when he came to work very early on Sunday morning. A former bag boy, he recognized the car as Opal's right away. She'd shopped at Lenny's for years. She was a notoriously lousy tipper, Dwayne commented gratuitously.

It seemed strange that the car would just be sitting there, and Dwayne wondered if it had been stolen. Thinking he'd check to see if the keys had been left in the ignition, he approached the automobile and saw Opal slumped sideways in the driver's seat.

Yanking the door open, he yelled at the woman to wake up. Then he noticed the yellow rope tied tightly around her neck. When he saw, at the same moment, the way her face looked, he exited hurriedly and upchucked his Sunday French toast on the roots of the eucalyptus.

A couple of hours later, Zack Hunter, well-known actor/celebrity, now the popular owner of the country-western tavern dance hall named CHAPS, was seen accompanying

Detective Sergeant Taylor Bristow into the Bellamy Park Police Station.

How did I learn all this? I caught a 9:15 A.M. news flash on my bedside clock radio while I was eating my organic oat flakes and black currants, and looking wistfully at a vase full of yellow tulips that had arrived the previous night from Marsh Pollock. Evidently he'd decided yellow was my color. I wondered if the flowers' tightly furled condition was meant to be symbolic. As soon as I was finished with breakfast, I intended calling him to thank him for the bouquet and to suggest we have lunch.

Once again, fate had interfered with what I laughingly call my love life. Maybe whatever might have developed between Marsh and me wasn't meant to be.

After slapping my face with water, I ran a toothbrush around my mouth, slapped a baseball cap over my sleep-tangled hair, then filled up Benny's water bottle and food dish. Still wearing the grungy old sweats I lounge around in, I drove my Jeep Wrangler directly to Bellamy Park PD. Zack was just coming out.

"Get in," I yelled, braking so abruptly my seat belt put a crimp in my right breast.

Zack pointed off to one side. "My pickup's over there, Charlie."

"We'll get it later. Hop in now."

There are times I get a certain note in my voice, and I have noticed that people will often do what I want them to. Zack was no exception. He hopped right in.

We didn't go far. Having noticed that instead of his signature black western shirt, black jeans and boots, he was wearing grey sweats and sneakers, which indicated that he'd left the house hurriedly, I drove a couple of blocks to the park.

I found a spot in the shade—it was going to be a hot, hot day—switched off the ignition and suggested we jog.

"I haven't had breakfast, Charlie," Zack complained.

"You can eat later."

The obey-me note was in my voice again. A minute later, we hit the trail that looped through the woods. Featuring bulging tree roots and toe-catching vines, it was rarely used. I didn't want anyone to notice us particularly, and I certainly didn't want anyone overhearing us talk.

"What were you doing at the police station?" I asked as we eased into a steady rhythm.

Zack looked as if he hadn't slept well, which was unusual for him. His eyes weren't red rimmed, as mine would have been, but the flesh under them looked bruised. The lines bracketing his mouth only showed up when he was stressed out.

"Taylor Bristow got me out of bed," he said. He looked at me sideways. "I guess you heard about Opal."

"I caught it on the radio. I figured I'd come to the station and find out what happened and why you were taken in."

"I wasn't taken in, Charlie, I was invited."

"Sure you were. No pressure involved. The honor of your presence is requested—black tie optional."

"Opal was *strangled*, Charlie. Just like Gerald Senerac. Her larynx was crushed. Her windpipe broken. It isn't funny."

I fought off a wave of nausea. "Sarcasm doesn't always qualify as humor," I explained when I could speak again. "The fact that Opal was strangled was on the news, by the way. Also that she was found in her car by a guy named Dwayne who works at Lenny's."

Zack nodded. "Same kind of rope was used," he contributed. "Same bowline knots."

I swallowed against another onrush of nausea as the still-vivid memory of Gerald Senerac's dead face popped up in my mind, superimposed by an image of Opal Quince as she must have looked when Dwayne found her. "Tell me you had an alibi," I pleaded.

It was Zack's turn to swallow.

I counted to twenty, in time with my pounding feet. Zack had not shown up at CHAPS the previous night—Savanna had told me he'd called in to say he didn't feel so good and he was going to turn in early. I'd understood why he might be feeling down after talking to Dr. Sugarman and hearing Alice's report about Senerac's quest for information. I'd felt bad for him.

"Where were you?" I asked, not mildly.

"I . . . went for a drive," he said.

"Is that what you told Bristow?"

"I'm—" He cut himself off.

"You didn't drive to Los Gatos to see Gertie," I said. "Please say you didn't do that."

"I didn't do that."

I breathed a little easier.

The trail narrowed and we had to go single file. We jogged in silence for a few minutes, our feet thudding on the dirt trail, stirring up dust. I concentrated on breathing through my nose. Breathing while running always feels terrific, like a liquid sweetness filling my body. The air smelled piney-clean. "Who *did* you go to see?" I asked when the trail widened again and I could come up alongside Zack.

He stopped running abruptly. So did I. "I didn't go to see anyone, Charlie," he said.

"You just went for a drive."

"I do that sometimes. Drivin' relaxes me."

"Is that what you told Bristow?"

He started jogging again. "Let it be, Charlie."

Muttering imprecations, I ran alongside him, noting that his mouth was zipped tightly. Totally, Mary Grace would have said. Which meant he was probably not telling the truth. While I was still wondering whether to coax or command him to give me a proper answer, we emerged from the woods.

Across the duck pond, in which panhandling mallards and Canada geese and mud hens competed to see who could squawk or screech the loudest, I saw the unmistakable lanky form and bare brown head of Taylor Bristow. He was standing next to my Jeep. His car was parked a couple of slots away.

"Hey," he shouted over the duck cacophony as we trotted up to him. "I recognized your Jeep, Charlie, didn't know Zack was romping in the woods with you."

"Not much in the mood for rompin'," Zack yelled back. "What I need is food."

"Breakfast," Bristow suggested, then bestowed his wide innocent smile upon me. "You're giving me the evil eye, Ms. Plato. You looking for hidden motives?"

He was wearing his usual casual clothes—a dark-blue knit shirt with well-washed and faded blue jeans. "Are you on duty?" I asked.

"Not so's you'd notice," he said ambiguously.

His and Zack's unanimous choice of eatery was of course Eggsactly, which featured large doses of cholesterol fried in generous helpings of bacon grease, served up as "home cooking."

Having given up on my morning cereal, when I heard the news about Opal, I was a mite ravenous myself, but the illustrations on the enormous menu were enough to raise my triglycerides. I finally managed to find a fruit platter hidden away on the back cover.

The "fruit platter" turned out to be chunks of grapefruit and canned pineapple, but was at least healthier than the bacon, sausage, eggs and home fries the guys ended up with.

"The thing I don't understand," I said to Bristow after the waitress finally quit hovering around Zack with her heart in her blue-shadowed eyes, "is how come Sergeant Timpkin hasn't shown up to toss Zack in the slammer. Is he on vacation?"

"In a manner of speaking," Bristow said, slathering butter on a slab of white toast he could have shingled a roof with. "Our friend Reggie is suffering from an acute case of conflict of interest, so to speak."

"He's off the case?" Zack said, cutting right to the core, which was most unusual for him. Being a murder suspect had really sharpened his wits. Maybe it was native cunning, stimulated by danger. Or else the character of Sheriff Lazarro, that valiant and brilliant sleuth, had once again taken possession of Zack's body.

Bristow shook his head. "No. However, it may yet happen. It seems the late Mr. Gerald Senerac at one time foreclosed on a mortgage held in the name of Reginald Timpkin. Reggie threatened to sue, and there were words on the subject in the presence of a brother law-enforcement officer."

"You?" I asked.

He shook his head. "I found out about the mortgage a

couple days ago, asked around the department. Officer Ben Sandford remembered the incident."

"You went *looking* for something on Timpkin," I said happily.

He placed a hand to his heart in mock shock. "Now why would I do such a thing, Ms. Plato?"

"To help Zack?"

He inclined his head. "Not a justifiable motive where the law is concerned. However, I have noted a certain obnoxiousness in Detective Sergeant Timpkin's manner. It has irritated me considerably for some time."

"Is there any chance *Reggie* killed Senerac?" I asked.

Bristow stabbed his fork in the air, declaiming, "Some, peradventure, have on them the guilt of premeditation and contrived murder."

"Henry the Sixth?" I hazarded as I speared the last piece of limp pineapple.

"The Fifth." He grinned. "There is no evidence to indicate that Reggie has guilt upon him."

"So now *you're* in charge of the case?" Zack asked, valiantly keeping up.

Bristow inclined his elegantly shaped head. "Not at this moment," he said. "I am but an interested party. Which does not mean," he added, with a stern look at Zack, "that I am not going to continue to pursue all evidence in this case, wherever it may lead."

"It won't lead to me," Zack said firmly.

"I sincerely hope not," Bristow said.

"I feel so bad about Opal," I said. "I think you feel worse when someone gets killed who you really, really didn't like. As if you gave them bad karma because of your nasty thoughts."

"An interesting theory," Bristow said, not meaning it for a minute if his raised eyebrows were anything to go by.

"Did Opal have any family?" I asked.

His mouth twisted. "Never married, no siblings, parents deceased. No friends either, as far as we can determine."

"That's awful. So sad to die like that, and not have anybody really care."

I caught a glimpse of myself in a large mirror on the wall and felt a chill pass through me.

I had friends, I assured myself. I had Zack and Savanna and Angel and even Bristow, and in a pinch, Rob would be there for me. My ex. Yes, I had friends.

The chill didn't go away.

Midafternoon, *Sunday* afternoon, a publisher called CHAPS from New York. He'd watched a CNN story about the candidates for city council dying off in our small but upscale town and wanted to offer Zack five figures to write his autobiography, with a little help from a British author noted for his best-selling true-crime books. The Brit came in on a conference call. He wanted to get the contract signed before Zack was arrested for Opal's murder, he said. "Is her name really Opal Quince?" he asked. "Priceless, abso-bloody-lutely priceless."

Dr. Rob Whittaker, plastic surgeon to the stars, also called. "Another dead body," he said gloomily.

"They do seem to propagate, don't they," I said breezily. I didn't feel breezy, you understand. I hadn't thought a whole lot of Opal, but I wouldn't wish murder on any human being, and this particular kind of murder sickened me. I wanted Opal restored to her proper place, haranguing the other candidates, writing nasty letters to the editor of the

Bellamy Park Gazette, peering through her thick glasses, clicking her teeth.

However, it annoyed Rob when I remained cheery in the face of disaster, so it had become a habit.

"How come you only call me when someone gets murdered?" I asked. "If our Sergeant Timpkin checked on our conversations, he'd think I'm murdering all these people so you'll pay attention to me."

"That's ridiculous, Charlie," Rob said.

Did I mention that my ex-husband is missing a sense of humor? I didn't notice that when I was in love with him. But then love distorts vision and causes the brain to wither. Take if from one who knows.

"I miss you, Charlie," Rob said.

He always, without fail, says one thing per conversation that causes my bones to melt. It's one of his most annoying habits.

"Hard to believe," I muttered.

"The office isn't the same without you."

Ah, that made more sense. He missed my office skills.

"New girl can't balance the books?"

"They're balanced okay—she's just no good on collections. She's not as forceful as you. I wish you'd come back, Charlie. At least you wouldn't be running into dead bodies all the time."

"Only limp ones," I said, picturing Trudi draped over the examining table.

A couple of producers called to offer Zack the lead in separate dramas. One of them assured Zack his people could shoot around trial dates, and would even put up bail if it became necessary. Didn't *anyone* take Sundays off?

Attendance doubled at CHAPS that night. We had to call in an extra bartender and a couple of waiters. Everyone wanted to have their picture taken with Zack, or get his autograph. Unfortunately for them, Zack wasn't there. It was his poker night.

I think I've said before that my brain has a weird habit of suddenly popping up things it recorded when I wasn't paying attention. Like a VCR that will tape one TV show while you're watching another, then play it back to you.

On Monday morning, while I was cleaning out Benny's cage, Benny occupied himself by happily tearing up a newspaper in the bathroom. It's his favorite thing to do. There aren't too many hobby choices when you're a rabbit.

Looking at the shreds he'd spread all over the tiled floor, I flashed on an image of Winston Jermaine at the first candidates' debate, the one Senerac had been killed after. Winston had spent a lot of time tearing up his program in front of the microphone, making crackling sounds that got on my nerves until Macintosh reached across Senerac and snatched the pieces of paper out of Winston's hands.

For some reason, the image was accompanied in my memory by a flash of light.

I tried to dismiss the whole picture as meaningless, but it kept poking itself back up, with a question mark attached. I finally gave in and called Macintosh.

I've mentioned before that CHAPS is closed on Monday nights. Usually we four partners take off in different directions, feeling that we see enough of one another the rest of the week. Fortunately nobody had plans for the evening. Even Savanna was free, Jacqueline having been invited to a little friend's birthday slumber party.

I was able to get Macintosh to bring over the tape of the first debate and set it up on our VCR in the little corral. I'd invited Bristow to join us. He accepted as soon as I mentioned that Savanna would be among those present. As I dimmed the lights, I noticed that they were holding hands, and I felt all misty eyed. I may be against romance for myself, but I can still enjoy it vicariously. Safest sex there is.

"What are we looking for, Charlie?" Macintosh asked as we all pulled chairs up in front of the television set.

"I'm not sure I know," I told him. "It has something to do with Winston shredding his program."

Bristow gave me a roll of his eyes, implying "why are you wasting our time like this?" but I ignored him. I could only hope my subconscious had really been on the job.

It was no easier than before to listen to Senerac's high-pitched, patrician voice delivering a fifteen-minute vituperative attack on Zack. What a snake he had been. Under the bright lights, the skin was drawn tight over his facial bones. I could see the faint impressions of ligaments and veins underneath.

Innuendos, suggestions, hints—these had been Gerald Senerac's weapons. Nothing in his speech about the issues at all. "A truly obnoxious man," Macintosh exclaimed, after the gaunt man concluded with a sneering comment about Zack Hunter's efforts to live up to his TV persona, Sheriff Lazarro, who always got his man—and the man's woman.

At the time I'd thought Senerac was just making a general accusation. Now the words had an ominously prophetic sound, and I wished I hadn't been so quick to invite Bristow along.

"Opal was just as obnoxious as Gerald," Savanna said.

"But neither of them deserved to be killed. Obnoxiousness isn't a capital crime."

"I'm not so sure of that, lass," Macintosh said, and there was a bitter note in his voice.

"What did Senerac ever do to you?" Bristow asked.

His voice was casual, but there was a stiffening to his posture that made Macintosh turn wary. Tilting his head back so he could look at Bristow through the lower lenses of his bifocals, he answered very cautiously. "I was referring to the dreadful things he said about my friend Zack," he replied, rolling every r to a fare-thee-well.

I don't think anyone was convinced he was telling the truth.

Had Senerac discovered Macintosh was gay? Had he threatened him with outing? Had Macintosh then strangled him and disposed of his body . . . in Zack's car? Why in Zack's car?

Savanna shivered as Opal began her speech. "I keep thinking what it would be like to be sitting in your car and have someone suddenly throw a rope around your neck and start pulling it tight." She glanced at Bristow. "What would you do, Taylor?" she asked.

"Bring my head back hard and break his nose," Bristow said grimly. "Reach back and poke his eyes out. Whatever's necessary."

I wasn't at all sure I'd have the wits to think of such tactics, or the will to carry them out.

"I'd faint," Savanna said with certainty. "I'd just go absolutely limp and pass out. I wouldn't even know I was dead until it was all over."

"Remind me to teach you some defensive maneuvers," Bristow said. "First one being—you have to get mad."

I was still staring at Opal on the TV screen. Her teeth were snapping away, her spectacles flashing. And there was Winston sitting between her and Senerac, nervously ripping his program apart.

Shushing everyone, I leaned forward, holding my breath as the tape advanced and Winston began to speak, still tearing compulsively. Now Macintosh was leaning across Senerac to take the papers out of Winston's hands.

And there it was, the flash I'd remembered this morning. A flash of gold. "Stop the tape," I yelled.

Nobody ever reacts quickly enough to an order like that. Macintosh had to rewind, then proceed frame by frame so I could figure out exactly what I'd seen.

"There," I said, and Macintosh froze the frame.

"Do you see it, Zack?" I asked.

Zack leaned forward, squinting. "What is it you want me—what the hey!"

"What?" Savanna demanded.

"Winston's cuff link," I said triumphantly. "It's a horse's head."

CHAPTER 17

"I don't believe it," Zack said. "Winny? Gertie's gettin' it on with Winny?"

"Whoa!" Bristow said. "Let's have some back story here."

Zack pointed at Winston's wrist on the TV screen. "I saw this cuff link in a photograph that was taken at Gertie Senerac's company party, end of June. The photo showed only Gertie, but she had her hand on the arm of a man who was wearin' a cuff link that looked exactly like this one."

"Zack asked her if she took Gerald to the party and she said no," I added. "She also let Zack know she was seeing someone else besides him."

"Charlie," Zack said, looking at me reproachfully and shifting his eyes sideways to Macintosh, who was staring at him in shock.

"This is no time for gentlemanly discretion, Zack," I told him firmly. "We have a couple of murders here, and you're still in the hot seat. We need to know who killed Gerald and Opal, and why. Macintosh isn't going to go around blabbing that you're sleeping with Gorgeous Gert."

Savanna smothered a giggle.

"Oops," I muttered.

Bristow's eyes had narrowed to gleaming amber slits. "You're still seeing that woman?" he asked Zack.

Zack shook his head and shot me another exasperated look.

Bristow wasn't through. "Judging by the preceding conversation, I take it you previously informed Ms. Plato about the existence of this photograph?"

Zack nodded.

"But you neglected to inform me, even though I asked you to dredge up from the depths of your soul every single thing you could think of that might have some significance in this case?"

"It was just a cuff link," Zack protested. "I didn't know who it belonged to, or if it was significant. And I don't believe it *is* significant. Gertie wouldn't ... sleep with Winny. He's an old man! He must be goin' on sixty. And she despised old Winny. Said he laughed like a horse."

"He does laugh like a horse," I pointed out.

"Like I said before, that man is loco," Angel said. It was the first time he'd spoken and we all stared at him in surprise.

I'd almost forgotten Angel's comment about Winston. "You said he had a bad aura," I murmured. "A dark aura."

Bristow snorted inelegantly. "I am not accepting auras as evidence."

Angel's facial structure tightened. I flashed Bristow a dirty look. "Angel wasn't offering evidence," I said. "He's sensitive to atmosphere, okay? A little sensitivity is a good thing in a man. You ought to try it."

Bristow gave me his wide smile. "I do confess my fault, and do submit me to your highness mercy."

How can you stay mad at a police officer who quotes

hakespeare at you? I smiled forgiveness and mercy at him.
I don't know that quote."

"The same Henry we touched on yesterday morning. The
fth. I apologize," he added to Angel. "What is it about Mr.
ermaine that disturbs you?"

Angel frowned and tugged on one end of his drooping
ustache, perhaps to stimulate thought. "He gets these
eird ideas about chaining himself to railings to stop the
ulldozers. Also, he pretends to be Zack's friend, but I think
e's more interested in hanging around Zack so people will
now he's Zack's friend. And also . . ."

He hesitated, glancing at Zack in an apologetic way
efore going on. "Charlie asked me to check around, see if
could find out anything about Mrs. Senerac."

"Our own homegrown private investigator operating
ithout a license again," Bristow said, frowning at me.

"So I asked around," Angel said. "Here and there."

Gina, I thought. *Gina knew something, but Angel doesn't
ant to get her involved.* Maybe *I* was getting psychic.

"Word around Bellamy Park is, Mrs. Senerac was . . .
oinking two of the candidates," Angel went on.

Zack looked uncomfortable. Good.

"Joke was her husband had put her up to wearing out
he opposition so Mr. Senerac and Miss Opal Quince could
in the election."

Now there was an interesting concept. I'd originally
hought Gertie was sleeping with Zack to get back at her
usband for whatever he might have done, or not done, to
er. And once Winston was added into the equation, that
eemed no less a logical approach. Except that I'd been
retty convinced Gertie was in love with Zack. Could she
e that good an actress? Well, sure, most women could fake

whatever reaction they deemed necessary. Maybe Gertie had faked being in love.

Mata Hari comes to Bellamy Park.

Or . . . here I closed my eyes, the better to think . . . had Gertie slept with Zack and Winston so there'd be a couple of suspects on hand when her husband met his death?

"Listen up, now," Zack said. "I don't believe for one minute Winny would kill anyone. He's a tough-lookin' old dude, I'll grant you, but he's pretty much just a nice old guy."

"It's often the nice guys who go berserk," I pointed out. "Afterward, the neighbors all say they were shocked, so and so was so quiet, so mild mannered, kept to himself. How often do they say, 'Well yeah, we're not surprised—he was forever blowing up at people'?"

I suddenly remembered that Gertie had told us Senerac was keeping a dossier on Winston, as well as Zack. He hadn't found *much* on Winston, she'd said. Which would seem to imply that he had found something.

"What?" Bristow asked. My face had given me away again, I supposed. I couldn't tell him about the dossier on Winston, without telling about the dossier on Zack. We still didn't know who had stolen those dossiers from Senerac's house. Could it be *Winston?*

"I was just wondering what possible motive Winston would have to kill Opal," I said. "I mean, if he *was* sleeping with Gertie, I could maybe imagine him killing Senerac so he and Gert could share the loot. It would be a stretch, but I could be convinced—*if* there was any evidence besides a cuff link in a photograph. But where does Opal fit into the scheme of things?"

Bristow shrugged. "When a second homicide follows a

first, one suspects the victim might have seen something, suspected something, and thus has become a danger to the perpetrator."

"You may be right," I murmured, thinking about it.

"Your accolades are always appreciated," Bristow said. He's almost as quick with sarcasm as I am.

I cornered Zack as the others were leaving. "I need to talk to you. But I want to think things through first. How about tomorrow morning, your place?"

"Sure, Charlie," Zack said in a lackluster way, which wasn't at all like him. He was putting on his cowboy hat, but not tilting it at its usual jaunty angle. Finding out about Gertie and Winston had evidently depressed him. With any luck, he might begin thinking twice before boffing every woman who flung herself in his path.

He attempted a smile. "I'll put the coffeepot on, Charlie."

I wanted to hug Zack, tell him that whatever Angel had heard couldn't possibly be true because I'd seen that radiant expression on Gertie's face when she looked at him, and that had to mean she'd gone after Zack because she wanted him for himself, not for any nefarious purpose.

But then I thought it wouldn't hurt him to spend a night thinking about people's motives. Including his own.

"I'll bring the bagels," I said, patting him on the arm. "Expect me about ten o'clock."

As it happened, I had to wait at Lenny's for a fresh batch of bagels to be finished, and it was 11:30 A.M. before I rang Zack's doorbell.

Which put me five minutes ahead of Detective Sergeant Timpkin and his search warrant.

Zack and I had barely finished greeting each other and

setting the bagels on a plate, the coffee cups on a tray, when
the doorbell rang. Zack opened the kitchen door to the nattily
dressed Sergeant Timpkin and three officers, one of whom
was carrying a camera.

"Oh goody, a photo op!" I exclaimed.

Sergeant Timpkin bunched his chin at me.

Both Zack and I examined the warrant. I'd never seen
one before but it looked official enough. It said that there
was reason to believe that on these premises certain prop
erty was being concealed, namely: yellow nylon rope such
as was used in the murders of Gerald Senerac and Opal
Quince, and also certain documents that were the property
of Gerald Senerac.

"Why would you think I have Gerald Senerac's prop
erty?" Zack asked.

Timpkin looked wise, but kept his own counsel.

"I don't have any yellow rope, either," Zack said as two
of the officers went in different directions from the main
hall. "I've never owned any."

"You never did match Zack's hair up with the hair you
found in the rope, did you?" I said. "What color was it? Maybe
you ought to be thinking about that, instead of harassing
innocent bystanders."

Timpkin gave me a look that said I'd be wise to keep my
mouth shut in his presence, if I knew what was good for
me.

"I understood you were off the case," I said, to show I
couldn't be intimidated.

Timpkin's woolly-bear caterpillar mustache writhed, but
then he clamped his mouth shut, inclined his head at the
remaining officer, turned on his heel and marched out of the

kitchen. The officer had evidently been assigned to keep watch over us desperate criminals.

I thought of calling the station to see if Bristow could ride to our rescue one more time, but decided it might be better to wait until Timpkin and his men got through with this fruitless search, and departed.

"Let's eat," I said to Zack as cheerfully as I could manage. "We know they aren't going to turn anything up, so we might as well fortify ourselves against whatever the day is going to bring."

We climbed up on stools at Zack's kitchen counter and started munching, the officer having declined Zack's offer of hospitality. Having a police officer with a gun on his hip keeping an eye on you tends to kill the appetite. We managed one bagel apiece and a couple of cups of coffee.

The young officer kept glancing shyly at Zack, as if he wanted to ask for his autograph, but he didn't speak.

After a long time, during which Zack prepared and perked another pot of coffee, it went quiet in the far reaches of the house. I could no longer hear the men tramping back and forth, opening drawers and closet doors. The lack of movement seemed ominous, especially as I thought I could detect the murmur of voices.

"Where are they?" I whispered. The young officer glanced at me but didn't say anything. I guessed it wasn't illegal to talk.

Zack cocked his head to one side. "One of the guest bedrooms? Maybe my den?"

Zack's den was a wonderfully macho room, all tricked out in wood paneling and forest-green leather upholstery. There was a full-size jukebox, a great entertainment center that included an enormous TV screen, a cabinet to display

Zack's Emmys, a pipe rack that was full of pipes, and books by the yard with nice leather bindings.

The footsteps started up again. The two officers came in and made a sweep through the kitchen. They were careful, polite, but also thorough.

Timpkin finally showed up holding a large evidence Baggie. With great ceremony, and also painstaking care, he slid the contents out onto the kitchen counter. A manila folder.

I knew what it must be the minute I saw it. I had to work hard to keep the knowledge off my face.

"Desk drawer. Top left. Office," Timpkin said, turning the file with his fingertips on the edges so we could see what was written on the front. "Zack Hunter."

"What is it?" Zack asked, looking completely perplexed.

Timpkin assumed his cop stance, complete with suspicious expression and voice. "You don't know?"

Zack's puzzled expression convinced me, but probably not Timpkin. "I don't own anything like that, man," Zack said. "I'm not into filing."

"This appears to be a minibiography of your past," Timpkin said.

"Where did you say you found it?" I asked. Not that I'd forgotten, I just wanted to distract the sergeant. I was afraid Zack might blanch if he realized what it was Timpkin had come up with. But evidently Sheriff Lazarro had departed Zack's premises, and Zack hadn't yet caught on.

Timpkin ignored my question. Taking a knife from a rack on the counter, he flipped open the file cover. A large envelope lay on top of a wad of pages, which appeared to have come off a laser printer. The envelope was addressed to Gerald Senerac, President, Bellamy Park Bank. There was no return address. No stamp or postmark. It had evi-

ently been hand delivered, or enclosed in a priority or
Federal Express envelope.

Zack looked bewildered for about three more minutes,
then light dawned and turned his expression sickly. "What's
an envelope addressed to Gerald Senerac doin' in my den?"
he asked.

Which I thought was a pretty good recovery. Lazarro
must have sneaked back in.

"I believe that's my question," Timpkin said. I was pretty
sure I could detect a smirk on his face. I was beginning to
develop a severe distaste for this man. He was the kind of
officer who turns honest citizens off the idea of community
involvement.

"I have no idea where it came from," Zack said.

Timpkin sighed audibly, but looked almost happy. "I
think it might be as well for you to accompany—"

"Zack's been downtown twice already," I pointed out
hastily. "There's never anything to hold him on. You want
to take him in, we're calling his lawyer. Nate Yoder, remember? You'll be lucky he doesn't sue you for harassment. He
just loves suing cities and states, and various and sundry
departments thereof. Why don't we first try to find out what
we can here? Wouldn't that be simpler?"

Without waiting for a reaction, I looked at Zack. "If
you don't know anything about the file, someone must have
brought it here without your knowledge."

Timpkin snorted.

"Listen," I said to him, "whoever put a body in the trunk
of Zack's car wouldn't shrink from putting a file folder in
his den."

Timpkin inclined his head and decided to humor me. He
raised his eyebrows at Zack, who leaned an elbow on the

counter and rested his chin on one fist like Rodin's "Thinker," a pose familiar to all viewers of *Prescott Landing*'s Sheriff Lazarro. Without a script, he didn't seem to know where to start.

"When were you last in your desk?" I asked to get him going.

"Four, maybe five days ago," he said after a minute or two. "I was lookin' for new checkbooks. You know—the ones you get in a box from the bank?"

"Did you notice any kind of folder at that time?" I asked.

Timpkin made a sound, like he was going to object to my arrogation of his duties, then subsided. Maybe the law enforcement handbook instructed detectives not to stop the flow once it was turned on.

"So who has visited in the last four or five days?" I asked when Zack shook his head.

"Melissa," he offered, his brow furrowing.

Flyin' Missy was really hanging in there. She'd been in and out for over a year.

"Lauren," Zack said after some more thought.

"Let's have some full names and addresses," Timpkin suggested, pulling his minitape recorder from his shirt pocket.

I wanted to kick Zack in the shins for his nonstop womanizing, especially where Lauren Deakins was concerned.

I suddenly realized that the address Zack was giving Timpkin sounded familiar. An apartment on Poplar Street. Whose apartment? Not Flyin' Missy—she lived conveniently near the airport. Lauren Deakins, aka Adoring Lauren, the fan with the terminal crush. Why should *her* address sound familiar? I must be thinking of something else. Poplar Street. There was a bakery, a store of some kind, a gift shop . . .

Wait a minute.

Zack's mystery woman. The woman he'd met at Paulie's Place the night after Senerac's murder. He'd given her a ride home, she'd given him coffee. *Only* coffee, he'd told Bristow. Then he'd written down her address and given it to the sergeant. Apartment 4, something Poplar Street.

He'd visited that child's apartment!

I ought to let Timpkin take him in for that, if for nothing else. I was definitely going to either call Marsh Pollock or drop by Dandy Carr's gym, I decided. I'd put him off long enough. Marsh was good company—as long as he didn't talk about farming.

"Anyone else?" Sergeant Timpkin asked.

"Did you play poker here Sunday night?" I asked, having been thinking of Marsh. "Zack has a bunch of poker buddies," I told Timpkin. "They call themselves the Sunday-night irregulars. Sundancer, our deejay; Marsh Pollock—he took over Dandy Carr's gym; and Macintosh, the TV guy."

Timpkin nodded. "My kids watch his show."

Kids? The man had kids? I found myself thinking of *The Sound Of Music*. The early part of the movie before Julie Andrews worked her magic on the Trapp children's father, as played by Christopher Plummer. He'd called the kids to order with a whistle, lined them up in the hall. I could imagine Timpkin doing that. I was getting as bad as Zack, relating real life to Hollywood epics.

"We played poker at Macintosh's house," Zack said.

So much for that trio of suspects.

"Winston came by," Zack offered abruptly.

"When?" Timpkin and I said at the same moment.

"Last night. After we watched that video, I came straigh home." He sounded as if he was expecting praise for goo behavior. "Winny dropped in around nine or so."

"That would be Winston Jermaine?" Timpkin asked, hi chin bunching up. "Guy who begged off the fishing trip? H a regular visitor?"

Zack shook his head. "I invited him over to ask—" H broke off abruptly.

I mentally filled in for him. To ask him if he'd been having an affair with Gertie. Something I'd meant to suggest when I came over this morning. If we hadn't been so rudely inter rupted.

"I wanted to discuss strategy with him. Election strat egy." Good recovery, Zack, I thought.

"We sent out for a double-cheese and pepperoni pizza had a couple beers," Zack continued.

Had he ever had his cholesterol levels checked? I won dered.

"Was Jermaine unattended at any time?" Timpkin asked

Police officers never seem to talk like real people when they're on police business.

Zack shrugged. "When I called out for pizza, I guess. used the kitchen phone. He was sittin' by the pool. Hot las night."

"The pool is right off Zack's bedroom, which is next t his den," I explained to the sergeant, forgetting for the moment that he'd just explored the whole house.

"And I suppose I went to the bathroom, sometime," Zacl continued. "Drinkin' beer . . ."

"Did you see Jermaine carrying anything?" Timpki asked, just as I was about to.

Zack shrugged again.

"He could have stashed the file by the front entry, brought it in when Zack was otherwise engaged." Now I was talking that way.

Timpkin twisted his mouth to one side. When Zack does that, he looks sexy as all get-out. Of course, Zack doesn't have a caterpillar mustache. Though even discounting the mustache, sexy used in the same sentence as Timpkin was an oxymoron.

He was nodding slowly now, tipping the folder carefully back into its envelope, his chin bunched tight enough to purse his mouth. "I'll have a few words with Mr. Jermaine," he said. "And with Miss Deakins and Miss Melissa . . ."

"Fresham," Zack said. "She's a flight attendant, remember, isn't always around. But there's no need for you to bother her. There's no way she'd—"

"Airplanes have to land sometime," Timpkin said.

Zack looked as if he was going to continue arguing against Timpkin's interviewing Melissa, so I rapped him pretty sharply on the nearest shin with the side of my boot. Sharper than I meant to, I guess, judging by his sudden hiccup.

"I didn't want you delaying Timpkin once he was in motion," I explained after Timpkin and his henchmen were gone. "He wanted to take you downtown again earlier."

Zack gave me a pained look as he hobbled to the refrigerator and took out a beer. "You don't have to kick so hard, Charlie. A simple tap is enough to give me the idea you want me to shut up."

"Hard to control," I said. "Especially when I'd just figured out that Lauren Deakins was the mystery woman you met at Paulie's Place, the night after the first debate, the night after Senerac was killed. You gave her a ride home.

She invited you in for coffee. Does any of that ring any bells?"

"I remember," he said.

"Do you also remember telling me you hadn't laid a hand on her?"

"I haven't, Charlie."

He popped the cap off the beer, took a long swallow.

I didn't know whether to believe him or not. What difference did it make anyway?

A teasing glint was making itself known in Zack's hard green eyes. "You jealous again, Charlie?"

If he'd been sitting next to me still, I'd have whacked him again.

"She was upset, Charlie, cryin' and all."

"When she came over here, or when you took her home from Paulie's?"

"Both. That night at Paulie's, she said she was lonely. Couldn't seem to make friends since she came up from L.A. Couldn't get a boyfriend because she isn't pretty. Couldn't even get a girlfriend, because she's too shy to just start talkin' to people."

"But not too shy to cry on your shoulder?"

"Charlie, darlin' . . ."

He started to move around the counter toward me. I held a hand up in a stop-where-you-are gesture. That brought on his bad-boy grin. He loves making me nervous. "When did Lauren come over here?" I asked.

He looked sheepish.

"Saturday night?" I suggested. "Saturday night when you were too sick to come into CHAPS? Saturday night when Opal was strangled? How long was she here?"

"Most of the night," he admitted. "I really was down,

Charlie," he insisted. "Had every intention of goin' to bed early. Then Lauren called, cryin' her eyes out again. Couldn't get her to lighten up. Finally, I said she could come over for a little bit. We talked, Charlie. That's all, I swear. She's a sweet little gal, Charlie. Had a tough life. Mother died when she was a baby, no Dad around, raised by grandparents. Poor kid doesn't have anybody in the whole world. Pitiful. I felt right sorry for her. I think she thinks of me as some kind of father figure."

I gave a fair imitation of Timpkin's snort.

He put his hand on his heart. "I wouldn't lie to you, Charlie," he said in his best John Wayne imitation. "I didn't do anythin' more than pat her shoulder a couple times, give her a box of tissues, let her talk it out. Kept tryin' to get her to go home, told her I was bushed. Finally got her convinced shortly before mornin'. Told her I'd talk to some of the other gals who come to CHAPS, introduce her."

I'd always admired his compassion. And I also knew he found it difficult to turn his back on a damsel in distress. "You're really not all that bad a guy, Zack Hunter," I said. I mulled for a minute. "If you were with Lauren all night, then you do have an alibi for when Opal was killed. Surely you realize you should have told Bristow that."

He nodded. "I did tell him, Charlie."

"You lied to me."

"Only by implication, darlin'."

I thought over everything he'd said while we were jogging. He was right. But he'd sure fudged on his answers. I decided to let it pass.

"So now I understand how come Bristow turned you loose and Timpkin decided against taking you in," I said. I shook my head at him. "You've got to stop being so secretive,

Zack. I can't solve this case if you keep stuff from me all the time. I need to know exactly—"

"We don't have to solve the case, Charlie," he said. "Bristow's on top of it, in spite of Timpkin. He has the resources and the know-how. There's no need for us to stay involved. And one thing's for sure. None of my fingerprints are on that folder."

"You could have wiped them off."

He squinted at me. "Surely there are better things we could be doin' than worryin' until we have to?" He started to move forward again.

"You're right," I said. "We should be on the way to Gertie Senerac's house."

He shook his head. "I'm not sure I want to be around Gertie anymore Charlie, all things considered."

"Because of Winston?" I'd forgotten that earlier he'd started to say he'd invited Winston over on Sunday, so he could ask him something. He'd caught himself and told Timpkin instead that he'd wanted to discuss election strategy, which might have fooled Timpkin, but had sounded ridiculous to me. Zack had no more idea of election strategy than my bunny. "You asked Winston if he was having an affair with Gertie?"

He nodded, his mouth tightening. "Seems like she came on to him same way she did to me. Never stood a chance, he said. Not that he was complainin', he said."

"I thought you didn't expect your women to be exclusive," I said flatly.

"Yeah, but *Winny?*" He sighed. "Thing is," he went on, "I phoned Gertie first, after we watched the video, before I talked to Winny. Asked her about it. She insisted she'd just told me that stuff about another guy to keep me interested. But then Winny admitted it. Which means she lied to me, Charlie. I hate that."

He shot me one of his zinger looks from under his eyelashes. "I think we should just hang out here today," Zack said. "Think things through. Let the police do their job."

"No, we *have* to go to Gertie's house," I said firmly. "We have to find out what's in those notes of Gerald's before Timpkin finishes going through them. He sees where you were treated for some kind of mental problem, he's going to be convinced all over again that you bumped Gerald off. If Gerald didn't leave any copies around, then there's not much we can do. But if he did, we'll be that much ahead, and can at least formulate a defense. Besides which, I want to know if Gertie set the police on you. Who would be more likely than her to plant that dossier here? Maybe she came across Gerald's briefcase. Maybe it was never missing."

I headed out of the kitchen and toward the front door, acting as if I expected Zack to follow. He did, grabbing for his cowboy hat from the hall table, putting it on, coming right up behind me before I could get the front door open. I could feel his warm breath on the top of my head. My hands went so sweaty they couldn't turn the doorknob.

"On second thought," I said weakly.

"Yeah, Charlie?" His hands came around my waist from behind, crossing themselves on my tummy, pressing gently, easing me comfortably back against him spoon fashion.

I sighed and went limp.

"You change your mind about going to Gertie's?" he murmured in my left ear. "You want to have a little R and R first, maybe?"

"Nope," I managed to say firmly, and finally wrenched the door open with sheer willpower. Yanking myself out of

Zack's embrace, I cleared the doorstep with a hop, skip, and jump that Benny would have admired.

"Didn't you just decide we *weren't* going to Gertie's house?" Zack said as I headed at a fast (cowardly) clip toward my Jeep.

"We aren't," I sent back over my shoulder as I climbed aboard. This was not exactly a lie. *We* weren't going to Gertie's house; *I* was. It had come to me that I was in a vulnerable state and shouldn't invite trouble by sticking around Zack. It had also come to me that I might be able to get further with Gorgeous Gert if she didn't have Zack to filter my questions through.

"I just remembered something," I said lamely. "I'm supposed to be somewhere else." In the grand cosmic scheme of things, that was probably true. "We'll go see Gertie tomorrow."

That *was* a lie. But Zack accepted it as truth. And had the grace to look disappointed that I was leaving as he waved goodbye.

CHAPTER 18

A wonderfully smart-looking young woman, with a petite figure, neat dark hair, and a European accent opened the Senerac front door to me. She was all togged out in a shiny black dress that needed only a little apron and a lacy hat with streamers to qualify her for the maid's role in a French farce.

Having eyeballed my jeans and cowboy shirt and boots, she was at first reluctant to let me in, but when I assured her my business was extremely important, she bade me wait in the entryway while she consulted Madame.

After a few minutes, she returned and ushered me without comment into the sitting room where Gertie was waiting to greet me. The sky was overcast, so the reflections of trees and sky from all the windows and mirrors weren't quite as overwhelming this time. But the room still looked like a stage set—a very extravagant stage set—rather than part of someone's home.

Gertie herself was still dazzling, though her expression told me she wasn't too terribly tickled to see me. (Visualize the lady of the manor greeting a refugee from some ethnically cleansed country. That's right, tips of the fingers extended, but not quite making contact.) Her makeup was perfectly applied. She was wearing a jade silk jumpsuit, which would have matched Zack's eyes.

Amazing. Do many women dress like that just on the odd chance that someone might happen by? Or do they own only dress-up clothes, and so they've never learned the proper way to lounge around?

"What is your business with me?" she asked, after gesturing me graciously to one of her designer chairs.

No kidding. That's really what she said. In nice round plummy tones.

"Coffee, if you please, Mimi," she told the maid while I hesitated, then added, "you might run those errands while Ms. Plato and I are visiting."

Mimi. Wouldn't you know! "What happened to Melanie?" I asked as Mimi nodded and exited stage left. That inquiring mind of mine is always on the job.

"Melanie is no longer in my employ," Gertie said.

Because Melanie knew something? I wondered, and made a mental note to mention the housekeeper's disappearance to Bristow.

Once Mimi delivered the coffee and made herself scarce, I told Gertie about Timpkin searching Zack's house. I carefully watched her face for signs of guilt.

If there were any, I didn't recognize them. She didn't even frown until I got to the part about the discovery of the manila folder.

"Gerald's notes about Zack," I explained.

The frown stayed, puckering the delicate skin above her nose. "How did they come to be in Zack's house?" she asked.

"Good question," I said.

"Someone is trying to incriminate Zack in my husband's death," she said after a minute's thought.

"You?" I asked.

Her horror seemed genuine. "What was in the notes?" she asked.

"Timpkin didn't seem to think it was any of our business." I looked at her directly. At least this time she wasn't treating me like a ventriloquist's dummy. Hard to do in the absence of the ventriloquist, I supposed. "Did Gerald have a computer?" I asked.

She nodded. "He used his computer for all his personal correspondence. And for drafting speeches. He often gave speeches."

I set down my cup and saucer on a glass-topped table, which didn't have a single smear on it. Incredible. Once in a while I polish up my bathroom mirror. Doesn't matter what I use, vinegar, newspaper, laundry-softener sheets, paper towels, linen cloths—I get smears.

Some people just have good housekeeping karma.

"Did Timpkin look in the computer when he searched the house?" I asked.

She looked puzzled. "Why would he do that?"

"To see what Gerald was doing at the time of his death. It might have had some bearing on the manner of his death."

She nodded thoughtfully, her perfectly bobbed and champagne-colored hair flowing smoothly forward and back. "I didn't watch everything the sergeant did, but he didn't mention anything about the computer, and there was nothing about the computer on the search warrant. Only the rope."

"If you didn't plant that dossier in Zack's house, who do you suppose did?" I asked abruptly, hoping she'd flush with guilt and admit all.

She looked bewildered. "I just can't imagine. Whoever stole Gerald's briefcase, I suppose."

"The mysterious footprint?"

She nodded.

"I'd like to look, if I may," I said.

"In Gerald's computer?"

I leaned forward. "I need to know what Gerald had on Zack. Timpkin has the file. It's possible Gerald was planning to blackmail Zack into giving up the council race, or else he was going to reveal the contents of that file to the press. Either way, it could appear that Zack had a motive to kill Gerald. Timpkin is looking at it, even while we speak. No doubt your husband chronicled your affair with Zack and perhaps with Winston. Timpkin's probably going to want to talk to you again if he finds out you've been . . . *entertaining* Winston, as well as Zack."

She blushed. I didn't think I needed to inform her that Sergeant Bristow already knew about her affair with Winston. "In the meantime," I went on, "Zack needs to know what's in that folder, Gertie."

She thought it over and nodded understanding, then her beautifully shaped eyebrows rose in perfect arches. "You *understand* those machines? Computers?"

"Fairly well."

"I'm afraid I've never learned how to handle mechanical objects," she said, looking proud.

I was proud too—that I managed not to make disparaging remarks about objects she *had* learned how to handle.

She rose smoothly, which seemed to be the only way she knew how to rise. I felt like a spring colt in her presence, all long legs and bony shoulders.

No money had been spared in the creation of Gerald Senerac's office. A designer had been called in and had been

ordered to create the definitive bank president's office. He
or she had succeeded admirably.

The computer setup was behind the rolltop part of a
built-in desk against the far wall. The desk had evidently
been specially designed—there were dividers on each side
separating the laser printer and a flatbed scanner from the
central monitor. The computer itself—a minitower—stood
to one side of the kneehole.

Surprisingly, the computer wasn't state of the art—it
was a 386 model and a brand I'd never heard of. I discovered
when I booted up that it had an outdated DOS and Windows
and WordPerfect and a fairly small hard drive. Checking
the directory list, I found something called "election," which
seemed the most likely place to start.

There were no files in the directory.

"Very interesting," I muttered.

Gertie sat down on a chair behind me. Her perfume was
very subtle. It smelled expensive.

I tracked down a utilities program. Not one I was accustomed to. It did have a file named wipeout.

And one named undelete.

I thought of calling Macintosh, my computer friend who
always helped me out with computer questions. "I can stand
a computer on its head and make it do unnatural acts," he'd
informed me with a roguish twinkle in his eye.

But Macintosh might want to know what I was up to.
And the fewer people who knew that, the better.

Biting the edge of my tongue, I activated the program,
hoping I'd get everything but the first letters of the files
that had been deleted. I could make guesses about the first
letters, I thought.

Nothing happened.

I went to the DOS prompt and checked the C-drive for any lost files floating around.

Nothing.

"Somebody wiped out the directory," I told Gertie. "I can't seem to recover any of the files."

"Gerald probably emptied it himself. He never made copies," she offered. "He always felt it was too easy for copies of things to fall into the wrong hands. If you only had one copy you could keep track of it, he said."

"Great. Did he apply that reasoning to floppies, too?"

"I beg your pardon?"

I swiveled the chair around so I could face her. "Floppy disks. This computer has a three-and-a-half-inch floppy drive and a five and a quarter, too."

Her face was a lovely blank.

Without asking permission I started going through the desk drawers. They were tremendously well organized. And yielded nothing. Having learned Gerald's philosophy regarding copies, I decided it wasn't worth a marathon search. I'd just have to accept that I wasn't going to be able to recover those files.

About to switch off, I suddenly realized that the slot I'd thought was for a CD-ROM wasn't wide enough. Switching on a halogen lamp that was affixed to the wall, I read the name of a popular tape-backup system.

"Cassette tapes," I said to Gertie.

She frowned.

I got up and looked carefully at all the bookshelves. Then went through the desk again.

Nada. Zilch. Zero.

A nearby cabinet caught my eye. Inside it were rows of music CDs and rows of cassette tapes. Senerac had liked

Mozart. I liked Mozart. Imagine that—we had something in common.

Tape-backup cassettes do not look like music cassettes. None of these were what I was looking for. About to ask Gertie if Gerald had used a safety-deposit box, or had a safe on the premises, I suddenly remembered where my ex had kept *his* backup tapes.

"Gerald's car still around?" I asked.

Gertie nodded, arching her fabulous eyebrows again.

"The glove compartment," I said.

She led me through the back of the house and down a pastoral little lane to a garage, which reminded me of an airplane hangar I'd once gone to a dance in. There were four cars parked in there. Did she drive a different one every day? "Those two," she said, pointing.

I checked the glove compartment of the first, then the console between the seats. Bingo.

"Just about everyone who owns a computer worries about it crashing," I told Gertie as we headed back to the office. "Most people keep some kind of backup on hand, just in case."

Gerald had kept his entire C-drive on tape. I found the directory labeled election, restored it, and printed out the three files it contained. The stack of pages was somewhat fatter than the wad Timpkin had found and absconded with. Interesting. Did this mean that whoever had planted the file in Zack's house had held something back, or did it mean that person hadn't obtained all the papers?

Gertie rolled her chair closer and started reading. "How about I make you a copy for yourself?" I suggested. "I think I'd better take off with this copy right away and go over it with Zack."

I had no intention of showing it to Zack until I'd read the whole thing. I didn't want him taking it over and keeping any parts of it from me. I also wasn't going to make a complete copy for Gertie.

"Would it be possible to get another cup of coffee?" I asked sweetly, hoping she wouldn't feel the request was impossible to fulfill without Mimi on the job.

She did hesitate, but then agreed quite affably, and as soon as she was out of the room, I did a search through the documents, found the section on the Jaenicke Institute that I had expected to find there, and hurriedly deleted the parts that applied to Zack's treatment. Then I backed up the altered version to the tape, replacing the previous file. I was probably going to end up in jail like all those politicians who shredded documents and deleted items from their diaries.

By the time Gertie returned with fresh coffee, I was halfway through printing out the three files, minus, I hoped, all reference to the Jaenicke Institute and Zack's treatment there. If Timpkin leaked *his* copy to the press, my attempt to keep Zack's treatment secret would have been wasted, but I figured it had at least been worth a try.

I gave the backup tape to Gertie. "No point hiding this," I said. "Now that Timpkin has a copy, whatever's on there is not much of a secret."

She looked pale. "I didn't kill my husband, Ms. Plato," she said with great dignity.

I nodded, not sure if I believed her or not. Someone sure killed Gerald Senerac. As far as I'd been able to tell, Gertie had the strongest motive.

CHAPTER 19

So much for my plan to go to Dandy Carr's gym to dally with Marsh Pollock. I had only a couple of hours to read through the pages I'd printed out and it would be time for the partners' daily meeting in the downstairs office. Then I wouldn't be free again until late.

After fixing and eating a veggie-melt sandwich, I turned Benny loose and settled myself at my rickety dining table.

I flipped through the pages first to see what I had. Evidently, Senerac had investigated some stuff in person, had hired people to look into the rest.

Yes, he had discovered that Winston Jermaine was sleeping with his wife. Yes, he knew that Macintosh was gay. He'd instituted inquiries about Angel, but apparently nothing had come in before he died. There was even a page on me—my former marriage to a plastic surgeon with wandering instincts, my bout with anorexia, my stepchildren, my parents' Greek restaurant in Sacramento, my grades in college, for heaven's sake. Another page dealt with Savanna and *her* ex—and the fact that *he* was gay.

The man had obviously been obsessed with gathering information. What on earth had he planned to do with it all?

The pages dealing with Zack were by far the thickest

batch. The print was crisp, but Senerac hadn't used a spell checker, and he'd made a lot of typos. Pretty soon I began to develop a headache, but I plodded on.

Senerac didn't say who his contact at the movie studio had been, but he'd learned about Zack fighting with Rudy DeSilva and being written out of the show. Evidently, he *hadn't* learned that the "firing" had been Zack's idea. But his informant *had* told him about Zack's stint in the Jaenicke Institute. I groaned. I wasn't sure if I'd deleted this brief mention of it from the backup tape.

Senerac had tracked down the same tabloid story I'd read and had scanned it into his record. Next came the stories of his visit to the Jaenicke Institute during Dr. Sugarman's absence and his interview with an unnamed woman who had to be Alice Waters.

I read quickly through the interview, none of which was news to me. In Zack's and my presence, Alice had confessed to her boss, Dr. Sugarman, that she'd told Senerac about Zack's abused childhood, the success of Dr. Sugarman's anger-management treatment, and the time when Zack had witnessed a man named Eugene Everard shoot a fourteen-year-old girl.

"Whoa!"

I didn't realize I'd shouted aloud until I heard Benny scurry into the bathroom, nails clicking on the tiles. I scurried after him. Poor little guy had shot back into his cage, and was huddling in the far corner with his whiskers twitching.

I coaxed him out and we nuzzled each other until he recovered from his fright, then I turned him loose again and returned to the table.

Why had I shouted? I'd remembered it was *Zack* who had told me about Eugene Everard and the shooting. No one else at the Institute had mentioned that incident. Not Sugarman, not Mary Grace Nolan, not Alice Waters.

But Alice had told Senerac about it.

My guess was that when Sugarman sent for her she'd realized her job was on the line. For self-preservation, she'd held back some of what she'd told Senerac.

Was it important that she'd told Senerac about the shooting? After all, on that occasion, Zack had done his civic duty, even if belatedly. He had picked out the man in a lineup, made a statement in court. Hero stuff.

Senerac could hardly have used *that* against him. So it didn't really matter that Alice Waters had withheld information, did it?

I read on. Senerac had evidently thought the shooting incident *was* important. He had hired someone in Los Angeles to track down subsequent newspaper accounts and then had scanned them into his dossier.

There was a fairly clear picture of Zack at seventeen. Skinnier, with longer hair, still a work in progress, but with the promise of the sexy good looks he was now famous for.

There was a picture of Everard, too. Apparently a school picture taken some time previously. The guy had been nineteen at the time of the shooting. He looked about fifteen here. Some of the print on the following page had bled through when the page was scanned, so it wasn't too clear. I remembered Zack mentioning Everard's big nose. His hair was pretty long also. Stringy. He was as skinny as Zack had been.

The fourteen-year-old girl had been very pretty. African-American. Carrie Dougall. She'd had a sweet smile.

Drugs. Would there never be an end to them and the death and destruction they brought? A fourteen-year-old girl dead. A nineteen-year-old boy shut up for life. No—he had died in a prison riot, Zack had said.

I had thought the Eugene Everard story was finished, but when I turned to the next page, I discovered it was still going on. Senerac's hired help had tracked down several later editions of the newspaper. Everard, it seemed, had had a girlfriend who was pregnant at the time. She had given birth to a premature baby girl and had died doing so. Drugs were mentioned as a causative factor. The baby was receiving treatment for addiction, but was not expected to live.

I thought of the opening sequence in Macintosh's television show for kids. It showed ripples emanating from a pebble thrown into still water. So many people had been affected because one lowlife was annoyed that a fourteen-year-old girl had "cheated" him out of $25.

As I turned pages, it became evident that Senerac had become distracted by the Eugene Everard story. He'd even copied the story of the trial and subsequent sentencing onto his computer. There was nothing new about the baby.

I stopped turning pages and sat back. Something was bugging me and I couldn't decide what it was. You know how it is when you wake up in the night with a brilliant idea about something and you don't want to take the time to write it down because you're too sleepy, and besides it's so brilliant you know you won't forget it? And then in the morning, all you remember is that you had a brilliant idea?

It was like that. There was something in my mind that wanted to come through, but couldn't quite make it.

Closing my eyes, I massaged the back of my neck.

The phone rang, startling me. And Benny. He scooted back into the bathroom, lickety-split. He had a low terror threshold. "It's okay, Ben," I called after him. "Nobody ever said bunnies had to be brave."

"Okay, then I won't even try," Marsh Pollock said in my ear. I realized I'd pressed the Talk button on the cordless phone a little prematurely.

I laughed, not at all displeased by the distraction. "I was going to call you," I said.

"Sure you were."

Well, I couldn't blame him if he was miffed. I'd kept putting him off with one excuse after another.

"I wondered if we could meet somewhere for dinner before you open tonight," he said. I may have mentioned once or twice that this man had a very sexy voice. Gravelly. Seductive. It made the little fine hairs on my arms stand up like wires.

"I'm going to be pretty busy today," I said regretfully. "We usually meet around three in the office—Zack and Angel and Savanna and me—so we can discuss what needs to be done before opening time. Today, Angel and I have to change the events board that advertises the bands we'll be featuring on the next four weekends. That means we have to take down the last band and move the next three up and add in a fourth. It's a rotten job, but somebody has to do it. We take turns. Except Zack's usually missing when he's supposed to be helping on it. The indoor signboard has to be changed at the same time," I added, when the other end of the line remained silent. "And I have yet to enter last night's bar receipts in the computer."

"Okay, Charlie, I get the picture," Marsh said.

"No, you don't," I said hastily. "You're thinking I'm giving you the brush-off, and I'm not. Honestly. I do want to see you, and I love the flowers you sent. I want to spend some time with you—it's just . . ."

"The timing's all wrong," he quoted.

"Exactly." I thought of inviting him to come to CHAPS for the evening. We could have dinner in Dorscheimer's. But I was feeling pretty stressed from reading Senerac's records, and I didn't really feel up to making nice for a whole evening.

"I'll try to get over to the gym soon," I promised. "I really would like to see you, Marsh."

"Uh-huh."

A definite note of disbelief.

"How's the sleuthing going?" he asked.

No way was I getting into that on the cordless phone. I was always afraid someone would pick up what I was saying on a radio scanner. "Not much time for that either," I lied, taking an easy out.

"Uh-huh."

"Sorry, Marsh," I said, meaning it.

"I'll talk to you later, Charlie," he said and hung up.

I felt a mixture of guilt and relief. "I'll make it up to you, Marsh," I said aloud. "Just as soon as we get Zack free and clear of all suspicion, and the police find out who killed Senerac and Opal Quince."

I groaned as I went into the bathroom to reassure Benny again. None of the above was going to happen quickly. What man was going to hang around patiently waiting while I played amateur sleuth? My love life was going to continue to be nonexistent for the rest of my life.

I almost decided to call Marsh back and insist he come to CHAPS, but it really didn't seem fair—given the state of my mind. Also, I didn't think I could bear to listen to him talk about farming after a day like today.

Before I could get back to the papers, the phone rang again. This time it was Matilda, my gynecologist's elderly receptionist, letting me know Dr. Hanssen had received the results of my recent pap smear.

My heart started pounding when I realized she was speaking in the hushed voice she reserved for the imparting of bad news.

"How come you got the results so quickly?" I asked. "You told me it would take a week."

"We put a rush order on it," she explained.

I tried to digest that. "Is it cancer?" I asked. "Why did you put a rush order on it? Why didn't you tell me you were doing it? I'm not ready for this."

"We don't *know* that it's cancer, Charlie," Matilda said soothingly.

I hate being soothed when I'm agitated.

"It's definitely class three," she said. "All that means is that there are some suspicious cells. It's probably perfectly okay, but Dr. Hanssen wants to do a cone biopsy, just to be on the safe side. As a precaution."

"I'll come in and talk to him."

"Well, of course, Charlie. It's perfectly understandable that you'd want to do that. There's no need for you to make an appointment—just come in when you can."

I must be going to die if she was willing to fit me in. Matilda was usually rigid about schedules.

"Don't put it off, Charlie," she said gently before hanging up.

I *was* going to die.

My headache didn't get any better. Which was hardly surprising. I was in a grouchy mood the rest of the afternoon

and into the evening. Zack suggested I go to Dorscheimer's
and eat a good medium-rare steak. Angel kept darting worried glances at me. I wondered what color my aura was, but
was afraid to ask. It was probably black, I decided. Black
for mourning. Black for depression. Black for death.

Savanna assured me she'd gone through similar scares
twice and had been perfectly all right. When Bristow showed
up off duty, she sent him over to the minimart to buy Advil
for me. He was very amiable about running the errand.
Proof of Savanna's effect on him. When he returned, I took
him aside and told him about Gertie's housekeeper leaving.

He nodded, apparently not surprised. "She went to Idaho
to take care of aging parents," he said.

"You're sure of that?" I asked. "You've checked to make
sure there *were* aging parents, and she did get there safely."

He nodded, then narrowed his amber eyes to a slitty
glint. "May I ask why you were visiting Mrs. Senerac?"

"Just happened to drop by for coffee," I said airily, wondering what the penalty was for lying to a police officer—
even if he was off duty.

Angel and I taught a couples dance called The Horseshoe
and then the Tush Push—a line-dance. I hate the Tush Push,
mainly because I don't have much tush to push.

The worst thing about a job like mine is that you have
to smile all the time, whether you feel like it or not. After
a while the face muscles get paralyzed. I tried to look like
I was having a good time, but I felt jangly and disoriented.
I kept probing my brain to see if I could uncover the thought
that still wouldn't quite come through.

After the lessons were over, I climbed on a stool at the
main bar and ordered a beer from Angel. I'd thought maybe
Marsh Pollock might show up, and though I wasn't sure I

anted that, I was sort of disappointed he hadn't. Women
e not always of sound mind where men are concerned.
ou may have noticed.

Adorin' Lauren was hanging around Zack as usual. Gaz-
g at him from a short distance away, wearing her uneven
ll black skirt again. Which was at least a lot less suggestive
an her black-leather number. She had on a ghastly little
le-blue fuzzy sweater that looked as if it would shed. Zack
as leaning gracefully against a pillar—he was really good
graceful leaning.

I wanted to tell him I had copies of the papers Timpkin
d taken from his house, but then he'd want to see them, and
hadn't finished reading. There was a lot more on Everard I
dn't read yet.

I was beginning to feel sorry for Adorin' Lauren. Unre-
ited love was a painful thing to watch. I tried to remember
I was in love when I was twenty-one. Yeah. Sam Palmer—
bodybuilder who had worked so hard on his body he'd
eglected to develop his brain. Sure had been good to look
, though.

He had returned *my* affections, however. Apparently
ack felt some responsibility for the girl, but that was all.
he did hold herself quite well, no rounded shoulders. And
ie had pretty hair that was a nice shade of brown. Eye-
rows that worked well for Brooke Shields, but looked much
)o heavy for this girl's thin face. And that nose. The sort
f girl that in school we'd have said had a nice personality.
xcept that Lauren didn't even have that going for her. She
eemed naive—shy—maybe a little on the simple side.

"Not what you'd call a boss babe," Angel said, picking
p my empty glass and raising his eyebrows.

"No more," I said. Beer wasn't going to stimulate m recalcitrant brain—it was more likely to put me to sleep.

"Lauren, you mean?" I asked.

He nodded. "Too bad about the nose."

He turned away to serve a customer, asking him afte he ordered to show his ID. I turned to look at the youn man. He looked old enough, barely, but Angel had an instinc for such matters. Unless they had white hair and a walker most of our patrons were carded at the entry—we didn' want any trouble with the law. But when Angel was susp: cious he went through the procedure again.

He rubbed a thumb over the boy's reluctantly presente card, then passed it on to me. "You gotta problem wit that?" the kid asked, trying to look cocky, and not quit succeeding.

"Not at all," Angel said. "It's a great job. Had one lik it myself once. Very neatly done. Congratulations."

It took me a minute to see that the picture, which cer tainly looked like the boy, had been glued on top of a preex isting photograph. As Angel had said, it was well done— the plastic had been resealed quite expertly.

According to the date of birth, the boy was thirty-one Which didn't seem too likely.

I handed it back to the kid.

Angel pointed at the exit, thumb and finger cocked lik a gun. The boy got the message. Sighing, he slid off the stoc and headed out.

Something weird was happening inside my head. Syn apses were opening and closing. Data was being processed "What?" I asked, cocking my head to one side, the bette to concentrate.

Angel gave me a worried look. But about then Zacl

moseyed over and asked me how I'd feel about doin' a two-step with him. I could feel poor Lauren's hopeless eyes watching. It would be better for her to give up hope, I thought magnanimously, and went into Zack's arms.

We danced well together. Zack was smooth. Very smooth. I wasn't all that bad myself. Something very sexy about a male and female body moving in unison, in public, with people watching, in this particular case with envy. Like taking part in an X-rated movie.

My jangled, disoriented mood mellowed dramatically and rapidly.

So it wasn't until the next morning that I realized the importance of everything that had happened while I sat on that bar stool guzzling beer.

CHAPTER 20

When it came to me it was as plain as the nose on Lauren Deakins's face. I had paid particular attention to Lauren's nose soon after noticing Eugene Everard's nose in the newspaper photo that Senerac had scanned into his report on Zack.

I woke up the next morning thinking about Lauren's nose. At first I thought, *no she couldn't be related*. Lauren was over twenty-one, and Eugene Everard's baby had been born nineteen years ago. And then I remembered Angel pointing the kid toward the door the previous night. IDs were faked all the time. Lauren's might have been good enough to fool Angel, but that didn't mean it was legitimate.

I did a light-aerobic workout with hand weights, hoping the resulting endorphins would help my brain decide on the best approach, then showered, shampooed, dressed and ate breakfast.

My hair was still damp when I called the drugstore where Lauren worked. My hair is at its best when it's wet—heavy enough to lie in romantic spirals. As it dries, it crinkles. Too bad I can't keep it wet all the time.

Benny was on my shoulder, happily inhaling shampoo vapors.

"I'm at work," Lauren said when I invited her to join me for midmorning coffee.

"It's important," I told her. "Zack wants to talk to you."

"I'll try to make it," she said immediately. Somehow I'd known that she would.

While we waited for her, Benny happily hip-hopped around the loft, making sudden rushes at dust bunnies under the bed, and I read through some more of Senerac's journal. He'd made some interesting notes about Detective Sergeant Timpkin. Senerac had apparently applied a little pressure—trying to get Timpkin to make some inquiries about Zack. Having foreclosed on Timpkin's house, Senerac had felt he had an edge.

Timpkin had insisted on following the letter of the law. A police officer did not investigate without probable cause, he said. Spending time in a mental institute was not a crime.

"You think the voters of this city would agree with that?" Senerac had said.

It was no business of his what the voters thought, Timpkin had answered.

Senerac must have been unbelievably frustrated. Good for our Reggie, I thought. I also thought that Senerac would hardly have endeared himself to Timpkin with that attitude.

Was foreclosure on a mortgage, and attempted pressure to interfere in a man's private affairs, sufficient motive for murder? In a world where tourists were shot because they just happened to be there, or kids killed kids to get their name-brand sneakers, or men shot women for dumb traffic maneuvers, possibly any minor gripe would serve as a motive.

Benny scuttled into his cage when the doorbell extension sounded off like a Klaxon in my loft. The noise makes Benny's whiskers twitch for a good ten minutes, but it's the only way I can hear that someone is at one of CHAPS' entries.

"I said I wasn't feeling well," Lauren told me when I answered the door.

Her boss would have believed her. Her face was pasty white. Did she suspect that I suspected her of being involved in our murders? She followed me upstairs, and accepted a cup of coffee and a seat on my lumpy sofa. "Where's Zack?" she asked.

"He'll be here right away," I said.

She looked around. "This is nice," she said.

God knows what her apartment looked like, if she thought my loft looked nice. I'd deliberately refrained from buying good furnishings because I'd made a vow never to get attached to *things* again.

"It's real homey," she added, sounding wistful. I didn't want her sounding wistful. Wistful was a hair's breadth from vulnerable. Vulnerability aroused sympathy.

Lauren's hand trembled as she lifted the cup to her mouth. Apparently, she did suspect *something*.

I had intended acting forceful, like the nasty half of a bad cop/good cop duo. But she looked so young, and so homely in her white ruffly blouse and old-fashioned black jumper, the scenario no longer appealed to me.

Calling up an image of a velvet glove, I smiled at her over my coffee mug. "Zack told me you've been having trouble making friends in Bellamy Park," I said.

She looked as if she were going to burst into tears. Because I sounded sympathetic? Or because Zack had told on her.

"I know how it is, coming to a strange place," I said. "I haven't been here all that long myself. I was living up in

Seattle, Washington, for a few years, though I was raised in California—in Sacramento. But I always liked the Bay area."

She nodded.

I plunged, trying to sound as if I knew my next statement for a fact. "You were raised in California, too, I understand. Los Angeles."

She looked uncertain, but nodded.

My heart thumped.

"Zack grew up in Los Angeles," I said.

Her only response was a slight twitch of her shoulders.

"He didn't like the area he lived in. How about you?"

She shrugged. "It was okay. Boring."

A stubborn expression had formed itself around her mouth. As an interrogator I was pretty much a bust.

Trying a different tack, I shook my head slowly from side to side. "You sure don't look like you're twenty-one," I said, trying to sound sympathetic. "I bet you get carded everywhere you go."

"Uh-huh."

"I used to get into places with a fake ID when I was eighteen," I lied. I'd never actually had the courage to do that. My parents had drummed into me that the law was the law and should be obeyed. They were such great people, so loving and demonstrative, that I didn't rebel, I just accepted. "My parents never caught me," I went on. "Not that they'd have done anything to me, they were terrific parents. How about yours?"

"I was raised by my grandfather," she said stiffly, then started looking from side to side, as though trapped.

I nodded wisely. At least I hope I looked wise. "I believe Zack told me your mom died when you were a baby."

"When I was born," she said.

Everard's girlfriend had died giving birth to a daughter

"And your dad? He died, too, didn't he?"

She averted her eyes, frowning. Time to zigzag again.

"I think you have a fake ID, Lauren," I said firmly
"Angel's pretty sure of it. Zack's convinced. He told me t•
ask you. We'd prefer you told us the truth voluntarily. W•
don't really want to go to the police."

"The police?" she whispered.

"As I understand it, you're actually nineteen," I said.
Her face flamed.

No need to press the point. I was looking for more tha•
proof of age here.

I set down my cup and looked directly at her. Her fac•
was all splotchy now, her eyes about to overflow. "I know
who you are, Lauren," I said. "I know Deakins isn't you•
real name. It's Everard, isn't it?"

Her mouth pursed to an o the size of a breath freshener
Then her whole face collapsed, as if her bones had dissolved
It wasn't pleasant to watch. "I don't believe you're as craz•
about Zack as you want him to believe," I said, steelin•
myself not to show sympathy at this point. "I think you hav•
some other purpose here. What is it? Revenge?"

A sob found its way out of her contorted mouth.

"I *am* crazy about Zack," she insisted. "I loved him i•
Prescott's Landing. I love being around him." She looke•
at me in a pleading way, which tugged at my guilt complex.
"Zack's not coming, is he?"

I shook my head. She sniffled for a while. I got up and
handed her a box of tissues, feeling like a heel. After mopping
up, she said very quietly, "I didn't want to do it, Charlie. I

hated doing it. I begged and begged, but he said I *had* to do it because I was the only family he had left."

He?

"Who?" I demanded, then added as inspiration struck. "Your grandfather? He wants revenge because your mother died?"

She shook her head. "It wasn't that grandfather who brought me up. It was my dad's father. My dad never knew his mother—just like me." Her mouth twisted, and another sob burst free.

I stared at her while my brain went haywire. What was buzzing through my mind was the fact that Macintosh was probably the right age to be this girl's grandfather. Macintosh had brought his children's television show to San Francisco just a few months ago. From *Los Angeles!*

Wait a minute. Macintosh didn't have a big nose—well not as big as the one in the newspaper photograph. Though the angle of a photograph often made a difference. And the lighting. Shadows. But Macintosh was gay.

Yeah. Like no gay man ever got married and had kids and grandkids.

Macintosh was around sixty. Eugene Everard would have been thirty-eight if he'd lived. Thirty-eight from sixty-two was twenty-four. Old enough to be a father.

What about Winston Jermaine? Where had *he* lived in the past. Neither Zack nor I had met him until he ran for city council. Had he ever said where he'd come from? He was the right age to be this child's grandfather, too.

"You didn't want to do *what?*" I demanded as my memory backed up a few paragraphs.

"My dad didn't kill that girl," she said, her heavy eyebrows frowning ferociously. "You've got it all wrong. Every-

body got it all wrong. Zack was the one who killed that gir
in Los Angeles. My dad tried to save the girl, tried to stop
Zack, but Zack put the blame on him. The police believed
Zack because the girl had cheated my dad out of money
They said my dad wanted to make an example of her. As if
he'd kill someone for stealing $25 from him. My mom was
so upset when my dad was arrested, she went into labor
early and died. I nearly died, too. And my dad was sent to
prison for something he didn't do. And it was all Zack's
fault."

She'd worked herself up into a state of indignation, which
was almost believable. She obviously believed what she was
saying. Or was trying to believe it.

I shook my head. "You've been sold a bill of goods
Lauren. Your father shot that girl. There's no doubt about
that, whatever your grandfather told you. The question is
did you help your grandfather kill Gerald Senerac and Opal
Quince?"

"I didn't kill anybody," she said, her voice verging on
the edge of hysteria. "All I was supposed to do was make
sure Zack—"

She broke off and looked wildly from side to side.

It was pretty easy to fill in the rest of her sentence. She
was supposed to make sure of Zack's whereabouts at the
time of the killings. Though she hadn't been with him when
Senerac was killed. He'd been with Gertie. Maybe she'd
made sure of *that*. She'd been with him when Opal was
strangled. Was she supposed to supply him with an alibi?
That didn't make sense.

"I'm sure the police will understand you were pressured
into whatever you did," I said soothingly. "If you tell them

he truth, they'll take your age and the fact you were lied
o into consideration . . ."

I wasn't at all sure the police would do anything of the
sort. But that wasn't what made me trail off. "Why on earth
would your grandfather kill Senerac and Quince?" I blurted
out, more to myself than to Lauren. "Senerac and Quince
weren't involved in your father going to prison."

She looked almost as bewildered as I suddenly felt. "I
don't understand why you keep talking about my grandfather," she said. "What does my grandfather have to do with
anything? He doesn't even live in Los Angeles anymore—
he moved to Idaho."

I gaped at her. "You said *he* made you do it. Who did
you mean if not your grandfather? Who killed Gerald Senerac and Opal Quince? You know, don't you?"

Whatever color had been left in her face disappeared, as
if someone had suddenly drained all the blood from her body.
She swayed on the sofa, and I was sure she was going to
faint. "Put your head down between your knees," I said
sharply. When she did that, I ran into the kitchen area to
pour a glass of water.

I heard the downstairs door slam, just as I turned off
the faucet. Cussing out loud, I put the glass down and hurtled
down the stairs after her. By the time I reached the parking
lot, she was gone.

Zack, I thought and hared up the stairs.

His phone was busy. I called the operator and asked him
to break in for an emergency. He finally agreed, but then
came back to say the telephone appeared to be off the hook.
Quite possibly Zack was entertaining one of his doll brigade
and would be engaged for hours.

I called Bellamy Park PD.

For once, Detective Sergeant Bristow was where he was supposed to be.

Before I could even begin filling him in on my interview with Lauren, he jumped on me. "Is Zack with you?" he demanded.

"Zack's apparently at home, his line's busy," I told him. "Is there a problem?"

"There's going to be. Timpkin just informed me Zack's alibi didn't stand up."

"Which alibi, the one with Gertie or the one with Lauren?"

"The one for the night Opal Quince was killed."

"Timpkin talked to Lauren Deakins?"

"This morning, early. She denied being with Zack at all. She said he asked her to say he was with her, but he wasn't; and she didn't think it was right to lie to the police, no matter how much she'd like to help Zack."

That made sense. If Lauren had been detailed to make sure of Zack's whereabouts that night, all she had to do was deny all knowledge when Zack produced his alibi, and Zack would be lost in space with no visible means of support. More damning than if he hadn't used her as an alibi in the first place.

"Where's Timpkin now?" I asked.

"Obtaining a warrant."

"Did he tell you about finding Senerac's notes at Zack's house?"

"Seems he had an anonymous tip that he might find something of interest in Zack's den."

An anonymous tip from Lauren probably, or whoever she'd referred to as family. Had Eugene Everard had a

brother, maybe.... "That didn't seem a little too pat to
him?" I queried.

Bristow sighed, but didn't comment. But his breathing
sounded a little friendlier.

"Zack didn't kill Opal Quince," I said. "Someone connected with Lauren Deakins did. She just left here while
my back was turned. I was trying to get out of her who put
her up to hanging around Zack, but she says it wasn't her
grandfather. But she did say, 'I didn't want to do it. He
made me do it because I was the only family he had left.' I
wonder if she just said that to make me think someone else
was involved. You know, she's a pretty big girl, she could
maybe have strangled—"

"Ms. Plato, what is it that gives you the idea you have
the authority to conduct a criminal investigation?"

"I've watched all the reruns of *Murder, She Wrote*." I
thought that would leave him speechless, and it did. "What
do you know about Macintosh?" I asked while I had the
chance.

"The TV guy? Where does *he* fit in your confused scenario?"

"Can you run a check on his background? To see if he is
who he says he is."

"One was already conducted. Because of his work with
children. He checked out okay."

Should I say anything about Macintosh being gay? There
didn't seem much point.

"You'd better keep talking," Bristow said.

It was my turn to sigh. Then I told Bristow everything
I knew about Zack's background, and the Jaenicke Institute,
and Senerac's dossier, and Eugene Everard. I explained
Everard's relationship to Lauren Deakins and his death in

a prison riot, and that Lauren had bolted out of my loft when I asked her who killed our two victims.

He had some choice words to say about people who suppressed important information. None of the words were Shakespearean—unless you count the word meddling, which appeared frequently, accompanied by some very pejorative adjectives.

"*I* called *you*," I reminded him when it seemed the spate wasn't going to reach closure during my lifetime.

"So go on," he said resignedly.

"That's it," I said. "Over and out. You don't want me to meddle, I'm through meddling. I won't even mention that I surely deserve some credit, *and* some consideration, after volunteering all this information, which I dug out from various sources, who were not at any time contacted by your Sergeant Timpkin."

Bristow heaved a sigh, which echoed hollowly through the telephone cable. "I'll get back to you, Charlie, soon as I have something to report."

It took him an hour. He had talked to a contact at San Quentin about Eugene Everard. "Everard was pretty thick with a guy who set fire to his own business," he said. "The fire killed the guy's wife and three firemen. The guy's business was a marina."

The significance in his voice escaped me, and my bewilderment must have traveled through the phone line. "The rope that was used in the stranglings," he said. "Bowline knots used as handholds. Everard's buddy could have shown him how to tie them—you have a lot of time on your hands in prison."

"But Everard died in a—"

"Don't get ahead of the story, Charlie." He paused as

though expecting me to protest, but I kept my mouth shut and he continued. "While it's true Everard was involved in a prison riot some years back, a riot, in fact, which led to the biggest lockdown in living memory, and it's true he sustained major injuries to his face and one shoulder, it is not true that he died."

My heart moved up a couple of inches in my chest and started rattling around.

Bristow went on. "He had to have several operations and—"

"On his face?"

"On his face."

"Plastic surgery?"

"In part, yes. Evidently the damage was fairly extensive."

"So what you're telling me is he's alive, and we don't know what he looks like. Is he also out of prison?"

"He is indeed. As of last November."

"And he just walked away?"

"He had served his time." He paused. "My contact's faxing me a picture as soon as he finds one. They've got someone new in the office and she doesn't know her way through the files yet."

He paused. "One thing we do know, though anyone can dye his hair, or shave it off if he wants, Eugene Everard's hair went grey while he was serving his time."

I suddenly felt empty, and colder than I'd ever felt in my entire life—even when I sprained an ankle skiing at night on Washington's Crystal Mountain and crawled through the snow for an hour before someone saw me and got hold of the ski patrol. Echoing in my mind was the memory of Bristow saying, "If the murderer *chose* the Lexus *knowing* it was Zack's car, then he's not likely to be someone who's too fond of Zack. I'd say it's probable he holds a humongous grudge against Zack."

Eugene Everard had cause to hold a grudge against Zack. Or thought he had.

"Was it a grey hair that was found trapped in the rope fibers?" I asked.

"It was indeed. Our Reggie had noticed Zack had one or two grey hairs—which is why he leaped to the decision that it might be one of his. If you happen to know someone with grey hair—not exactly a rarity in Bellamy Park—someone who might also be the right age to be Eugene Everard, then you might consider letting me know."

"Marsh Pollock has grey hair," I said flatly. "What do you know about *him?*"

"Zero," Bristow said, sounding surprised. "I've never met the man. I know of him, but I don't use the gym. Never did. I run every day and work out at home. I've heard Zack mention him, but he's never seemed . . . significant. He wasn't involved in the campaign."

He paused. "Lots of guys have grey hair, Charlie." He hesitated. "What do *you* know about Marsh Pollock?"

I certainly wasn't going to give intimate details. "He said he used to be a farmer in Minnesota. Talked about it in detail. A lot of detail. He sounded like . . ." I shuddered and started again. "He sounded *just* like an encyclopedia."

"You ever see him with the girl?"

"Lauren? Not that I . . . wait a minute. Once. The day we found Senerac's body in Zack's car. Marsh was in my office, talking to me about something—that I should use his gym for my workouts. Lauren popped her head in to see if Zack was there. Marsh turned to look at her. She seemed about to burst into tears, but I thought that was because she couldn't find Zack. My God," I exclaimed as a thought occurred to me. "Lauren ran out of here over an hour ago. If Marsh is the killer and she told him I was on to her, he could be at Zack's now. Maybe that's why the phone's off the hook. No, it was off the hook a minute after she left—but still . . . I'm going over there."

I hung up before he could object and grabbed my car keys. I was going to slap my cowboy hat on over my hair but I couldn't see it immediately, so I dashed out of the loft without it.

I don't think my feet touched the stairs on the way down. I just sort of grasped the banisters and slid down the steps as if they were a ladder, then I slammed out of the street-side door and bounded toward my Jeep.

I had one hand on the Jeep door when Marsh Pollock said, "Hey, Charlie!"

CHAPTER 21

"What's the hurry, Charlie?" Marsh asked.

He was wearing sweats and a blue nylon parka with the Dandy Carr logo on the left breast. He looked athletic, healthy, buff, and extraordinarily handsome. Until I saw the glacial lack of emotion in his vivid blue eyes and felt myself shudder.

Just in case he didn't know that I was on to him, I summoned up a smile, which probably looked as stricken as I felt. "I just heard from my gynecologist, Marsh," I said hurriedly. "Dr. Hanssen. He says I have to have a cone biopsy, whatever that is. I have some cells that . . ."

I stopped in the face of his mirthless grin. "I have to get there as soon as possible," I said, hanging in there.

"I'll go with you," he said.

He was around the other side, climbing into the passenger seat, before my trembling fingers managed to get the key into the ignition.

"Oh, darn," I exclaimed. "I just remembered something. I don't have the insurance forms. I'll be right back." I fumbled for the door handle.

"I think you'd better stay put, Charlie," Marsh said, and I followed his glance down to his right hand, which was lying asually on his muscular thigh, holding a pistol pointed in ηγ direction.

I stayed put. Frozen, actually.

"Katy told me, Charlie," Marsh said.

"Katy?"

"She changed her name for her new ID. Same time as I hanged mine. She chose Lauren because she thought it ounded glamorous." He lifted the gun a centimeter. I emembered a TV show where someone wondered if a pistol ιad a bullet in its chamber. I thought Marsh's pistol probably lid. "Let's go for a drive, Charlie," he said.

"I need to teach you some defensive maneuvers," Bris- ow said in my head. He'd been talking to Savanna, but it vas my brain that had gone blank the minute it took in the presence of that pistol, my brain that could have used the advice.

On the way out of the parking lot, we passed Angel :oming in. As his battered but polished old pickup passed, caught his wave out of the corner of my eye, but stared tonily ahead, praying he would notice that my aura was a errified green.

I remembered Angel and I were supposed to interview potential new bartender this morning—that's why Angel vas coming in early. He was going to be miffed that I'd left. But would he wonder why I'd missed the appointment? Vould he wonder enough to think something funny might be going on? Probably not.

"Turn right," Marsh said. "Keep it down to the speed imit. Anything you might try would be stupid, so don't do t."

He kept giving directions until we were out of Bellamy Park and headed through the hills toward the coast. My

brain came out of its stunned state and went into overdrive
presenting wilder and wilder escape plans. I'd read recently
that three thousand people drive their cars into trees every
year. The statistician hadn't mentioned whether or not they
survived.

I thought of jumping out of the Jeep while it was in
motion, but that scenario didn't hold a lot of appeal. I thought
of watching for a state patrolman and committing some
infraction of the rules so he'd chase after us. I even hoped
a passing cop would notice we weren't wearing seat belts.
But of course there wasn't a cop in sight. There wasn't much
of anybody in sight. A light drizzle was falling. The sky had
turned dark. Symbolic. I reached to turn on the wipers and
lights, and Marsh jerked the gun up another inch.

I could jam on the brakes and hope Marsh would go
through the windshield, and I wouldn't. I thought of leaning
on the horn, but had an idea Marsh might regard that as a
stupid move and react by shooting me. Besides, would anyone pay any attention to a woman in a Jeep leaning on a
horn?

"I had to shoot that girl," he said after a long silence. I
couldn't believe he was still justifying his actions nineteen
years later. "Not just because she stole money from me, but
as an example to the people who worked for me. I employed
a lot of people, Charlie, most of them baseheads—users. The
only law they understood was the one of fear."

I understood fear. I was experiencing a particularly viru-
lent form of it at the moment.

Could I jab an elbow in his chest, causing his finger to
squeeze the gun's trigger and discharge a bullet into his
own personal parts?

All he had to do was jerk his hand up a half inch and I wouldn't need that biopsy, after all.

"Where are we going?" I asked. My voice had gone rusty, as if it had been left out in the rain.

"You'll see."

He was going to take me down some long abandoned road into the woods and shoot me. He'd got away with two murders, why not a third?

"I'm not planning on shooting you, Charlie," he said, as if he'd read my mind; his voice as gravelly, as seductive, as always. "Guns aren't my weapons of choice. My gun helped convict me last time I used one. Besides, guns make blood, which tends to splatter on the person doing the shooting— I had some of that before, too. And guns make a noise. People turn their heads to see who's shooting. Zack turned his head. If he just hadn't turned his head . . ."

He was silent for a while. The steady rhythm of the wipers sounded incredibly loud. I could almost smell my own fear. My hands gripping the steering wheel felt sticky and cold. I had never felt so helpless in my entire life.

And I'd never seen the roads so empty of traffic. Where was everybody? It wasn't raining *that* hard. It must be getting close to lunchtime. Was the entire population having sandwiches at their desks?

The few cars were all speeding past, occasionally honking angrily at me for sticking to the speed limit. I kept hoping a truck would overtake me on one of the downhill grades, so I could gaze up in anguish at the driver.

"Nineteen years, Charlie," Marsh said. "Lost my girl. Lost my baby daughter. Lost my business."

"Business? Drug trafficking hardly belongs on the Fortune five hundred list," I said, then wished I hadn't. This was hardly the time to make wisecracks. I needed to be friendly, understanding, wily.

But he didn't take offense. Turning slightly sideways on the seat, gun still pointing my way, he said very seriously, "It makes as much or more money, Charlie. I had it made. My whole organization was set up and functioning just the way I wanted it. Money was rolling in. My girl was pregnant. I wasn't like most guys, panicking at the thought of being a father. I *wanted* to be a father. And one stupid female took it all away from me, aided and abetted by your buddy Zack. Katy had to grow up without a mother or a father, my dad had to take care of her, on his limited income. I had to spend twenty years in hell."

I guess there aren't too many criminals who accept responsibility for their own actions. It had probably never occurred to Marsh Pollock, aka Eugene Everard, to blame *himself* for throwing his life away.

I glanced at his handsome profile, the straight nose, the curled grey hair, and thought of the photo I'd seen of him in Senerac's dossier. He'd come out of prison much better looking than he went in. Maybe San Quentin should advertise: Come on in for a complete makeover, courtesy of the state of California. Whoever had smashed Marsh's face had done him a favor. He had also pumped a lot of iron while he was in the lockup. When he wasn't studying up on the crop situation in Minnesota.

I remembered him saying he hadn't married because of circumstances beyond his control. I understood the comment, and its irony, much better now. Not too many opportunities for romantic meetings in San Quentin. But probably plenty of opportunity for the alternate offers he'd said he'd received.

"I used to watch Zack on television," he said, looking directly at me, his hand steady on the pistol. "Saw all those stupid old movies he made, watched every commercial, tuned in to *Prescott's Landing*. Good old Sheriff Lazarro. There was one episode he and this woman went dancing and had this romantic interlude. I kept thinking and thinking about that episode, him dancing with that beautiful woman after making me lose everything I had."

The bitterness in his voice attested to his harboring thoughts of revenge all these years.

"Knew all along I was going to get even one day," he went on. "'Hey, Lazarro,' I'd say. 'Go ahead and dance while you can. Dead men don't dance.' And then I saw him in the TV interview when you found that skeleton in CHAPS' flower bed, so I knew just where to find him when I got out."

"But you killed Senerac and Opal, not Zack," I said. Even in the depths of terror, my inquiring mind wants its facts kept straight.

He didn't answer for a moment, he was peering through the windshield. He nodded after a while, then directed me to take the next turnoff.

He *was* going to take me into the woods and shoot me. Trees arched over the dirt road, which wasn't much more than a lane, narrow and winding and full of potholes. The Jeep bucked and bounced. Maybe I could jar the pistol out of Marsh's hand.

"I did mean to kill Zack for what he did to me, Charlie," he said. "You're quite right about that. But then I got to thinking about one time I visited a farm when I was a kid." He laughed. "*Not* in Minnesota. One day, I watched a calico cat playing with a tiny shrew, trapping it and letting it go, running after it, catching it in her mouth, letting it go again. Finally crushed its head in her jaws. Then walked away, game over. I thought that was the greatest thing."

He nodded several times. "Don't you see, Charlie, it was more fun hanging out with Zack, watching him, knowing one way or the other I was going to get even. All I had to decide was how and when. When I had to kill Senerac, it occurred to me that it would be more fitting if Zack went to prison, especially for something he didn't do. So I stashed the body in Zack's car, hoping he didn't have a good alibi. Hoping at least to make him sweat and wonder who hated him enough to do that."

I glanced at him again. He was smiling. Looking gorgeous. His voice was just as sexy as ever. But he had become a monster. No, the monster had been in there all along, I just hadn't recognized it in its attractive packaging. I remembered the chemistry between us making me breathless. Well, I was breathless now, all right—and maybe about to be more so.

"Pull over," Marsh said and I saw an opening in the trees to the right. As I parked the Jeep, I saw a weathered cabin— not much more than a shack—at the end of a short pathway.

"Lauren and I met here from time to time, so I could remind her to keep tabs on Zack, and she could report to me," Marsh said as he walked me briskly down the path through the rain.

"She didn't want to do it," I said.

He laughed. "I know that. But what had she ever done for her old man before? She owed me. And she knew it." He squeezed my arm. "Besides she *liked* sticking to Zack like flypaper. Good old sexy Sheriff Lazarro turned her on.

Can you believe that?" He grinned at me. "Turns you on, too; huh, Charlie?"

I shook my head. No way was I getting into a discussion of my feelings for Zack with this maniac.

"You never did say why you killed Opal," I said as he opened the cabin door and shoved me roughly ahead of him.

"Later," he said. "Right now you have to make a phone call."

"From here?" I looked around, hoping to spy something I could use as a weapon. The room was almost bare. It had a couple of folding chairs, a camp cot, a card table, a few pots on the kitchen counter. An iron skillet on the propane-gas stove might do in a pinch. An open door led to a dim and dingy-looking bathroom.

I remembered a novel I'd read recently in which the heroine clobbered the bad guy in a sensitive area with her heavy shoulder bag. Unfortunately I'd run out of CHAPS with only my car keys, which were now in my jeans pocket. If I gripped them tightly, thrust them in his eye . . . I shuddered at the thought.

Marsh took a cellular phone out of his parka pocket and handed it to me, gesturing me to the table and one of the chairs. Sitting down opposite, he kept the gun pointed my way.

"Call Zack," he said. "Tell him you need him to come here. Give him the directions." He laughed. "No need to mention my name."

"I called Zack earlier," I said. "The operator told me his phone was off the hook."

"We can keep trying," he said. "I've waited twenty years, I can wait a little longer."

I shook my head.

"What?" he demanded, holding the pistol in a more aggressive manner.

"I won't do it," I said.

He lifted the gun, and I felt my innards bunch up in a knot, which might never come undone. "You have to do it, Charlie," he said. "The man took my whole life away. This is where I get it back."

"Go ahead and shoot," I said. What was I thinking? Where did all this bravado come from? "You're obviously planning on shooting me. So go ahead. I'm not bringing Zack out here to a trap."

He sat back, gazing at me with what—to my disgust—seemed to be admiration. "It's too bad we couldn't make a go of it, Charlie," he said. "I wasn't fooling about wanting to be with you. You're a whole lotta woman, my opinion. Zack thinks so, too—main reason I started going after you, thought it might work into something I could use against him. But then I found out you weren't gonna let Zack do what every red-blooded man wants to do with a woman. Yet I still wanted to see you."

Was I supposed to feel complimented?

He glanced at his watch. "There *would* be enough time—except Lauren might start worrying and she's not all that reliable, you know?" His gaze turned sensual, and I felt another chill sweep over me. "Nah," he said. "Too risky. I'm not sure I'd altogether trust you in a clinch, Charlie."

"Wise of you," I said.

He laughed. He seemed to be happy all of a sudden. His face was flushed with pleasure, his eyes sparkling. I suppose if you've spent twenty years of your life planning revenge, you enjoy every moment of the final denouement.

With the gun, he gestured for me to get up and walk into the bathroom, pointing out the bolt on the kitchen side of the door before waving me inside. "No lock inside, Charlie," he said as he closed the door.

He was right. Nor was there any loose piece of furniture that I could use as a brace under the doorknob. There *was* a window. A very small window. But I was skinny. And agile. I climbed up on the pot and examined it without much hope. It had been painted shut years ago. I tried chipping at the paint with my car keys, but unless I was willing to give it a year or two, there was no way I was going to make enough difference. I took off a boot and tried beating it on the thick frosted glass. A high heel might have made enough impact, but then again, maybe not.

There weren't any drawers where I might have found a tool. No medicine cabinet. Just a small square mirror, which showed me a scared but defiant face, which was pink with effort; a filthy sink; and a disgustingly mildewed shower, which didn't have glass doors or a curtain. I might have been able to unscrew the lightbulb and use it as a weapon, if there had been a lightbulb.

I began to feel claustrophobic. The mildew was getting to me.

I was also still feeling helpless, which was not something I was accustomed to. Most of the time I was pretty well in control of my life, but right now I had no idea how to get out of the mess I'd gotten myself into.

I stared at my stupid pink face in the mirror. If I got out of this alive, I was going to enroll in a school for terrorists. Not that I wanted to terrorize anyone. I just wanted to know how to protect myself. I didn't ever want to feel this useless again.

Marsh opened the door and gestured me out. "Sheriff Lazarro's galloping to the rescue," he said happily. "I told him we were both in trouble and needed his help, told him I couldn't say any more. Gave him directions. I could almost hear him yelling, 'charge!'" He laughed. There was an edge to his laughter now. I wasn't sure he was in any better control than I was.

I had two choices as I saw it. I could stay calm and watch for a more obvious break in his control, then rush him for the gun. Or I could fall apart.

I walked back to my seat at the table, hoping he'd sit on the other side. If I could distract him I could maybe heave the table forward, knocking him off balance.

He'd read my mind again. Pulling a chair well away from the table, he sat down in it and grinned at me. "Maybe there'd be time now, Charlie," he said. "It'll take Zack a while to get out here."

"You were going to tell me why you killed Senerac and Opal," I said and breathed relief when he seemed willing to consider the question.

I prompted him. "I knew Senerac had kept a dossier on Zack. I imagine it was you who planted it in Zack's house?"

He nodded. "Nothing to it. I showed up at his house before the poker game with a couple of fishing magazines I'd discussed with him, offered to drive him to Macintosh's place. While Zack was locking up the back of the house, dropped the magazines in the den—put the folder in the desk drawer."

Typical Zack. I'd asked him if he'd had the poker game over and he'd said no. Truthfully. Obviously, he hadn't even remembered that Marsh had been in the house.

"Did you tip the police off that the papers were in Zack's house?" I asked.

He laughed shortly. "Somebody had to do it."

Zack would be glad it hadn't been Gertie. If I told him. If I was alive to tell him.

"How'd you know about the dossier, anyway?" Marsh asked. "Gertie tell you?"

I nodded. "I found a copy on a backup tape. I take it you were the mysterious stranger who entered the house the night Senerac was killed."

"Guilty as charged," he said with that knowing smirk of his.

"I understand you left a little message on the rug."

He looked blank. I guess he hadn't noticed the poop. "Let me guess," I said. "I didn't read all of Senerac's notes, but he was obviously interested in Eugene Everard. He discovered you were Eugene?"

"Hired a PI who made contact with someone I'd known inside. Guy who helped me build the paperwork for a new identity. Traced me to Bellamy Park."

"Senerac was trying to blackmail you?"

He laughed. "All Senerac wanted, he *said*, was to get Zack off the candidate list, so he could get on the city council. For nefarious reasons of his own." He grinned at me. "Most people have nefarious reasons of one kind or another, Charlie."

I shook my head, but I wasn't about to argue philosophy with him. "Nasty piece of goods, Senerac," he went on. Talk about pots running down kettles! "I was pretty sure if he got me to do what he wanted, he'd be going after me next. Anyhow, Zack was *mine*. I didn't want anyone horning in on my territory. So I agreed with everything Senerac said about us joining forces to stop Zack from running, then I walked behind his chair, pulled the rope from the drawer I'd left it in—I liked playing with it, Charlie, pulling on it, imagining I had Zack's neck in there, so it was always handy—so then I walked behind him and . . ." He demonstrated with both hands, using the pistol to show how he'd crossed the ends of the rope before pulling it tight.

I felt sick and probably showed it.

He looked pleased.

He went on talking, and I noticed that his voice had become monotonous. It worried me. All the same, I could imagine the scene as Marsh described bringing a tarp from the gym's utility room, wrapping Senerac in it and carrying him out through the rear door of the gym to his own car, stashing him in the trunk. No easy task for most people, but no problem at all for someone as buff as Marsh Pollock.

The parking lot was surrounded by shrubs and trees, very private, very dark with the outside lights turned off.

"Zack gave me quite a problem," he said. "It occurred to me immediately, of course, that I could make Zack look responsible. Thought I could break into his garage, leave the body there, call in a tip to the police. Zack wasn't home, so it looked possible, but the area was very brightly lit. So then I thought it would be much more interesting to put the body in the trunk of Zack's new car and see how long it took him to find it. Not so much chance of him establishing a definite alibi that way. I drove around for a while before I remembered the motel he'd told me about, the one that catered so discreetly to love's young dream. A nice dark alley. And I had a good set of keys I'd made while I was nside. Senerac was in that trunk before a shadow stirred. Took a hell of a chance, all the same. Anyone could have walked by. Gave me a rush. Jammed the trunk catch so it would delay things. Worked even better than I thought, what with Zack going fishing and all."

I found myself wishing I had a tape recorder. Stupid thought. As if he'd leave it on me after he shot me. Besides, if I recorded him without asking his permission, the courts would probably decide it was inadmissible. "Opal found out?" I asked.

He made a face. "Not exactly. I told you that stupid old bitch had been bugging me ever since I got to Bellamy Park. Wanted me to insist my patrons should dress in what she considered proper street clothes, before leaving the premises. So I wasn't too concerned when she came over to see me after Senerac got himself killed."

I was interested and unnerved by his choice of words. *Got himself killed.* He was still avoiding all responsibility.

"Seems good old Gerald Senerac had *confided* in Miss Opal. Told her everything he'd found out about Zack *and* me. Very self-righteous about it all, she was. Told me she was going to report me to the police for being an ex-con, ought to be a law that citizens be warned. Unless I promised to make dressing rules for my customers, the way she'd told me. So I promised I would, followed her to Lenny's Market, and finished her off before she could even get out of the car. Couldn't take a chance on her running into a crony and spilling all she knew. Didn't want to off her in my office— might have had to redecorate again, like I did after Senerac was bumped off."

I swallowed.

He laughed, enjoying my discomfort.

And then he held up a hand, and cocked his head to one side, listening.

I heard it, too. The sound of a truck door slamming.

"The cavalry has arrived," Marsh said.

CHAPTER 22

"Let's see how Zack plays Custer's Last Stand, shall we, Charlie?" Marsh said quietly. He grabbed my upper arm in a viselike grip and hauled me to my feet. "I'm afraid you'll have to listen to it from the bathroom."

I couldn't meekly go into that room and let him shoot Zack. Come on, I begged my brain, give me some inspiration. We're talking serious life-and-death stuff here.

Just as I reached the door, I heard Savanna's voice saying, "I'd just faint. I'd go limp and pass out. I wouldn't even know I was dead until it was all over."

Maybe it was inspiration, maybe it was foolishness, but I didn't have anything better to work with. I took hold of each side of the doorjamb and let myself go weak in the knees. "What? What the hell are you doing?" Marsh demanded.

"I feel funny," I muttered.

Putting his left arm around my waist, he held me up and started pushing me forward. Remembering something Bristow had said, I let myself lean forward from the waist, as though surrendering to his superior strength, then suddenly brought my head back sharply. I felt it make contact. Marsh said something he must have learned in prison. It hadn't come out of any encyclopedia I ever saw.

Bristow hadn't mentioned what would happen next. I found out. Marsh threw me into the bathroom. I landed on my knees and hit my head with a sickening smack against the pot, just as Sheriff Lazarro flung himself at the cabin door and broke it in. It had to be Lazarro—Zack would never have risked bruising his beautiful bod.

Marsh turned, cussing, gun in hand. "He's the killer Zack," I yelled as I twisted myself around, lunged for Marsh's ankle and yanked with all my might. I came close to dislocating my shoulders. I might as well have tried to topple a lamppost set in concrete. But at least my maneuver distracted Marsh enough that he glanced down in irritation and kicked out with his foot.

Lazarro, taking in the scene with a lightning swiftness that had to have been discussed and rehearsed with Rudy DeSilva many times, hurtled across the room. He grabbed the gun barrel and forced it upward, brought his knee up in Marsh's groin, then, as the man began to fold, delivered a beautiful right uppercut to his jaw that knocked Marsh Eugene right over the top of me and into the shower stall where he crumpled instantly to the floor.

"Wow!" I exclaimed.

Zack turned his fist over and showed me the rock he'd picked up outside. "Learned that little maneuver in the 'Whatever happened to Molly' episode of *Prescott's Landin',*" he said laconically. "Lucky I always did my own stunts."

He went to the door and whistled. Next thing I knew Bristow and Timpkin came hurtling in, guns drawn, chins up. I could have kissed them both. Yes, even Timpkin.

Instead, I kissed Zack. Well, I'm getting ahead of myself. The first thing Zack did when he came back into the room was to help me to my feet, then fold me into his arms. "Are you okay, Charlie?" he demanded.

I didn't appear to have a voice. It had been known to desert me on other dangerous occasions. Maybe smacking my head on the pot had damaged whatever part of the brain controlled speech. No, that wasn't right. I'd managed to yell a warning to Zack immediately after.

It didn't matter anyway. Right then, it just felt good to be held. I could feel Zack's heart beating steadily against my chest, and I felt like a newborn baby must feel when its mother holds it close. Comforted. Safe. Not a worry in the world.

Yeah, I know, it's a cliché all the way. Strong man comes to the rescue, takes the damsel in distress in his manly arms.

There are times when strong manly arms feel pretty good, even to a feminist. And *I* was the one who'd made it possible for Zack to catch Marsh off guard, don't forget. I hadn't been all that helpless after all.

In the meantime, blood was seeping out of the corner of Marsh's slack mouth. "Looks like he bit his tongue," Bristow said laconically, then began to inform Marsh/Eugene of his rights. Marsh stared at him blankly. His nose was bleeding, too, I noticed. Maybe he'd need to have it rebuilt again. "May need a little medical help before we can get the message across," Bristow said.

Timpkin went to call an ambulance. When he came back, he and Bristow checked Marsh over carefully, during which time Marsh regained full consciousness and came up fighting and cussing, using some extremely colorful language. After a brief struggle for dominance, Timpkin hauled out a pair of nun-chucks from inside his jacket and whipped them around one of Marsh's wrists, bringing it up behind his bac with a rapidity and skill that brought an admiring "Whoa! from Zack.

A couple of minutes later, the two lawmen had Mars cuffed and escorted him outside, Bristow happily Miranda izing as they went.

The kiss? I was coming to that. "I was scared half t death, Charlie," Zack murmured in my ear. "If anythin' hap pened to you . . ." Words failing him, he gazed into my eye his green eyes glinting with emotion.

So I put a hand on each side of his face and I kissed him I had kissed him on the cheek a few times since I'd know him, but this seemed like a special occasion, so I kissed him on the mouth.

Let me tell you, kissing him on the mouth was bette than kissing him on the cheek. This man knew all abou kissing. This man could enter the Olympics of kissing, i such a competition existed. He'd beat all the other countrie hollow. I could see him standing at attention on the dai hand on heart, gold medal on a ribbon around his neck. Wel maybe I was suffering just a little from post-traumatic stres disorder complicated by concussion. Whatever, my hand had moved around to the back of his neck, and his arms ha moved around me.

What a wonderfully adaptable thing a body is—it ca go from abject fear to extreme pleasure in the time it take for two sets of lips to meet.

"Well, give it to me with both barrels," Zack said whe we finally surfaced. You may remember Sheriff Lazarr repeating this saying ad nauseam during his *Prescott'*

Landing days. Hang in there. With any luck, eventually, the memory will fade.

"Are you able to talk?" Bristow asked, twitching his eyebrows at me. I hadn't noticed that he'd come back in. Nor had I heard the ambulance arrive, but I could hear the sound of voices now and see movement beyond the open door.

"We'll get back to this later," Zack said, transmitting one of his zinging glances from under his eyelashes. "Let me mark my place." Lightly, delicately, he touched a finger to my mouth.

I sat down on the chair I'd recently occupied, my knees having threatened to go out from under me for real this time. "You need CPR?" Bristow asked, his deep voice edged with amusement. "Water maybe?"

I shook my head. "I wouldn't trust any container in this place to be free of germs. And I wouldn't be too sure about the quality of the water itself."

I took a couple of shaky breaths. "Marsh was going to kill Zack. And me. He said he wasn't going to use a gun, so you may find some yellow rope around."

Bristow nodded. "We've a crew on the way, we'll see what we can find."

"I think maybe Marsh was going to kill me first, then make it look like Zack did it and took his own life," I said. "Or the other way around. I don't know. But one way or another, we were both slated to be dead. Which was what Marsh had planned for Zack in the beginning."

I went on to fill Bristow and Zack in on the change in Marsh's plans and how they had included Lauren. Timpkin listened, too, after he bustled back in, having turned Marsh over to the emergency medical technicians.

"Foul deeds will rise, though all the earth o'erwhelm them to men's eyes," Bristow intoned when I paused for breath.

"I can't believe it," Zack said. "Marsh and I played *poker* together."

"Sometimes people kill people they've had sex with," I pointed out. "People they're married to, even. People kill their mothers, their fathers, their kids. Why *not* a fellow poker player?"

Impervious to sarcasm as always, Zack merely shook his head. "Marsh bought the gym from Dandy Carr. He was one of the guys. He ..."

"Did you ever hear the story about the wolf in sheep's clothing?" I asked.

He frowned. "The kid who kept crying wolf until nobody believed him?"

"No. The same author, but I meant the fable about the wolf who covered himself with the skin of a sheep so he could mingle with the flock and choose himself a plump lamb for his dinner."

He mulled that over for a while, forehead furrowed wisely in true Lazarro style. "Marsh was acting like my friend so he could get close enough to do me some harm?"

I was proud of him. "At first he just wanted you dead. He used to watch you on *Prescott's Landing*, saw you dance with what's-her-name in one episode."

"Molly Carstairs," he said with a reminiscent note in his voice, which told me Molly had probably belonged to his doll brigade.

"Whatever," I said briskly. " 'Dead men don't dance,' Marsh would say when he thought about you and Molly. But then when he got out of prison, he found he wanted to rolong his pleasure in the job. So he waited and watched. nd when Senerac found out who he was, and had to be one away with, the idea of framing you arose."

"Eugene Everard," Zack muttered. "Marsh didn't look nything like Eugene Everard."

I explained that.

Then Bristow told me he'd received the promised faxed hotograph right after I'd hung up and shown it around at he station. Someone had recognized Marsh Pollock. Pollock rasn't at his gym. Bristow had gone to Zack's, only to find .ack was just leaving to see what kind of trouble Marsh nd I had gotten ourselves into.

"It didn't take a genius to figure out what Pollock had lanned for you and Zack," Bristow said, his amber eyes linting. "Just to be sure, we called CHAPS and talked to Angel. He said he'd seen you driving away, but you hadn't een him."

So much for Angel's psychic powers.

"I was hoping he'd read my aura," I said.

Bristow shook his head once, as if to clear it. "Angel was erturbed that you didn't even look at him. Said you were vith Marsh Pollock and that didn't surprise him because 1e'd known you were sweet on the guy."

"I wasn't exactly sweet on him," I said. "I thought— vell, I thought he was attractive. I found out he wasn't." I ighed. "I've been fooled before. I guess I don't have much ense when it comes to men."

I looked at Zack, who had a quizzical expression on his ace. "So after you talked to Angel you came straight out 1ere?" I asked.

"Taylor and Reggie drove me," Zack said. "They held •ack so as not to spook Marsh."

I could accept Zack calling Bristow by his first name. H
and Zack had been friends for some time. But *Reggie?*

"Reggie insisted on going to Zack's house with me," Bri
tow said.

Timpkin actually smiled, making his little caterpilla
mustache twitch like it was in shock. "Felt bad. So sure
was Zack Hunter killed those people. Only thing keepir
me from arresting him was lack of enough evidence to ge
a warrant. Couldn't arrest him without a warrant—riske
tainting any subsequent evidence. Fruit of the poisone
tree."

"But you didn't let Senerac push you into investigatir
Zack when you didn't have probable cause," I said, remen
bering Senerac's notes.

He nodded, growing faintly pink around the cheekbone

Bristow was eyeing him in a mildly jaundiced wa
"Remind me to discuss with you why you didn't infor:
anyone of Senerac's interest in my friend Zack," he said.

Timpkin swallowed and stroked his mustache to sett
it down.

Bristow turned his attention to me. "I trust this exper
ence has taught you a lesson, Ms. Plato."

"It certainly has," I said briskly. "I'll never trust blu
eyes again."

The amber eyes gleamed balefully.

"I'll never do it again, Sergeant, sir," I said hastily. '
will leave police business to those who are trained to serv
and protect."

He gave me his irresistible Michael Jordan smile, the
said he thought Zack and I could probably leave and mee
up with him and Timpkin at the station.

Once outside, Zack decided he would drive my Jee

Wrangler back to Bellamy Park. I didn't argue. I was still feeling shaky. He glanced back over his shoulder after we climbed aboard, as if to check that we were out of sight of the cabin. Then he looked at me fondly, his green eyes glinting. "That was some kiss, Charlie. Can't remember that we ever kissed like that before."

"That was a first," I agreed.

On guard, my brain said.

"You think maybe another kiss like that might be kinda nice?" Zack asked. "Nobody around. Quiet. Trees. Romantic."

I could hardly think of this place as romantic after what I'd gone through. Which is probably what saved me.

"You caught me at a vulnerable moment before, Zack," I said carefully. "I have no real desire to kiss or otherwise get sexually involved with a man who treats women as if they're all lying on a conveyor belt set up to drop them off in his bed."

"Fascinatin' idea," he drawled, moving infinitesimally closer. "You're not like other women, Charlie."

"No, I'm not." I edged away a couple of inches. "So would you give them all up for me?"

"All of them?"

"Gertie, Melissa, Molly, whoever else, Lauren—well, I guess Lauren might be joining her dad in jail—though I hope they'll go easy on her—she didn't have a whole lot of choice."

I wasn't sure he'd know what I was talking about, but he was nodding wisely as Sheriff Lazarro had been wont to do. "Taylor Bristow filled me in about Lauren on the way out here," he said.

"So tell me this," I said while he was still ruminating on

the other women in his life, and the sacrifices involved i
my question. "Why was your phone off the hook when
tried to reach you this morning?"

"I was havin' a meetin', Charlie," he said. He still ha
an absentminded air.

"Sure you were."

He started the engine, still looking distracted, put hi
foot on the accelerator. "I guess I need to tell you abou
that meetin'," he said as he drove onto the road. "I may b
havin' to take off again. Rudy came up to see me this mornin
Brought John Donatelli with him. You remember us talki
about John?"

I nodded. "There really was a meeting?"

He shot me a sideways glance, mischief brimming in hi
green eyes. "What did you think I was doin', Charlie?"

"Let me guess," I said, ignoring the innuendo. "Rud
decided your experience as a politician had qualified you fo
his *Honorable Mr. Scott* series." I let out an angry breath
"You can't just walk out on things, Zack. You've got a whol
campaign committee already in action. There's no doubt i
anyone's mind that you're going to win the election."

He nodded. "That's the thing, Charlie. I've been doin
some thinkin'."

"Whoa! Should I notify the media?"

"*Why* would people be votin' for me, Charlie?" he asked

I stared at him. He had an unusually serious expressio
on his lean face. He really wanted an answer.

We'd turned onto the highway, I noticed. I felt relieve
to be away from that awful cabin. Later on, I was probabl
going to have a few nightmares about that cabin, and Marsh
Pollock, and how near Zack and I had come to death. Bu
right now, Zack was asking a serious question, whicl

equired a truthful answer. "The women think you're sexy, ack. The men think you're a hero. They all know you're a elebrity. Then there's the fact that for seven years you ere their favorite law-enforcement officer. You solved all our cases, right there in the viewers' living rooms. The bad uys were all sent to jail, or shot. People like that idea. They xtrapolate from it. If you could do it on TV, maybe you ould do it in real life."

"But you and I know I'd never make a good politician."

"You might grow into the job."

"Hardly seems right, when most of the time I've no idea vhat I'm doin'. Janice—now, she seems to have a handle on ll of it."

"Have you been sleeping with Janice, too?" I asked.

"Get your mind out of my bed, Charlie," Zack said with sideways grin. But I noticed he avoided the question.

"Janice has the same kind of ideas you have about what vould be best for Bellamy Park," he went on. "We met and alked and I got to thinkin' maybe I ought to step down and et her go ahead. She'd be good at the job, don't you think?"

I sighed, thinking of all the work I'd put in, of the dozens f disappointed people I'd have to face. "Yes, she would be :ood," I allowed.

"It's just not the same as fightin' Senerac and Opal Quince," Zack continued. "There were principles involved here. But there aren't with Janice. She and Winny could andle the job without me—along with the good people lready on the council."

I studied his face. He had his solemn Sheriff-Lazarro- eaches-a-decision expression in place. "You're really seri- us about this? You're not just quitting because Rudy wants ou for his stupid series?"

"Rudy's given up the idea of the *Honorable Mr. Scott,*" he said.

"Really?"

"Really."

"Well, then." I relented and smiled at him. "I have t͏ say I think you're doing the right thing, Zack, under th͏ circumstances, but only because the opposition isn't what͏ was."

"So do we stop for that kiss now?" he asked, settling hi͏ cowboy hat at its sexiest angle and giving me the benefit ͏ the slanting eyebrows and bad-boy smile, which never fa͏ to perk up some interest in my nether regions.

"You were telling me about that meeting," I said hastil͏ noting that we were about to turn off toward Bellamy Par͏ "If Rudy's given up on *Mr. Scott,* why was he meeting wit͏ you?"

"That's the excitin' part, Charlie," Zack said. "He want͏ to revive *Prescott's Landin'*. He wants to bring old Sheri͏ Lazarro back on the job."

"How can he do that?" I demanded. "Lazarro's dead.'"

"Not so," Zack said, shaking his head. "Old Lazarro, h͏ got run over by a bus. Everyone *thought* he was dead. Bu͏ all this time he's just been badly injured and lyin' in a com͏ Now he's come out of it on account of some new drugs th͏ town doc discovered. Even his arthritis is cured. Rudy͏ talkin' 'bout Lazarro havin' a near-death experience. That͏ be the first episode, he says."

There have been many times in my life that my min͏ has been boggled, but never to such an overwhelming degre͏ as at that moment. Perhaps part of it was that I'd had so͏ of a rough day. Or perhaps I felt so flabbergasted because͏ knew, even while my mind was busily boggling, that *Presco͏*

Landing's former audience would swallow the story whole, and take Zack back to their bosoms with cries of joy.

"Home again," Zack said, pulling my Jeep into a parking slot across from Bellamy Park PD. The light rain had stopped at some point. The sky was high and blue, with just a few wispy clouds. I gazed at the planters that stood around everywhere in the downtown area, admiring their riotous collections of marigolds and salvia, daisies and petunias. But though I was glad to see them, very glad of this proof that I had returned alive, the flowers seemed blurred—as though I was looking at them through an unfocused lens.

Still stunned, I allowed Zack to help me solicitously from the Jeep and put his right arm around me to escort me across the road.

A TV crew was emerging from the police department, looking down in the dumps. Probably because Bristow and Timpkin hadn't arrived yet.

Seeing Zack, the cameraman raised his camera and taped our approach. The reporter started yelling questions. Zack straightened his already straight shoulders, tipped his cowboy hat at its winningest angle, and lightly stroked the faint zigzag scar on his left cheek.

I could hear the voice-over already. "Local hero and television celebrity Zack Hunter is seen here helping one of his employees into the police station, having heroically saved her from a deranged killer."

CHAPS would be full again tonight.

Please turn the page for
an exciting sneak preview of
Margaret Chittenden's newest
Charlie Plato mystery
DEAD BEAT AND DEADLY
now on sale wherever
hardcover mysteries are sold!

CHAPTER 1

"Back off!" I yelled.

"Louder," the instructor said.

I filled my lungs with air, exploded it out through my mouth. "BACK OFF!"

"Yo!" he said. Leaning forward, he added in a conspiratorial whisper, "It's a euphemism, you know."

I kicked his shin, just the way he'd demonstrated in lesson one. I knew how to do that before the lesson of course; I've practiced on Zack.

"You're a quick study, Charlie," the instructor said with a weak grin. He turned his back on me and looked around at the other nineteen women standing in a circle in the middle of CHAPS' main corral—aka the dance floor. Some of them wore sloppy sweats like mine, some were tricked out in bicycle tights and tank tops, Patty Jenkins had on a spandex bodysuit.

P.J. was a regular at CHAPS—which is the country-western tavern/dance hall where all this activity was taking place. CHAPS belongs to me and my three associates, Angel Cervantes, Savanna Seabrook, and Zack Hunter.

Ever since her divorce, P.J. had been conducting a serious man-hunting expedition, trolling the length and breadth of the San Francisco Peninsula. After showing up in sweats for the first lesson, she had discovered to her obvious joy that our instructor was an ex-military policeman with serious muscles. Hence the switch to figure-hugging spandex. It hadn't done her any good. So far, the only woman the instructor had shown extra interest in was Gina Giacomini, who managed Buttons & Bows, the Western store in CHAPS' foyer. Gina was a character in her own right, outrageously punk, bluntly outspoken. Her spiky hair had been red and green through the holidays; it was now striped blond and magenta, which dramatically set off the black lipstick and nail polish she'd taken to wearing lately, and the assortment of earrings that circled each of her ears.

Our instructor was playing with fire there, though he probably didn't know it. Gina was Angel Cervantes's girlfriend, and Angel had muscles, too. More on that later.

It had taken me a few months to find a qualified instructor who would agree to teach self-defense to women. I'd been referred to this one by Macintosh—one of Zack's poker and fishing buddies. The instructor's name, swear to God, was Duke. Duke Conway. In his parallel life he was an auto mechanic. He had dark hair, sharp features, and blue eyes that were possibly almost as vivid as mine. His kung-fu outfit looked like black pajamas. He had earned, but was not wearing, a karate black belt.

"Okay, ladies," Duke said, making most of us cringe. "Ms Plato has shown you how it's done. Let's hear it."

"Back off!" the women said in voices varying in tone from squeak to weak bleat.

Duke sighed. "Ladies, ladies," he complained. "We are imagining a large male person who wishes to harm us physically, to rape us, perhaps, to steal our valuables."

I glanced at a woman named Estrella Stockton, a very
~~pretty~~ pretty Filipina who was wearing a surprising amount of gold
~~jewelry~~ welry with her white, satiny long-sleeved shirt and electric
~~blue~~ ue bicycle shorts. There were gold loops in her ears, rings
~~on~~ several fingers, and a flat woven chain around her neck.
~~A~~ wide gold clip held her luxurious black hair away from
~~her~~ face. She needed to be prepared to protect her valuables.
~~I~~ didn't have to worry a whole lot about mine.

Duke started walking slowly around the circle, making
~~eye~~ contact, explaining all over again that it was *okay* for
~~a~~ woman to get mad when attacked; it was *okay* to yell,
~~okay~~ to gouge and bite and kick and stomp.

Estrella was a thirtysomething like me. We were both
~~Asian~~. There all resemblance ceased. She was petite. My nick-
~~name~~ in school was Stretch. She had a perky bosom under
~~her~~ suspenders; my bosom is not a particularly noticeable
~~item~~ of my equipment.

I envied Estrella for her hair rather than her gold or
~~bosom~~. Mine was just as long, but orange. As in jack-o'-
~~lantern~~. And curly. Okay—frizzy.

Duke had cut Savanna Seabrook out of the pack. Savan-
~~na~~'s a truly beautiful woman, inside and out. Zack calls her
~~the~~ African-American version of Dolly Parton.

Yes, I'm talking about *the* Zack Hunter—the man of
~~every~~ woman's dreams—used to play Sheriff Lazarro in the
~~long~~-running drama series, *Prescott's Landing*. Zack owns
~~half~~ of CHAPS. Savanna and Angel and I own the rest. Zack's
~~away~~ right now. In La-La land. We'll talk about him later,
~~too~~.

"Okay, Miss," Duke said to Savanna. "This is the scenario.
~~I'm~~ gonna hit you and punch you." He put his hands loosely

around her lovely throat. "I'm gonna strangle you, throttl
you. What do you say!"

While Savanna mulled it over, I thought it would be inter
esting if her boyfriend were to show up. He's one of Bellam
Park's finest. Detective Sergeant Taylor Bristow. A Michae
Jordan look-alike, according to Zack. (Those of you who'v
met Zack before will remember that almost all of his refer
ences are to television or the movies.)

"Let's hear it," Duke demanded.

Savanna attempted a snarl that turned itself into a giggle
"Back off," she spluttered.

Duke rolled his eyes. "You got any kids?" he asked.

Savanna nodded. "A daughter. Jacqueline."

Savanna's a single mother. She finally got around t
divorcing her gay white husband a short time ago. Some c
us can sure pick 'em.

"How old is your daughter?" Duke asked.

"Three."

"Okay. Close your eyes."

Savanna quirked a bird-wing eyebrow at me. I knew wha
she was thinking: *you got me into this, Charlie.* She did a
she was told all the same.

"There's a guy breaking into your house right now,
Duke stated.

"Apartment," Savanna corrected, looking serene.

Duke gritted his teeth. "There's a guy in a ski mas
breaking into your apartment right now. He's got a gur
Your little girl's just coming out of her bedroom in her littl
nightie. She sees the guy, sees the gun. Scared to *death*
She screams for mommy, mommy. The guy grabs her b
the arm. You run into the room swinging a baseball ba
going for the guy, what do you shout?"

Savanna's eyes had flown open and widened. Her hands
urled into claws, reaching for Duke's eyeballs. "BACK
)FF!" she screeched, making the wagon-wheel light fixtures
ibrate.

"Works every time," Duke said smugly. "She-bear pro-
ecting her cub."

He strode to the center of the circle. "Okay, ladies," he
aid. "Repeat after me, loud: I can fight back."

"I can fight back," we shouted.

"Louder!"

"I can fight back," we yelled louder.

"I *will* fight back. I will *win*."

He pulled Gina out of the circle next and coaxed her until
he shouted really really loud. When she finally managed it,
e put his arm around her shoulders and gave them a
queeze. I glanced over at the bar, where Angel was taking
nventory. Yep, he was watching.

Duke gradually worked his way around the circle. This
ime, the only one to fail the "back-off" test was Maisie
Ridley, a pleasantly plump, middle-aged Englishwoman who
ust couldn't bring herself to raise her flutelike voice. She
vas a widow, she'd told me after the first lesson. She hadn't
nown the class would be all female. She was disappointed.

"There's always the instructor," I'd pointed out.

"That's true," she'd said thoughtfully. "He is quite good-
ooking isn't he? Certainly well built." She raised her eye-
rows at me. "Somebody told me Zack Hunter owns this
lace. Is that true? Zack Hunter, the actor?"

"He's *one* of the owners," I corrected. "I'm afraid he's
way right now." I'd disappointed her all over again.

The instructor had selected Estrella Stockton. "I can
ell, no problem," she said. Actually, it didn't come out that

clearly. Estrella had a bit of a speech impediment tha
affected certain letters. "No problem" sounded more lik
"No pwoblem." It was almost like baby talk, and Duke smile
at her in a paternalistic way that would have brought hir
serious grief if he'd done it to me.

But she was right, just the same. She could yell.

Estrella had kept herself apart from the other wome
during our first lesson just before the holidays, and durin,
this one. Even in the rest room, while everyone else wa
tugging off jackets, swapping jeans for sweats or gym short;
changing shoes, cracking jokes about Duke hitting on Gina
talking about what they got for Christmas, what they di
New Year's Eve, Estrella put on her bicycle tights in on
of the stalls, then exited without so much as a howdy.

"Estrella, isn't it?" Duke asked.

She nodded shortly.

"Okay, Estrella," Duke said. "You're really mad at me
I'm attacking you. You're much smaller than me, and yo
know it's no use fighting me. There's no way you can wir
No way."

"Okay," she said.

"Wanna know what to do?" Duke asked.

"I know what to do," she said. "You taught us last lesson
The knee in the gwoin thing."

"Yo! You were paying attention," Duke said, smilin
fondly again. He said "Yo!" quite often. I guess he wa
image-conscious.

He was right about Estrella paying attention. She wa
throwing her heart and soul into these lessons. Most of th
women clowned around, not really taking it all seriously.
took it seriously. As I indicated earlier, I was the one wh
arranged for the self-defense lessons in the first place. No

too long ago I'd had a near-death experience with someone who'd wanted to interfere with my way of life. Permanently. For a period of time that was actually brief, but seemed long, I had felt absolutely helpless. And terrified. I had vowed never to be helpless again. Next time danger came looking for me, I was going to know how to cope.

I wondered if Estrella had felt helpless at some time or other. A couple of times during the first lesson, I'd thought she was following Duke's instructions a little too strenuously—as if she was venting some deeply buried anger.

Duke had his hands on Estrella's shoulders and was encouraging her to grab hold of his arms and bring her knee up. "Put your head down and push," he told her. "Push me backwards, get me off-balance, bring your right knee up, make like you're going to get me right in the family jewels. Up, down, up again, push!"

Estrella's face tightened into a mask. Pretty soon, she had Duke stumbling. About her fifth knee raise, she connected.

Duke let out a yell and went white.

Somebody's giggle was quickly suppressed.

Estrella let go at once and said she was sowwy, weally veally sowwy. But her dark eyes held a glow of satisfaction that had no hint of apology. Maybe she had noticed that paternalistic smile after all.

"That's enough for today," Duke said hoarsely, and limped off to lean on the edge of the stage and do some power breathing.

The women crowded around the bottles of Pellegrino water Angel had set out on the bar. Angel had gone missing, I noticed. I looked around for him, saw him in the entrance, leaning against the wall, still watching Gina. She was chat-

ting away to P.J., who had also been after Angel for a while
P.J. had given up. Gina was hanging in there. She and Ange
had been going together for a year or so.

Angel Cervantes is a tough-looking hombre, relatively
silent, fiercely private. Think of a man-size mahogany sculp-
ture, cheekbones to die for. Long black hair pulled back and
tied with a leather thong. Pancho Villa mustache. White
western shirt, form-fitting blue jeans. Don't forget the cow
boy hat made of the finest straw.

Now add spaniel-mild brown eyes. Yeah, that's the sur
prising thing about Angel—he's an incredibly gentle man

"You all done?" he asked, as I passed him on my way to
the rest room.

"It's more that Duke's done for," I said.

Angel's smile appeared rarely, but in this case it showed
great satisfaction. "Lot of spirit in that little lady," he com
mented.

I have to explain something here. While I object to
woman being called a lady or a girl, I've learned to accep
"little lady." I spend a lot of my time around hat hunks, ak
cowboy wanna-bes, who usually adopt the mannerisms an
some of the speech patterns to go along with the Stetson an
boots. Being called little lady is part of my job descriptio

By the time I came out of the stall, the rest room wa
crowded. Everyone was laughing and congratulatin
Estrella on her performance. She looked pleased but wasn
saying much. I stood next to her as I washed my hands. Sh
had pushed her sleeves up, ready to do the same. My ga
caught by the light glinting on her rings, I noticed ugly dar
bruises on her left forearm. Four of them, finger wide.

"Those bruises look pretty recent," I said quietly, as th
other women straggled out.

Her mouth tightened. She didn't look at me. "My what d'you call it—depth perception—is off," she said. She had difficulty with the "p" sounds too—a minor hesitation, but she didn't let it slow her down. "I walk into doors all the time."

"Really?" I looked in the mirror and fluffed up my hair as an excuse for sticking around. It's too frizzy to fluff, so I mainly just made it look messier. "Looks like a handprint to me," I said evenly. "Four fingers."

She had her hands under the air dryer, palms up. I could see the thumbprint now. She turned her head and saw me looking.

"You want to talk about it?" I asked.

She sighed, twitched her sleeves into place and buttoned them. "My husband," she said in a resigned voice. "He beats me all the time."

"Leave him," I said right away.

She gave me a cynical sort of glance.

"I'm serious," I said. "Nobody has to stay in that kind of relationship. There are shelters, agencies that can help you."

She shook her head. "I'm not an Amewican citizen. And I have only lived in this countwy for eighteen months. I leave him, he divorces me, I have to go back to the Philippines. I like it here. I don't wanna go back. I will never go back." She was very intense.

"I'm not sure that's so anymore," I said. "I seem to remember reading that there's a battered-wife clause in the immigration law. If you can prove you've been abused, you could get permanent-resident status. You might look into that."

She didn't look as thrilled by that as I would have

expected. She simply shrugged and pulled on a down parka. "I'm okay," she said. "I'm taking this self-defense course so I can pwotect myself."

About then Gina came in. She must have been visiting with Angel. She went into a stall without saying anything. She'd probably realized Estrella and I were talking private stuff. Gina's a bit brash at times, but she can be discreet, too.

"How did you hear about the course?" I asked Estrella, being discreet myself. "You don't live around here, do you?" Most of the women had come from the Granada apartments on the other side of Adobe Plaza, or from one of the businesses in the area.

She pulled a lipstick from her jacket pocket and applied it with confident strokes. "The instwuctor. He came by my salon, asked me to put a poster in the window."

I was immediately distracted. "Salon?"

"I'm a stylist at Hair Waising. It's a hair salon."

"Hair—" Oh, Hair *R*aising. "I know where that is. The Fairview Mall, right?" I could feel my eyes lighting up. "Could you do anything with *my* hair?"

She looked at me in the mirror, squinting professionally. She was really a very good-looking woman. She didn't smile much though. I suppose if a man was constantly beating up on me, I wouldn't smile a whole lot either.

"What you need to do is apply an antihumectant to your hair while it's still damp," she said. "Plus, you should use a diffuser to dwy it." She lifted a hank of hair away from my shoulder and studied it, frowning. "Your hair is natuwally like this?" she asked.

"I'm afraid so," I said humbly. "I tried cutting it short once, but I looked out of balance. I'm too tall for short hair."

I had looked like Orphan Annie, but I wasn't going to
admit that.

Estrella pursed her lips. "We could work some Fwizz-
'wee thwough it. Twim these ends."

She sounded like a toddler, the way she talked. But her
ideas sounded wonderful.

Pulling a card holder out of the front pocket of her gym
bag, Estrella handed me her business card. "Call for an
appointment. Tell Felicia to make it with me personally."

As we left the rest room, I asked her to wait, dashed
into CHAPS' office, and brought out one of my own cards.
She looked at me inquiringly. "If you decide you need to
talk to someone or you need help, call me," I said.

Estrella laughed shortly, but she put my card into her
jeans pocket as she headed for the exit.

"Estrella's going to have a go at my hair," I told Gina,
as she walked past me.

"That's nice, Charlie."

"Is anything wrong?" I asked as Gina unlocked the door
to Buttons & Bows. Gina was usually very upbeat and
friendly. Always ready to stop and chat, especially if she
thought there was any gossip to share.

She shrugged, entered the store, and closed the door
behind her. Maybe she and Angel had a fight, I thought. I
hoped Angel hadn't acted jealous because of Duke's interest
in Gina. She hadn't encouraged the instructor at all. It was
none of my business, of course. Which didn't mean I wouldn't
be giving Angel the third degree if this state of affairs continued. My mind, like nature, abhors a vacuum.

I walked over to the main entryway and looked out
through the side window. Duke's van—a squat black monster with Duke's logo painted on the sides—was already

gone. Three of the women were smoking and talking at the foot of the steps. Apparently they invited Estrella to join them, but she shook her head, crossed the parking lot to gold-colored Mercedes, and slid into the driver's seat.

A *Mercedes*. I wondered how much she was going to charge me for doing my hair, then decided that whatever was, it would be worth it.

Estrella drove away, and I wandered back to the office thinking about the accounts I needed to balance, wondering if there was a good movie on anywhere. Monday night was the only night CHAPS was closed. I ought to do something for excitement other than cleaning my pet rabbit's cage.

Sitting down in front of my computer, I booted it up and prepared to work, thinking that if it wasn't such a cold wet January day, I'd whisk myself off in my Jeep Wrangle drive down to Carmel maybe.

I thought I might call the hair salon after lunch and set up an appointment with Estrella before she forgot every thing she was going to do for me.

I also thought that if a man beat up on me, I'd beat him back.

I kept beating on the clock radio to shut off the alarm but the noise wouldn't stop. Finally realizing it was the telephone that was ringing, I grabbed the receiver and fell back on the pillows with it. For some reason I thought might be Zack calling. I hadn't heard from him in a month or so. "What?" I snapped. I do not wake up easily. Or joyfully And I was mad at Zack for not calling for a month. He was one of CHAPS' owners after all. Business could be going down the tube for all he cared.

"Charlie?"

The voice was masculine, but it wasn't Zack's drawl. This voice was deep. Vibrant. An actor's voice. A name rose out of the sluggish bog that is my waking brain. Bristow. Taylor Bristow. My friend, Zack's friend, Savanna's boyfriend, detective Sergeant Taylor Bristow. Who occasionally performed in Shakespeare in the Park with that same vibrant voice. "What time is it?" I demanded, noting there was no daylight filtering around the miniblinds.

"Six-fifty, Charlie. Are you awake?"

"No."

"Concentrate woman, I need your help."

I sat bolt upright, adrenaline streaking through me. What's wrong, something's wrong? Savanna? Are you with Savanna?"

"Nothing's wrong with Savanna. Savanna's fine."

"Something's happened to Jacqueline? Listen, I can be there in half an hour, tops. I'll just . . ."

"Charlie!"

I shut up.

"I'm down by the old creek bed that's part of the border between Bellamy Park and Condor. Still called Flood Creek even though it dried up years ago. Where the bridge crosses. You know where that is? It's not twenty minutes from HAPS."

"Behind the discount stores."

"You got it. I want you to come down here and see if you can identify a body."

"Somebody's dead?"

"A woman. Yes."

"Just because I've come across a couple of bodies in the past, you think I'm acquainted with every corpse that turns up in Bellamy Park? What makes you think I know this woman? What did she die of?"

His patient sigh came clearly over the line. "You sure are cranky in the morning. She had your card in her jeans pocket. Only piece of identification on her."

"Estrella Stockton," I said at once.

"How can you be sure?"

"I gave her my card yesterday. She put it in her jeans pocket. She's in my self-defense class. Filipina? Long dark hair. Slight build. Maybe 5'4"?"

"Got it in one."

"I gave her my card because she told me ..." I broke off, threw the covers aside, and swung my legs over the side of the bed. In his cage alongside, Benny, my Netherland dwarf rabbit, stood up on his hind legs and pushed his nose against the mesh. I stuck a finger through and rubbed the velvety brown fur between his ears. It's one of his erogenous zones. He started vibrating with pleasure.

"How did she die?" I repeated.

"She was murdered. Stabbed."

"I'll be right there," I said.

ABOUT THE AUTHOR

Margaret Chittenden lives with her family in Ocean
.ores, Washington. She is the author of three Charlie Plato
ysteries: DYING TO SING, DEAD MEN DON'T DANCE
d DEAD BEAT AND DEADLY. Meg is currently work-
; on her fourth Charlie Plato mystery, which will be pub-
hed in 1999. She can be e-mailed at *megc@techline.com*
d her web site address is http://www/techline.com/~megc/

BOOK YOUR PLACE ON OUR WEBSITE AND MAKE THE READING CONNECTION!

We've created a customized website just for our very special readers, where you can get the inside scoop on everything that's going on with Zebra, Pinnacle and Kensington books.

When you come online, you'll have the exciting opportunity to:

- View covers of upcoming books
- Read sample chapters
- Learn about our future publishing schedule (listed by publication month *and author*)
- Find out when your favorite authors will be visiting a city near you
- Search for and order backlist books from our online catalog
- Check out author bios and background information
- Send e-mail to your favorite authors
- Meet the Kensington staff online
- Join us in weekly chats with authors, readers and other guests
- Get writing guidelines
- AND MUCH MORE!

Visit our website at
http://www.kensingtonbooks.com